Reunion Safari

Books by Caro Ayre

African adventure Series

Feast of the Antlion
Reunion Safari

Crime Fiction

The Mallaig Link
Smoke Screen

Psychological Romance

Never too late

Family life fiction

Breathless

Reunion Safari

By

Caro Ayre

Greenham Hall Publishing
TA21 0JJ

Reunion Safari

This is a work of fiction. Names, characters and incidents are the product of the author's imagination or are used fictitiously. Any resemblance to persons, living or dead is entirely coincidental.

ISBN 978-0-9572224-8-9

Greenham Hall Publishing
Greenham
Wellington
Somerset TA21 0JJ

I want to thank my family for their support with my writing. I know I get lost in my story, and that perhaps I am not always there for you.

And I'd like to thank all the people who have helped by reading, correcting, answering strange questions. Without your support I would never complete a book.

CHAPTER 1

Kenya - Saturday 21st September 2013

Sandra Harriman loved her daily ritual of lunching with Martin when he got back from his morning drive. Today he was late. Something must have distracted him, hopefully nothing serious.

The delay gave her time to soak up the amazing view, one that evoked happy memories. Mount Kenya stood majestic and cloudless as it did on the first day she visited Martin Owen's family home, Chui Farm, nearly seven years ago.

Martin bounded up the wooden steps, brushed her cheek with a kiss, and dumped his camera, phone, and keys on the wide ledge beside his seat. Rupee, the mongrel he gave the children so long ago, followed him and flopped onto the floor by her feet.

"Sorry I'm late," Martin lowered himself into the chair. "I got chatting to Murumbi. A plant you're interested in has flowered."

He reached for his camera and pressed a few buttons, selected the image before handing it to her. "He said you wanted to see this desert rose."

"Wow, what a beautiful colour. This is the first bloom I've seen. Your mother told him it was special, and I can see why. I really should try to paint it. But not sure I can get in the right mood. I'm glad you got a photo. Maybe, I can work with that after the baby comes."

She handed the camera back. "I'll go down later. He's doing a great job pulling that area back into shape. I'm so glad you persuaded him to work for you." Martin had come across the old gardener sweeping leaves at the Mount Kenya Safari Club when he came back to Kenya and begged him to return to Chui Farm. Murumbi was the perfect candidate for the job of restoring Martin's mother's garden, as he had been there at its creation.

Juma, with his normal quiet footsteps, approached with Martin's customary cold beer. "You need to listen," he said, placing the portable radio on the table. His bringing the radio and his serious tone were a forewarning the news would not be pleasant.

"Thank you." Sandra still found it strange having servants pandering to their needs.

Martin switched on the radio. The unwelcome sound of gunfire shattered their peace. It echoed against the stone wall of the house behind them. The unsettling impact made worse by the h ushed tones of the reporter speaking as if his life depended on keeping his presence secret as he related the carnage unfolding in front of him.

It took a while to discover his location. The broadcast was coming live from the Westgate Shopping Mall. Sandra shuddered. Only last week she and Martin had gone to Nairobi and wandered round the shops in that mall, to buy nursery things to prepare for their child.

Was the news more horrifying because she could picture where this atrocity was unfolding?

She checked Martin's reaction. He had gone rigid, his face drained of colour, his hands clinging to the armrests, knuckles white with tension. Their eyes met. She recognized the despair behind the blankness. The blank look that told her past events had returned to haunt him. These episodes had become less frequent in the last few years. She guessed how he would react. Going for a drive had been his way of coping, but she wished he'd talk to her instead. He never spoke about his time as a war photographer and what had made him quit the job. When the memories returned, he would withdraw. It was his way of coping.

"I'm going out."

The chair legs scraped on the wooden floor as he stood to leave. Grabbing his keys, he bent down to kiss her and muttered. "You'll be okay?" She nodded, no point in trying to stop him.

Martin stumbled down the veranda steps and vanished round the corner of the house, his camera forgotten in his rush. Rupee scampered after him, claws scratching the polished wood.

Sandra refrained from begging him to stay. She wanted to pretend Juma had never come with the radio. Too late. Hearing the gunshots had wrecked Martin's mental peace. Peace that he'd fought so hard to find.

Early in their relationship, she had learned that solitude was his need when the memories awakened. He'd return after an hour or two, calmer and in control. The only way she found to help was to avoid listening to the news when he was around, as distressing reports of conflict around the world were triggers for his nightmares.

Today was different. His leaving without his camera unsettled her. The camera was an extension of his being, which he seldom left behind.

Sandra listened to the horrifying broadcast as Martin's dust trail faded. She wanted to switch off but felt compelled to keep tuned in. Her horror at the emerging news was nothing compared to the terror that those involved were experiencing.

Her baby kicked. She put her hand reassuringly on her bump. Keeping calm for the next few weeks was vital. The life inside was too precious to jeopardize by having a stressed parent. She switched off the radio.

Martin's departure gave her time to reflect on the implication of the attack. All they had done to preserve Ol Essakut as a conservation ranch was at risk.

Before she did anything else, she must reassure all the guests staying on the ranch they were safe. Then she'd make contingency plans to cover their existing bookings. People all over the world would cancel their safari because of this, especially if the embassies advised against traveling to Kenya. Cancellations would be a disaster for everyone employed in the tourist industry.

The house phone rang. Juma brought the phone out to her. It was Hank, a co-founder of the conservation consortium.

"I need to speak to Martin. He's not answering my calls."

Sandra wasn't surprised. Hank, supposedly retired from the media world, was still very involved. He would expect Martin to cover the events at the mall. Should she beg him to leave Martin alone? No. Martin had to make up his own mind. She shouldn't interfere.

"He's gone out. I don't know when he'll be back."

"I'll come over and wait for him." Hank's determination was something she was used to. "We can talk about plans for guests when I get there."

The last thing she needed was Hank bossing her around. It had taken a couple of years to prove to Hank that she, along with Martin and Simeon Mugo, her appointed manager, were more than capable of running the consortium without his help. But, to avoid him trying to interfere, she be prepared with lists of actions she should take. She figured Hank would arrive within the next half hour.

First, she'd ask Martin to contact his old school friend, Sean, who was due to arrive on Thursday with Oliver and Edward, and their families for a long overdue reunion. Martin was the best person to persuade him they would be safe. They had booked months ago, before she knew she was pregnant. The timing wasn't great for her, but it had been too late to change their dates.

She and Martin had hoped to spend a few days in Nairobi with them before they went to Tsavo. After which they were all coming to stay at Ol Essakut. Doctors' orders meant she would miss that first part of their stay.

Instead of a few days in Nairobi, they could fly to the coast. The house at Diani was set up for unexpected guests, and Amina, Simeon's girlfriend, was down there. She'd text her and ask her to stay on. Plans for the surprise party at the end of their trip could wait.

A fresh cloud of dust appeared in the distance, heading towards the house. From the speed and direction, she knew it was Hank. He'd want Martin to go to Nairobi to cover the most significant event to have occurred since his return to Kenya.

Knowing Martin would be pressured into taking the assignment terrified her. She took a deep breath. She must not let her pregnancy dictate her emotions. Her greatest fear was that the damaging mental trauma that brought him home to Kenya would resurface.

Hank's need to be involved in everything drove her mad. Martin had warned her, once a newspaperman, always a newspaperman. Which was true as far as Hank was concerned. His influence in the media circles and his embassy connections meant he would never quit working.

Hank had come to Kenya to run the Africa desk, and been so entranced he opted to stay on and manage his boss's vast estate, and bought the adjoining property for himself. These two estates, and two others, had been linked with Ol Essakut when the Ol Essakut Wildlife project was created by Nick Harriman. Sandra had to fight to keep control after Nick's death, to provide for her stepchildren. She had won the battle for control when Martin had added his support and his family property, Chui farm, to the group.

While Sandra hated the thought of Martin accepting this assignment, photography and journalism was in his blood. This would be hard to refuse.

Could he cope with live gunfire again? Having witnessed his daily struggle to adjust to the quieter pace of life, she feared it could wipe out all the progress he'd made.

Hank didn't know about Martin's bad days or his struggle to push the past aside.

Deep down she knew, pregnant or not, whatever Martin chose, she would have to accept his decision and not put barriers in his way.

Sandra heard Juma greeting Hank. Bad enough she had to face Hank, but was relieved his wife hadn't come with him. Despite working together, because of their large stake in the estate, she didn't need her input.

Sandra forced a welcoming smile.

Hank paced the length of the veranda, clearly annoyed at Martin's absence.

"Avoiding me won't work. I won't give up without a fight." He plonked himself down beside Sandra. "I suppose you're going to oppose this?" Hank's deep southern American accent was stronger than normal.

Sandra ignored the comment and asked Juma to bring hot coffee. Then she faced Hank. "You know perfectly well Martin will decide for himself."

Of course, Hank had never seen Martin during one of his nightmares, as he writhed in the bed, reliving horrors of such intensity that made him scream. Martin brushed her off if she asked about the dreams, but once let slip, it was the suffering of children that haunted him.

"Isn't there anyone else you can ask?"

Hank shook his head. "No. There's no one with Martin's experience to produce a balanced story. Kenya's tourism will go through the floor again, without sane reporting to counteract the current horror media coverage. We must do something. Don't worry, I intend to go with him for support."

The reasoning was sound. But would getting Martin to take photos and write about awful things revive his half-buried memories?

While they waited, he quizzed her about her plans to deal with the current tours, and made suggestions about the best way of making the future bookers feel secure.

Martin returned, looking composed. He flashed an apologetic look in Sandra's direction, enough for her to understand he intended taking whatever job Hank proposed. She forced herself to mouth, "Okay," and got a grateful smile from him, which did little to reassure her.

"Hank, forget the long speech. I'll go, but I'll need a couple of things."

"Fire away," Hank replied.

"A new phone, for starters."

Hank pulled one out of his pocket and placed it in front of him, along with a few cards with the number on. "It has full internet access, and all the normal apps needed so you can access your contacts if you want to. I have more equipment in the car."

Martin nodded, picked it up, and shoved it into his pocket.

Then, in a whisper said, "Will you be okay?" She nodded. "And the kids?" The crack in his voice was enough for Sandra to gauge his concern.

"Don't worry about them. Jenny will bring them back from riding later. I'll tell them you had to go to Nairobi. We can cope fine," she answered, glad the twins were still at home and not at boarding school in Nairobi. Martin had hated boarding and was determined to find an alternative solution for his children. The result, a private venture supported by a few other families with similar concerns. It was home schooling with a twist, run by a couple of well-qualified teachers, with classes spread over a few locations offering a varied and exciting learning experience.

He touched her shoulder. “I don't expect I'll be gone long. The drama will probably be over by the time we reach Nairobi.” His effort at cheerfulness was unconvincing.

“I hope so,” she said, wanting him to believe she was happy with his decision.

“I'll leave this with you.” He placed his phone in its battered leather case into her hand. “All the Ol Essakut stuff comes in on this. It would be better for you to deal with it while I'm away.”

“Can you call Sean before you go to explain the situation? I think they should go to the coast instead of staying in Nairobi.”

“I've already spoken to him. He won't back out. He'll accept whatever you arrange. The coast idea is brilliant. Amina can look after them. I've spoken to Simeon, and he's warned her to keep a low profile.”

“Do you think Amina is in danger?” Sandra was appalled at the thought. But even more appalled that she hadn't considered her Somali friend and colleague might be at risk because of terrorism links with her home country.

“Better to be safe than sorry. Mob culture is unpredictable,” Martin said. “If you have questions about the party, ask Simeon. He'll know what's needed.”

There was something odd about the conversation. Martin calling Simeon, without prompting, reminded her of when the twins were plotting to take themselves off on a trek. They had behaved oddly at breakfast and gone off to play. Instead, they'd packed their school bags with a few toys, and set off on an adventure. Murumbi, the gardener, spotted them and followed. He didn't have to go far as hunger drove them home.

Martin had looked forward to these visitors with more enthusiasm than any group they'd hosted in the past. It would be such a disappointment if the terror attack got in the way.

Martin bonded with the men of the group at college on a ski trip. Then joined them for city breaks, and beach holidays, and on to an annual house party. Martin was a regular participant if his work commitments allowed, but hadn't joined them since his return to Kenya. He assumed the dynamics would be different, with marriages and growing children swelling the numbers. Sean, Edward, and Oliver kept the tradition alive, taking turns picking the venue.

This year had been Sean's turn, and he set his heart on a once in a lifetime three-week family safari trip to celebrate their 20th year of holidaying together. At the last minute, he'd added a surprise party to the trip. A challenge as she didn't know what they were celebrating, but Martin suggested she plan the event as if it was her own wedding.

CHAPTER 2

Sat 21st September 2013

Listening to the radio report triggered an unexpected reaction. For the first time in years, Martin experienced the same surge of adrenalin that sustained his front line work. He hadn't expected to experience that buzz of anticipation again, and needed solitude to process exactly what it meant.

Part of him felt bad about abandoning Sandra to listen to the unfolding drama on her own. Would she try to stop him if he wanted to cover the story? Would she understand his need to face his fears? If anyone knew how much he had struggled to find peace, it was Sandra. But this was a chance to prove to himself he could cope. Would she give her blessing? Was it too much to ask, with the baby on the way?

He headed to his favourite viewing point and, whilst scouring the distance for movement, mulled over the options open: admit defeat, or test himself.

Decision made; his next action was to call Simeon. "Hi, I'm guessing you've heard the news?"

"Yes, I've spoken to Amina and warned her to keep a low profile for a few days. She'll be safe enough at the coast. I'll fly down at the weekend to bring her home. I'd go today, but the new recruits have just arrived. Unless you need me to come back now."

Martin loved Simeon's commitment to his ranger recruiting program. Turning ex-soldiers and ex-poachers into a crack team to fight the war against the ivory poachers in the district was the perfect use of his military training.

"No, stay where you are," Martin said.

Then Martin called Sean about the three-week safari. Sean would need to reassure Oliver and Edward they would be safe.

"Hi Sean,"

"Hi, what's up? Don't tell me you're worrying about my best man's speech?"

"No, nothing like that." Sean's ability to look for the fun in everything was unfailing. "There's a terrorist attack happening in Nairobi. I just wanted to warn you, and let you know it shouldn't be a problem regarding your trip. We may have to alter your itinerary to avoid staying in Nairobi."

"I hadn't heard. But if you say it's okay, that's fine with me. Are you going to cover the story? It's been quite some time since you've covered anything dangerous."

"Seven years," Martin replied, surprised that Sean kept tabs on his work. The only stories he'd tackled since that time had been about tourism, wildlife conservation, and how modern life impacted the pastoral tribes in northern Kenya.

"How are the wedding plans going?" Typical Sean to leap from one topic to another without ever waiting for answers.

"Fine, except I still haven't asked her." He expected Sean would react.

"You're mad."

"Probably, I'll ask her on Monday, on her birthday."

"She'd better say yes. The others are excited about the wedding."

"We'll be in touch about the changes."

"Never mind that. Get on with that proposal." Sean answered.

"I will. Don't worry."

Once he disconnected, he thought about Sean's comment. Yes, he was mad to have left it so late. No one knew what Sandra had endured for the last seven years. He had been a broken man when he returned to Kenya to sell the family property. Sandra had nursed him back to a near normal mental state.

No one would understand the surge of emotion that hit him when he heard that radio broadcast. Or that it would trigger the unexpected need to test himself under pressure.

As he was speaking to Sean, he saw the dust trail. Hank had called. He'd ignored his calls and his texts. Martin guessed Hank was driving like a man on a mission, no doubt to bully him into covering the events at the mall in Nairobi.

Since his involvement with Sandra and the Ol Essakut conservation project, he'd spent a lot of time with Hank, because he owned a large stake in the project. Hank was a forthright American with dogged determination to get things done his way. Though he'd met his match in Sandra. She never allowed herself to be bullied into something she didn't feel happy about. Gradually the confrontations dwindled, as Sandra proved to be capable of running the estate with Simeon, her manager. Fear that her inexperience made her unsuitable for the task, was swiftly dismissed, and respect given despite the occasional difference of opinion.

Martin knew taking this assignment would be risky. He was grateful to Hank for his tenacity in making him keep on photographing and writing. The first article he'd written after returning to Kenya had been necessary to save Ol Essakut. Writing it renewed his love for the country of his birth. But Hank hadn't stopped there; he'd regularly commissioned articles on the local tribes. Work which helped with his recovery.

This task would be different. This time, there would be pressure. Could he handle it? Maybe, maybe not, but perhaps with Hank covering his back, using all his contacts, he'd cope. The last few lingering doubts about the sanity of his accepting the assignment vanished.

The only other hurdle was getting Sandra's blessing. How would she react? Was it fair to ask her at this stage in her pregnancy? Probably not. With luck, the siege would be over by the end of the day.

He drove back to the house, wondering how much resistance he'd face.

As he approached them, Hank sprung to his feet.

"About time," he said. "We need to move fast if you are going to take pictures worth printing."

Martin checked Sandra's reaction to Hank's assumption he would go. She gave a tiny shrug, and with a nod of her head, mouthed the word, "Okay."

Did she guess he'd need her approval before committing himself to the job? He wanted to hug her, to thank her for her support, but was terrified that doing so would undo his resolve.

He squeezed her shoulder gently, while Hank prattled on about the arrangements he'd made.

When Hank drew breath, Sandra touched his hand. "Can you call Sean? We could send them to the coast to avoid them being in Nairobi until things settle down."

"Perfect plan. I've already spoken to him. He'll go along with whatever we suggest. Amina is staying down there. Maybe she can look after them. It'll be good for her to have company."

He didn't mention Sean's questions about the wedding or his reaction to finding out he still hadn't proposed. Sean was right about him being a fool to leave it so late. But he could hardly pop the question right now. No, he'd stick with his original plan and excused himself. “I'll fetch my equipment.”

“I'll come with you.” Sandra offered, as she edged herself to the front of the chair to stand.

“No. Stay with your feet up. I won't be long.” Her disappointed look added to his guilt at holding her at arm's length, but he couldn't risk a touching farewell. “I need to concentrate, or I'll forget something vital. You know what I'm like.”

He wasn't sure she did, but it was true he needed to focus as it was so long since he done front-line reporting. His hands shook as he pulled out his battered camera case. First, he emptied everything onto the bed and sifted through the contents. In amongst the spare films, light meters, torches, a range of lenses and filters and his old somewhat scratched and battered Leica was a velvet-covered box.

He picked the box up and opened it, remembering when he had hidden it in the camera box. Just handling the ring calmed him and clarified his thoughts. Years ago, when he proposed, she turned him down. They were both struggling to adjust. Too much had happened in their lives. Fear stopped him from trying again. Now, with the baby due, he had to take the risk. He moved over to the desk, pulled out a sheet of paper, sat down, and wrote. He folded the paper, placed it with the ring box in a large envelope, which he sealed and addressed and placed on the bed.

Now he could sort his camera box. Maybe he was crazy, but he loved working with his father's old camera and film. The quality of an image was special. Something digital cameras didn't capture. He put it aside. For this assignment, he needed modern digital equipment, extra memory cards, batteries, and all the gadgets that went with them. He packed a small overnight bag with a change of clothes, including a jacket and tie, in case he had to put in an appearance at the club. With bags in hand, he took a detour via the kitchen to find Juma. He trusted the cook to give the envelope to Sandra on Monday morning. Though, with luck, he'd be home before then to celebrate her birthday.

There was a tense silence on the veranda when he returned.

Hank wasted no time in rising and saying. "All set? I'll drive. We need to leave now if we want to reach Nairobi before dark."

Martin knew better than to argue.

Sandra sat quietly. He wanted to hug her, but was afraid if he did, he would change his mind about leaving.

He slipped behind her, bent to kiss her forehead, and whispered, "I love you. Please don't come and wave me off. I'll be back soon. Give the children a kiss from me."

With a nod to Hank, he moved away. Sandra stayed motionless.

"Will you be okay until Jenny gets back with the children?" Martin would feel better knowing she was not alone. She smiled and nodded.

Then, with a flick of his wrist, he instructed Rupee. "Stay."

He strode to Hank's vehicle, praying for a swift end to the whole situation.

Hank's offer to drive was a mixed blessing. A vehicle in Nairobi would be a disadvantage. Traffic in the capital was bad on a normal day. The chaos this incident would create was unimaginable. The entire city would be in gridlock.

Martin was pleased to see Enuto, one of their best Samburu trackers, was sitting in Hank's Land Rover, waiting for them to go. Having an extra person around, someone trustworthy who could look after his kit while he was working, would be handy. He greeted him, shook hands, and climbed in.

Hank was a bullish driver, who drove as if he owned the road; an attitude most other Kenyan drivers have, resulting in a few close shaves. Too many for Martin's liking. But for once, Hank drove at a sedate pace. Possibly because he was trying to gauge Martin's preparedness for what they faced. The radio continued to give updates. Now the reports said that hostages were being held. No one knew how many.

There were more roadblocks than usual. The queues were longer than those witnessed during the election troubles and the attitude of the police differed. For once, they were less focused on extracting cash from the drivers. Martin saw some Somali passengers being pulled from a matatu and facing harsh treatment. This increased his fears for Amina. He hoped she would be sensible and heed Simeon's advice and stay close to the house in Diani until Simeon joined her.

Hank talked his way through the roadblocks, waving his press card and sweet-talking the men imposing their power over the travelling public. Praising them for their diligence made them more willing to wave him round the spiked barriers placed across the road.

Near to Thika, Hank turned onto a side road. Hank seemed confident he'd find a way through the maze of dirt roads and get near to Westlands this way.

"Everything will be at a standstill, so I'll drop you off on a side road. You'll have to walk to get closer."

"Good plan," Martin agreed.

They drove past vast expanses of pineapple plants, some tiny, others bearing spiky topped yellowing fruit, ready for the canning process. Then through a coffee plantation, with the beans, turning red and ripe for picking. Soon they wiggled on down red dusty tracks through the waist high tea fields, and towards the densely populated Banana Hill area on routes that Martin doubted would be on any navigation system or map.

The closer they got to Muthaiga, the denser the traffic became. They came to a standstill. It was obvious the people on the roadside were aware of the situation. There was palpable tension in their movements, as if expecting danger to follow them.

Hank eased through a police roadblock, and got stuck a few hundred yards further on.

"I think this is as close as I can get you," Hank announced, as he unfolded a rather battered map. "We're here. If you walk down this road," he said, pointing to a spot on the grubby, creased paper, "you'll eventually join Peponi Road. Follow that and it will take you close to the action. Enuto will go with you to help mind your stuff. He has a mobile and cash."

Martin used his phone to take a snapshot of the page.

"With luck, we can all keep in touch." Hank continued, "I'll head to Muthaiga Club. There's no sense in trying to drive further. I booked rooms for us, so we have a base to work from. He shoved a neat rucksack towards Martin. There's an iPad for your reports. Everything on it backs up to the cloud, which I can access. All our phones have trackers linked. If you get separated, you'll be able to find each other. I've added earphones in case you forgot them and there's a dictation program to record any comments you make, and I've thrown in a couple of full battery packs. If you need anything, just shout and I'll get it to you."

Martin understood from that comment that Hank intended to sit it out at the club. His being supportive meant providing useful gadgets. Martin wasn't sure he liked being tracked, but if it made Hank happy, then he'd live with it.

“Thanks. We'll talk later.” He squashed a fleece into the rucksack before slinging it over his shoulder. “I'll leave the rest of my other stuff with you.”

Enuto picked up the camera box and the pair of them started the long walk towards the action.

CHAPTER 3

Saturday 21st and Sunday 22nd Sept

Martin and Enuto often walked together in silence in the bush. Marching through the suburbs felt odd. Martin remembered the first time they met. Enuto begged for a job after his employer, an unscrupulous character, met his end while trying to kill a rhino. The result was a lengthy discussion about whether they could trust him with his history of being involved with poachers.

Simeon saved the day. He pointed out that if they didn't trust these skilled trackers and keep them gainfully employed, they'd help the poachers. Under Simeon's care, Enuto and his cousin Barnard had become valued staff members on the conservancy, and gained the respect of the staff at Ol Essakut.

Martin had never seen Enuto in anything other than his tribal dress. Today, dressed for a trip to town, he wore a tattered pair of multi-pocketed walking shorts, probably discarded by a visiting tourist, a faded t-shirt, a well-worn green fleece, and the obligatory car-tyre shoes. His shuka slung over his shoulder, and the short fighting stick he always carried, tucked under his arm. That, along with his pierced earlobes, kept his Samburu identity intact.

"How's your wife?" Martin asked.

Enuto grinned and extended his hand out in front of his belly. "Like Mrs Sandra. Baby, come soon."

Martin congratulated him, remembering the day Enuto brought his wife up to the house to meet them. Her nervousness was so obvious. She wore the most elaborate bead necklaces and walked two steps behind him, trying to make herself invisible.

Sandra managed, in her magical way, to put the girl at ease, making her giggle about something.

"That's good," Martin said, hoping that his wife was having less trouble than Sandra with her pregnancy. Thinking about it made him regret the crazy impulse that made him desert her to take on this assignment. He'd missed Sam and Emma's birth and wanted to be there for this one.

He looked at Enuto and recognized he was out of his comfort zone. In recent years, the change in attitude to people keeping their tribal traditions had improved. On the ranch, they actively encouraged the old ways, though with a few exceptions. Killing lions to prove bravery was no longer a ritual of growing up. Instead, the young men were being taught how to protect their old foe by learning to track the animals, and using radio-controlled devices linked with modern mobile phones, so they could warn the local herdsmen to avoid those areas.

The old expectation of tribesmen being illiterate was no longer the case. Now many were university graduates who returned to their tribal land and used their knowledge for the good of the area. They were adapting modern technology, working with it, while still respecting most of the old traditions. But changes regarding women were slower.

Enuto had missed out on a formal education regarding reading and writing, but he was a master of practical skills, and unrivalled as a tracker. Martin's children, Sam and Emma, adored him and constantly begged to go off into the bush with him to learn his skills.

Martin thought Enuto was unlikely to discuss problems if there were any, and would prefer their accustomed, comfortable silence. Idle chatter would not make either of them any less guilty about leaving their partners at home. Sandra's pregnancy had been tough. Swollen legs had kept her confined to the house with her feet up for the last month.

He pulled out his phone and called her.

"Sorry I took off so quickly. I didn't want to leave you, but I hope you understand. I need to do this."

"I know," she answered.

"I didn't want you to be left alone. I take it Jenny's back with the children."

Sandra reassured him they were, and that everything was fine. The twins had gone outside to play, and Jenny was fussing over her.

Jenny was like a grandmother to Sam and Emma. Everyone was overjoyed when she moved into the guest cottage on his property.

"I miss you," he said.

"Are you sure you can handle this?"

"Yes. You mustn't worry. Enuto is with me," he said, knowing exactly what she would worry about. "Hank dropped us off on some back road, and we're making our way there on foot. Traffic is, as expected, gridlocked. We'll be there soon. I'll call later. Love you."

The route on the map took them through a typical area of the suburbs, filled with houses built in the fifties. Mainly bungalows surrounded by thick prickly hedges with watered lawns, shade-giving trees, and sweet-scented flowering shrubs. Plots had been sub-divided, and blocks of flats built on them. Most properties had watchmen on patrol.

The tension was visible on the faces of passers-by. When asked for information, their reluctance to speak showed the fear the attack had generated.

It was almost dark when they reached the police cordon, where they found clusters of people huddled together in groups waiting for news of colleagues and friends. Some had a haunted look, a sign they had witnessed unforgettable scenes.

Martin didn't stop to speak to them. He wanted to circle the complex, then find out who was in charge. And how many people were trapped.

He picked a spot under a tree, removed his rucksack. Enuto nodded his approval of a spot of shade. Martin thought he'd be pleased. There was a stall on the other side of the road selling tea and snacks. Enuto put down the camera box and shrugged off the rucksack.

"Chai?" he said, pointing towards the stall. Martin nodded and watched him stride off. Martin dug into the camera box, stuffing his pockets with the things he'd need. He took a photo of the back of the mall and sent it to Hank to show his location.

He inched forward towards the policeman blocking the way, listened to what he said to everyone trying to get past him. The man took his job seriously and was not letting anyone through. Martin moved in close and asked how long he'd been standing there. The policeman responded in a more friendly way, and the conversation became more general. Martin produced the press card Hank had given him and panic hit. Could it have expired?

"Is it possible to go over there?" He pointed to the cordoned off area about fifty yards away. "I need to speak to the officer in charge."

The policeman studied his press card. After deliberating with a colleague, he waved him forward with strict instructions to stay close to the wall that edged the gap.

Martin moved off cautiously, keeping tight to the wall, trying not to upset the amenable policeman. When he reached the other side, he explained his mission to the officer guarding the crossing point with the same courtesy used earlier. He presumed they were traffic cops, who were terrified by the ongoing drama.

A crack of gunfire made everyone dive for cover.

His heart thudded, but instinct kicked in, and he lifted his camera in readiness. Seconds later, a group of people came running from the building in their direction. Two were being dragged along. Martin snapped a few shots before they reached relative safety and were surrounded by police and medics and a crush of reporters. He stayed where he was and let out a slow breath. The first hurdle was over. He hadn't frozen. It was a comfort to witness people coming out.

No point in trying to get closer. The victims were stressed enough. He'd complete the circuit and get back to Enuto.

A few yards further on, he bumped into a reporter he knew from past assignments. The man had been inside when the attack began. Footage he'd captured on his phone was now being shown on all the major international news broadcasts.

After a quick greeting, he gave Martin a rough description of the initial exodus of shoppers. "Those left inside are too afraid to run to safety." He described how two plain clothed policemen had rushed inside and been gunned down. He believed the bulk of the hostages were in the downstairs supermarket. "I was lucky to get out alive."

Martin thanked him and continued his planned circuit. Where the vegetation had been flattened by the relentless footfall of people was easy. Other areas where foot-high posts, crisscrossed with barbed wire supports for low-growing plants designed to deter cars and people, had to be avoided.

Martin took photos as he moved until he reached a side street. One filled with police and army vehicles, and groups of armed men standing waiting for instructions.

He quickly pushed his camera round to the side. The armed forces usually objected to being filmed, and he didn't want to stir up trouble.

There was an air of uncertainty over who was in charge. Politicians appeared. Those he recognized belonged to the 'be seen brigade', always looking for publicity or an opportunity to line their pockets. After posing for the press, they would scurry back to their fancy cars and depart. Martin risked taking a few shots from a distance, for personal interest rather than for publication.

Further on, he found a second side road. Another convoy of army vehicles waited. Was this the solution? Did this rag-tag mob in camouflage jackets look as if they could stop the carnage inside? Martin had his doubts. He'd encountered many soldiers while working round the world. This bunch struck him as undisciplined, and incapable of dealing with a complex hostage situation.

Armies had often surrounded him in the past. But these were the scariest. They looked like teenagers. Most had that wide-eyed look of people high on bhang.

With his camera lowered, he got closer, hoping to find a senior officer. Their commanding officers were having a heated discussion with the police authority over who should lead the operation. Martin couldn't help thinking perhaps the people inside the mall were safer with the terrorists than with this lot. Friendly fire was not something you'd expect. But with leaders arguing over superiority, it was a real risk.

He continued round the outer perimeter until he got back to where he started.

Enuto proved to be rather resourceful. He'd made friends with a samosa seller and bought a few for their evening meal. Martin thanked him and tucked in gratefully.

Sporadic bursts of gunfire kept Martin alert as they sat there in the orange glow of a distant streetlamp. Being a hero was not for him. He recognized his avoidance of the injured people who escaped was down to fear. Fear of rekindling the memories he'd tried to erase for years.

Knowing that his friend had taken some extraordinary footage early on meant that new images would never displace those. The television stations would replay the same clips. He checked the computer that Hank had provided to confirm this. The solution was to focus on the human interest of members of the crowd.

All around the complex, people waited. He wanted to find out who they waited for.

He called Hank, who listened to his report. Hank offered to come over.

"Don't bother, I doubt much will happen tonight, and we've found a place to hunker down. They haven't sorted out who is in charge." Martin said, hoping Hank would accept his decision. Enuto's undemanding company suited him fine.

"Okay. Let me know if you need anything."

Enuto and Martin agreed to take turns to sleep. Not that they'd get much with the intermittent gunshots close by.

CHAPTER 4

Nairobi -Sunday 22nd September

As dawn broke on Sunday, Enuto disappeared for about half an hour, reappearing with a tin mug of steaming sweet chai and a sugary bread roll. Martin gratefully wolfed down the roll and washed it down with the tea.

Warmed by the tea, and a call with Sandra and the children, Martin set off on another tour round the perimeter of the building.

The crowds were increasing, and there were growing clusters of wailing relatives, all desperate for news. People who had made their escape the previous day had come back to wait for news of their missing friends and workmates. Shop owners watched their livelihood disappear, while employees waited and wondered about their futures or if they'd ever get paid.

Martin found he could pick out the people who witnessed the bloodshed. Their stance, the shock in the eyes made them stand out. Those he approached with extra care, seeing death, played havoc with the mind. Some were ready, almost eager to pour out the details of what they'd witnessed, including graphic descriptions.

Martin fixed his focus on the face of the person in front of him, rather than on the words spoken. He put the camera into video mode to avoid their memories seeping into his core. He jotted down one or two phrases of their story to identify them later.

The moment they finished their harrowing tale, he'd let someone else comfort them. Then, he'd forward the recording, erased the images from his camera and move on.

It was an unusual way to work. But the best he could do in the situation. His footage would give Hank something to work on.

He made forays back and forth along the front of the building. Occasionally, he turned his camera on the waiting crowds. On one pass, a tall man ducked behind a tree as the camera focused on him. The movement caught Martin's attention. Was the man evading the camera, or simply moving away?

A sudden burst of gunfire sent everyone ducking for cover, and the police frantically pushed the crowds back to get themselves further away from the shooting.

Martin was on his way back to Enuto. His camera battery was running low, and he needed a break. He passed the convoy of twitchy troops. They seemed less disciplined than on the night before. There didn't appear to be anyone in charge.

Then he spotted the disturbingly familiar mystery man. His height made it hard for him to melt into the crowd. Martin replaced the lens cap on his digital camera and let it hang by his side. He pulled out his phone, set it to record a video, and pretended to be deep in conversation. Striding forward and back, swapping hands with each turn, he prayed the lens angle would capture the bystanders.

The charade over, he checked if the man had moved. Their eyes locked for a second. Martin shivered. They had met before. Where? When?

Instinct told him to keep moving. He took a turn to the left and made a wide detour, to make sure he wasn't being followed. At a street stall, he bought a bag of crisps and checked the road behind. No one was in sight. He dug deep into his memory archive. Who was that man? Why did his presence feel so unsettling?

He plonked himself down on the low wall next to Enuto. The sun was scorching hot, but he couldn't stop shivering.

"You no look good. I get you tea?" Enuto didn't wait for a reply before heading off.

Martin took a deep breath to regain his composure. He needed to check the phone footage. The bright sunlight made it hard, so he hunched over the screen to shade it with his body and played back his recording.

"Yes. Got you," he muttered. With shaking hands, he isolated the important section and studied it again. Yes. The face was familiar, but where and when was the encounter?

Enuto returned with a much-appreciated cup of sweet tea. Martin cupped his hands around the enamel mug, to hide how much they were shaking rather than for the warmth.

"Enuto, can you take pictures on your phone?"

"Yes. Simeon, show me."

"Let me see how good you are. Take a picture of those people." Martin pointed to a small group standing near the tea stall.

Enuto shrugged, pulled his phone out of one of the many pockets in his shorts, and wandered towards the group. And with much laughter, they posed for him, and he came back grinning. Eager to show Martin his pictures.

Now Martin set him a fresh challenge. "Can you film them without them knowing?"

Enuto looked puzzled.

"Set the camera on video and pretend to be talking to someone while you film them. Like this." Martin got up, set the phone video rolling, and strolled past the group, pretending to talk to someone on his phone. He returned and sat down, and showed Enuto what he had filmed.

Enuto grinned, suitably impressed.

"You have a go now."

Enuto went off to test out this strange method.

His first attempt failed. All he got was pictures of the jacaranda blossom up above everyone's head.

Martin jokingly pointed out that his height was a problem.

Enuto kept trying until he worked out the best angle to hold the phone to keep the people in the picture.

Martin then got Enuto to forward the pictures to him. This he did easily. Then Martin made him delete the footage. Enuto looked puzzled, but Martin said it would fill the phone memory capacity, which would stop him from being able to take more photos. Enuto nodded. He understood.

"There's another more important reason." He had Enuto's full attention now. "If you film the wrong person, like a soldier or a policeman, and they stop you. They will find nothing on your phone to cause trouble."

Enuto, like many Kenyans, had little trust in the police, or the armed forces, grinned. Outsmarting the authorities was something he'd enjoy.

Instruction over, he got Enuto to look at the pictures taken earlier on his phone. He scrolled through the phone video, froze a frame including the elusive character, zoomed in, and let Enuto study the face.

"I need you to take a better picture of this man." Enuto grinned enthusiastically at the challenge. It beat sitting around acting as a guard for Martin's possessions.

"Be careful. I don't want him to know you are taking a picture of him."

Over an hour later, he got a blank message from Enuto. It was the signal that he'd uploaded a video.

Martin checked. Success. A brilliantly clear picture any professional photographer would be proud of. Now Martin was certain he'd photographed the man before.

His back-up hard drive of all his photos was in his holdall Hank had taken to the club. He had to go to check when and where he had seen this man before.

He replied with a blank message. Enuto knew that meant to keep watching the man and only take pictures if the man spoke to anyone.

Then he called Hank.

"Hi, I could do with a break. I need a shower and a decent meal. You said your wife had joined you and brought Barnard with her. Any chance you could come and pick me up and drop Barnard off to keep Enuto company?"

"Why the urgency?"

"I need to check something on my backup disk."

"Fine, just remember the club rules."

Martin knew what he meant. The club still banned business discussions in the bar and dining areas. They had a room set aside for business matters.

"I'll send him now."

No need to give them directions. Hank's tracking device would take care of that.

He called Enuto. To tell him that Barnard was coming to join them, but he would be back in the morning. While he waited for Barnard to arrive, he called Sandra. He was still feeling guilty for leaving her when their baby was so close to being born.

CHAPTER 5

London - Monday 23rd September 2013

Oliver Weatherby boarded the train at the usual time, carrying the resume he had spent the weekend working on. Kim wasn't happy that he'd spent so much time on his computer, but she didn't know what he was doing. She was on a mission to get everything in order before their holiday.

The news reports of the terror attack in Nairobi put her in panic mode. He'd promised to get an update from Sean when they met for lunch, and tried to convince her that Martin wouldn't let it impact their trip. There was a no cancellation policy on their tickets, so he was keeping his fingers crossed the situation wouldn't alter their plans.

Kim thought he was heading for work, but it was nearly two weeks since the half-expected redundancy notice had hit his desk. He'd decided not to tell anyone until after the holiday. He didn't need the pity of his friends or to dampen their mood.

Sean, who was busy out of town, had agreed for him to use his flat as a postal drop, and handed him the keys without asking questions. Sean probably assumed he was having an affair rather than needing a refuge where he could make calls to recruitment agencies and talk to his bank in privacy. A nearby gym also came in useful to fill the hours while he waited for replies to his applications for work.

Today he had his first interview, and he was nervous. It was a step down the corporate ladder. The salary was adequate to cover the mortgage, but at this point any job was better than none.

Halfway through the interview, he knew it was a mistake. He didn't want the job. He was a qualified vet who hadn't touched an animal for ten years. His passion for animals had pushed him to go through five years of study. Then he'd been side-tracked away from the live animals into pharmaceuticals. Now he was free to do what he loved.

"I'm sorry," he said, standing up. "I don't want to waste your time. This job is not for me."

"I don't understand," the lead interviewer said.

"I want to work with animals rather than be behind a desk. It's what I trained to do."

He could tell from their expressions they understood. And probably had the same desire.

Escaping from the interview put him in a gleeful mood. He wanted to jump and shout to passers-by that he was a free man. Then reality kicked in. He had wasted two weeks chasing the wrong sort of job. Now the hard work must begin.

He entered the first coffee shop he came to, ordered a coffee, took it across to the small park opposite. He needed to change his job specifications quickly. Then work his way through the list of agencies and tell them to rethink his job requirements. They were unhelpful. Finding a job as a vet in the city was unlikely. He didn't mind. He hated the city.

Then he called Sean.

"Is lunch still on?"

"Yes, Edward's coming. There are changes to the Kenya trip. I'll tell you about them when we meet."

"Yes, where?"

Sean named an Italian restaurant where they often met.

"Great," Oliver said, "see you at one."

The restaurant was within walking distance, and Oliver looked forward to a leisurely lunch. Then he'd go to the gym before catching the train home. The best thing about his gym membership was the different establishments he could choose from. He didn't have to go to the one nearest his old office and risk facing his ex-colleagues.

He was undecided about telling Sean the news of his redundancy. Could Sean keep a secret? He wasn't sure. Perhaps not. Sean believed he was having an affair, even though Oliver kept telling him he was plotting a surprise for Kim.

Oliver arrived first, got settled, and ordered a glass of wine. His office had strict rules about drinking, which everyone flaunted on occasions. Edward rushed in, looking decidedly harassed. He muttered something about hoping Sean wouldn't be late because he had a meeting after lunch.

Oliver asked. "What's up?"

Edward looked startled, and after a slight hesitation, answered, "Nothing. I just need to know if the problems in Kenya will interfere with our trip."

His response didn't fool Oliver. There was more to Edward's tension than fretting about the holiday. "Sean says it's all sorted. Slight change of venue for the first few days."

"That's all? Have you listened to the news?" Edward snapped back. "Penny's been onto me three times today, asking if we'll have to cancel."

Sean arrived a few minutes later.

Edward waved the menu at him. "Can we order? I'm pressed for time."

The waiter was called and took their orders.

Sean said once that was done. "I'm guessing you've been following the news. The attack in Nairobi is still ongoing. But I've had a chat with Sandra and confirmed all the alterations to our plans. We won't be near any danger spots. I double checked with the airline. No refunds are possible, so if you decide you can't go, you lose your money."

"If Martin thinks we'll be safe, that's enough for me." Oliver said as he put his wineglass down. "Kim won't back out either. She's a wedding fanatic, and won't let some bloody terrorist win, especially after it's taken so long for Martin to find a wife."

Sean shook his head. "Keep your fingers crossed. He hasn't asked her yet."

"What?" Oliver couldn't believe that Martin could leave his proposal this late.

"Typical Martin. His commitment phobia is clearly still in place." Edward said. "Penny's worked up about security, but like Kim, she has no intention of missing a wedding."

"What does Fay have to say?" Oliver asked.

Sean made a weird face. "Fay isn't coming. She found out about Vanessa. and moved out. We're heading for divorce. So far, everything is friendly, and she says she wants nothing from the house, because she doesn't want to mess up the children's lives more than necessary."

"I've heard that before. Be wary, everything can seem sweet until the lawyers get involved." Edward said.

"No, I really think she means it. She says she likes Vanessa, after all she introduced us. Though I can't see their friendship surviving."

"How have the kids taken it?" Edward said as he cleared the last of his lasagne off his plate.

"Rosie's kicking off about coming to Kenya."

"I thought she was really keen on the idea." Edward pushed his empty plate away and put some money on the table to cover his tab.

"It's not the holiday that's bugging her. She doesn't like the idea that Vanessa is coming with us. Matthew's not happy, he's jacked in his college plans, and is heading off on some hare-brained gap year, intending to cycle his way as far round the world as he can go."

"Might be the making of him." Oliver hoped that this might help Sean accept Matthew was growing up.

"Sorry I have to dash." Edward pushed his chair away from the table. "Let me know of any developments."

"What's up with him?" Sean said as they watched him go. Oliver shrugged.

"Who knows? Maybe he's prosecuting someone and doesn't have enough evidence to make it stick. You know him, letting his job get to him. I'm more interested in why you need a covert address?" Sean asked.

"I told you; I was expecting some mail that I didn't want Kim to see."

"And here I was thinking you had succumbed to that lovely receptionist."

Oliver smiled. Nice one Sean. Sally would die of embarrassment if she knew Sean thought she was the significant interest in his life. Still, easier to let Sean think that than start a lengthy explanation.

"Just because you have an ongoing affair doesn't mean everyone does the same. How come you never mentioned Vanessa was coming with us until now?"

"I wasn't sure she'd come, but I finally convinced her it was a good idea. She's worried a new face might change the dynamics. Ridiculous idea."

Oliver said nothing. Fay, Kim and Penny had become close friends over the years, and they might find it odd accepting a replacement for Fay. He'd find out soon enough.

CHAPTER 6

London - Monday 23rd September 2013

Edward Standish was under pressure from several fronts. He'd spent the best part of a week arguing with his colleagues against proceeding with a prosecution case, trying to convince them there was not enough evidence to take the case to court.

The terror attack in Kenya had put the family holiday in jeopardy. And to top that, lunch with Sean and Oliver had slashed the time allocated for his planned farewell with Lauren.

He was halfway through his plate of lasagne when his mobile buzzed with a message. He skimmed the text, his heart sinking. Lauren. How the hell could he convince her this was not what he wanted?

"I've got to go," he said as he wolfed down the rest of his food. "Something has come up at work." A lie, but he needed an excuse to get over to her and stop her before she did something stupid.

Nothing with Lauren was easy. And even harder when Penny was continually sending texts about the holiday.

"I'm going to miss you," Lauren said as she stretched out on the bed and poured herself another glass of champagne. "Want some?"

Edward shook his head. He had to convince Penny it was safe to go to Kenya. Her latest text had been yet another, expressing her concerns. The last thing he wanted to do was to discuss his family holiday with Lauren.

The safari was one event he didn't want to miss. He couldn't back out. Not if he wanted an amicable divorce. Which was unlikely to be as uncomplicated as Sean and Fay's break up appeared to be.

Hearing Vanessa would come to Kenya instead of Fay came as a shock. He tried to imagine the reaction he'd get if he took Lauren on holiday instead of Penny.

That thought jolted him in the reality of his affair.

Lauren lay back in a most seductive pose as he dressed. He'd fallen prey to this move before. He turned away from her and concentrated on his shoelaces.

"My friend who works in an estate agent told me there's a fantastic flat coming on the market next week. I've arranged a viewing," she said.

How could he stop her? "I've already told you I can't commit to anything. If Penny gets wind of anything like that, she'll make me pay."

"Bloody Penny," Lauren muttered quietly, but not so quietly that he didn't hear. Her catty tone worried him.

"I have children to think of." He grabbed his jacket and keys, eager to escape before Lauren became clingy.

She eased herself off the bed, flung on a silky kimono, and blocked his exit. He kissed her and firmly put his hand on the door handle. He was leaving.

She followed him into the corridor, clutching his arm while he waited for the lift, and kissed him as the ancient contraption rattled its way up the building. It arrived, and the grill opened.

"Hi Vanessa," Lauren said enthusiastically to the raven-haired woman half hidden behind a huge oblong canvas she was trying to manipulate out of the lift. Bulky carrier bags hooked over her wrist hindered her. The soft rope handle of one of her packages caught on the door handle, and as she tried to untangle it, another bag split, scattering the contents all over the floor.

Edward wedged his foot in the lift door to stop it sliding shut on her, and automatically reached in and unhooked the shopping bag from the door handle. Meanwhile, Lauren took the canvas from her and propped it against the wall. They all bent down to pick up the scattered possessions. The painting was exquisite. He recognized the style with no need to be told the name of the artist. Vanessa Somerville. Then he caught her looking directly at him with a slightly puzzled expression.

His secret blown. He'd been so careful. The truth was out. He smiled. Of all the people to find out, Vanessa was probably the best. Discretion was her forte. Her affair with Sean had been very discreet. With Lauren wearing a skimpy kimono, pretending their relationship was different wouldn't work.

"Vanessa, this is Edward, the man I told you about. Vanessa's my new neighbour. She's just moved into the fabulous studio flat on the corner."

His heart sank. What had Lauren said about him?

Vanessa freed one hand and stuck it out to shake his. "Nice to meet you," she said, without a flicker of recognition. He liked that. Though it felt deceitful, especially knowing she was coming on holiday with Sean and the rest of the gang that week.

"Love the painting," he said, hoping that it would show her he was happy not to admit they were already old friends.

"Getting it ready for an exhibition in the new year."

"I'll take you." Lauren said with enthusiasm.

Edward nodded. No need to tell Lauren that he already had an invitation to the exhibition. Or that he already owned three of Vanessa's paintings. He stepped into the lift, waved, and hastily pulled the outer gate shut before Lauren had time to smother him with kisses, slammed the inner gate closed and pressed the button to descend.

The encounter left him feeling ashamed of his affair. While no one else had known, it had been fun. But could the relationship survive the pressure of going public? He doubted it could. He'd met Vanessa often enough, and had known about her affair with Sean for years, without it changing his relationship with Sean and Fay.

As he stepped outside, he realized that the difference was that Vanessa never made public displays of affection. He didn't think Lauren was capable of such restraint.

On the way home, he compared the two women, and with each comparison, he became less happy with his relationship with Lauren. He had to end it before it turned more complicated than it was. He pulled over into a lay-by and called her.

Her phone went straight to her message service. He hesitated. He could hardly dump her in a message. "Lauren, about that flat... For God's sake, do nothing until we've talked." He disconnected and drove on. He was a fool. The sex was great. But was it enough?

CHAPTER 7

London - Monday 23rd September

Penny Standish tore at her fingernails as she waited to be called into Doctor McKinnon's office. She winced as she realized she had gone far enough to draw blood.

She rummaged in the cavernous red bag Edward had given her for her birthday. Why he thought she needed something so vast was beyond her. He said it would be useful for travelling, especially for their pending trip to Kenya. Unconvinced, but not wanting to appear ungrateful, she didn't remind him that a neat, unobtrusive purse just large enough for essentials was more her style. Instead, lumbered with this monstrosity, filled with an accumulation of stuff that had amassed surprisingly quickly. She could lose an army, tanks, and all in it. She dug out a tissue to dab the offending nail, just as she was called to get her test results.

Doctor McKinnon greeted her warmly. He had been her doctor for years. The lack of sparkle in his eyes told her the news was bad.

"I thought you were bringing your husband with you today," he said.

"He doesn't need to know."

He held her hand. "I'm sorry, but I think he does."

She wanted to pull away. Walk out of the office and keep walking. Those few words confirmed her fears.

"The results are worse than expected," he said, almost whispering, as if that would make it less painful. He nudged her towards a seat, and continued, "You have an aggressive cancer." He paused, giving her time to take in this news. "I've organized for you to go in for surgery. The earliest date I can get so far is for Thursday next week."

"No," she answered. "Not then. We're going away for three weeks. And I'll have to organize the kids when I get back."

"Penny, this is serious. You shouldn't delay."

"I have to."

"Why?" he asked, peering at her over his half glasses. "What is more important than your health?"

"My sanity..." she said, the words coming out before she realized what she was saying.

His eyebrows lifted, and he settled into his chair as if he had all day to listen. "Explain."

Where should she begin? Did her suspicions that her husband was having an affair with the woman responsible for the massive shiny red bag at her feet matter? He'd only ever bought flowers and chocolates in all the years they had been married. Never something as expensive or as unwanted.

Her delay in replying prompted him to ask, "Why can't you put this holiday off?"

"It's an annual event. Edward and his two friends, Oliver and Sean, have holidayed together for twenty years. They take turns choosing a destination and making the bookings."

"So, where are you heading that's so special you can't postpone?"

"Kenya."

"Is it safe with that terrorist attack still in the news?"

"Shocking isn't it?" she answered. "But as a group, we've decided that terror attacks can happen anywhere in the world, and changing our plans makes them more successful. They've adjusted our itinerary to avoid

Nairobi. Edward's friend who lives out there will make sure we are well away from any trouble. They've been planning this trip for over a year."

"Kenya, I went there years ago. An amazing place."

"We'll be on safari most of the time, then staying on a conservation ranch near Mount Kenya. The children are so excited, I can't let them down."

Doctor McKinnon shook his head. "I understand. But I'd better tell you more about your operation and treatment."

She listened carefully as he outlined what to expect. None of it sounded pleasant. In fact, the whole thing was terrifying. He gave her a handful of leaflets for her and Edward to read in case she forgot what he had told her.

"I am sure Edward will want you to be treated as soon as possible."

"I won't tell him until we get back."

"Why not?"

"I can't wreck everyone's holiday by mentioning the big C word. Can you imagine the fuss they'll make? It would be unbearable. And, if it is as bad as you are making out, I want the children to have happy memories of me as I am now. If the truth comes out, they'll all turn into gibbering fools."

Doctor McKinnon rubbed his chin. "Maybe you're right. The extra weeks with the family might be beneficial, as long as you eat well and build up your strength." He paused and wrote furiously on his prescription pad. "Start taking these straight away. They'll help ease the discomfort, and the others will help build you up for the operation. Promise me you'll take them."

"I will."

"Good. I'll fix a date for the week you come back. I don't want to leave it any longer. The operation and the treatment afterward will be harsh. You'll need lots of support." He looked at her with an intensity that made her shift her position. "How are the boys?"

"Growing fast," she answered, nearly added growing away, which was closer to the truth, and her own fault. She had always encouraged them to be self-sufficient, which made them distant from their father. Something she had to put right. They needed to be more connected. Especially if her illness got the better of her.

Now she wished she hadn't missed so much of their childhood. She had returned to work in a local family law practice six weeks after the boys were born. Edward worked long hours too. She adored the children, and often she felt that she almost preferred spending time alone with them rather than with Edward. She had an au pair to help her, though she tried to collect them from school at least three days a week herself, and either her parents or Edward's parents helped on the other two days. Edward got the occasional moment alone with them at weekends.

Tears welled up. The fear of death made her realize how disconnected she had let Edward become from her and his own children. When she first guessed he was having an affair, she had been angry, then she had been philosophical about it. She hadn't put enough effort into the marriage, so it was hardly surprising he had sought comfort elsewhere.

"Edward and I have things to sort. The holiday will enable that."

If she died, someone else would take her place. What a scary thought. Fay was a perfect example of someone doing just that. She stepped in when Sean's first wife died and took charge of his two children. Heaven knows how they would have coped if she hadn't been willing to help. Thinking about that made her even more determined to ensure her family was in the strongest position possible to cope. Yes, it would be nice to think they would notice her absence, but she also needed to feel they could move on.

More terrifying was having to tell her parents. She wasn't sure which she dreaded the most. Her mother turning into an overzealous helpful fiend, trying to fight everything with every ounce of strength, or refusing to talk about it, while rallying round seeing to the children and monitoring Edward.

Edward's parents would most likely stay aloof, as they always had. Their behaviour was probably the reason Edward had so easily become disconnected from the boys. She was pleased that he didn't follow his father's example of pushing the boys all the time. They were competitive enough without encouragement. Edward was quite good at calming them down, taking some of the fierceness out of their challenges. His relationship with his father had always struck her as being very formal. He was not the type to have ever given him a hug, nor was his mother, though she had softened since the twins arrived. Penny had seen the joy on her face when the boys gave her a hug. The most contented she had ever seen her was when one of them fell asleep on her lap while the other rested his head against her arm, enjoying the proximity of uncomplicated love. Penny felt it unlikely that Edward's father ever gave the poor woman a hug. Maybe this illness would make Edward a closer and more tactile dad than she had let him be.

The more she thought about the family, the more her fear of death diminished. She would fight the disease with everything she could. Take the medications given and rest when she had to. And even give up her work to fight it. But more important, she'd get her family behaving as a unit, rather than four individuals, living in shared space.

CHAPTER 8

London - Monday 23rd Sept

Kim Weatherby squashed the lid of the suitcase down. She had packed too much. She flipped it open again, knowing she would have to be ruthless. Oliver would have a fit if she took an extra bag. The children's rucksacks were just big enough to hold their toys.

Motherhood made her want to cover all contingencies for the whole family. Especially when they were heading to a destination she knew little about, and one currently suffering from terrorist activity. Sometimes she felt she should have a separate 'just in case' case. Then she could happily shove in warm clothes, cool clothes, medicines, books to read, paper, paints, cards, sun hats, goggles, and enough sunscreen to cover an elephant. It was easier for her when it was Oliver's turn to choose the destination because she invariably ended up making the arrangements, which gave her more control.

The doorbell rang. She was happy to have a distraction from the paring down task, so hurried downstairs to answer it.

"Fay, what a lovely surprise," she said, as she gave Fay a hug. "I didn't expect to see you before we left. Sean said he'd see us at the airport, just before the check-in desk opens."

Fay pulled away, shaking her head. "He hasn't told you?"

"Told us what?"

"I'm not going to Kenya with you."

"What? Is someone ill?"

"No. Sean and I are getting divorced."

Kim was stunned. "You're kidding."

"No. But I'm angry that he didn't say something sooner. I assumed you'd call, but remembered you were busy with your exams. How did they go?"

"Better than I expected."

"When do the results come out?"

Kim couldn't believe Fay could drop a bombshell about divorce and be asking about her results. "Two weeks' time."

"I'm sure you'll pass. I'm so glad you went for that extra qualification. It will make a difference to your getting back into midwifery on your terms. What does Oliver think?"

"I haven't told him yet."

"I hope he appreciates your decision when you do. Anyway, back to Sean. I guess he hadn't had the courage to say anything."

"He might have said something to Oliver, but I've hardly seen him for days. Though he's usually good about passing on news." She pulled her friend inside and closed the door. "Come on in and tell me all about it."

Fay dumped her bag and coat on the chair in the hall, peered at her reflection in the mirror on the wall, fluffed up her hair with her fingers, and followed Kim. She perched on a stool alongside the swish breakfast bar that the kitchen designer had insisted would be invaluable, but rarely used. Kim filled the coffee machine, took out mugs, sugar, and milk, and then dug in the cupboard for chocolate biscuits, in case comfort food was required. Maybe Fay could do with something stronger than coffee.

"Sorry, I should have asked. Would you prefer a stiff drink?"

Fay smiled. "No, coffee is fine. I'm driving anyway." She waved her arm round. "Great make-over."

Kim shrugged. She liked the old kitchen, which was more than adequate for their needs. But Oliver, who never cooked, had been keen to have it extended and modernized. She gave up arguing with him over all the unnecessary gadgets he insisted on having included. She was still getting used to it. "Yes, Oliver's golfing friend designed it."

The machine burbled on and on. Kim contained her desired to dig for details. Fay would open up when she was ready. She filled their mugs and tore open the biscuit packet.

Fay hesitated, then with a guilty smile, reached out and took one. "I'm glad I came. I hope that Sean and I breaking up won't mess with our friendship."

"Of course, it won't. We've shared too much together to let that happen."

"Good, because I need your help."

"I'll do what I can," Kim answered, hoping that Fay's request would be reasonable.

"Look out for Rosie for me." Tears filled Fay's eyes. Kim could see that she was attempting to blink them back. "Leaving Sean was inevitable. But abandoning Rosie and Matthew after twelve years is heart-wrenching."

Kim reached out and touched her hand. "Of course it is. How did they take the news?"

Sean's children had been so small when their mother Jean died. Fay had stepped in and been there for them, and in due course Sean married her. Kim often wondered if Fay would have liked children of her own, but had never dared to ask.

"Not well. Matthew ditched his college plans and has set off on a cycle ride that will take about a year.

He's going with three quite sensible lads, so I'm not as worried about him as I am about Rosie."

"She's always been the sensitive one."

"Yes, and worse this year. She started self-harming. At first, I pretended I hadn't noticed. I tried to get her to talk. That failed, so I admitted I knew about the cuts. She still won't open up to me, or agree to talk to a professional. Sean's not listening. He's convinced she'll grow out of it. Probably because it's easier than finding a solution."

"Any chance of you patching things up with Sean?" Kim asked.

"No way. I expect Vanessa will move in after the holiday. You remember her, my artist friend?"

Kim gulped and reached for another biscuit. "Vanessa Somerville, the one who painted that picture?" She pointed to the picture over the fireplace.

"Yes, that's the one. He first met her at a charity event for the hospital about six years ago. We had been friends for years. Strangely, I don't blame her for our bust up. Things have been horribly wrong at home for ages. It was bound to happen. Sean sleeping with Vanessa was the least of my problems."

"What does Rosie think of her?"

Fay sipped her coffee and after a pause answered, "Difficult to say. Rosie's blanking me. I know she's met Vanessa in the past. But I'd say she's indifferent. Yes, that would probably describe it best. Trouble is, she has become indifferent to just about everything. Maybe Vanessa will get through to her better than I can."

"When did all this happen? Why didn't you tell me there were problems?"

"I guessed a long time ago and pretended I didn't know until Matthew lost his temper and thought it was his duty to tell me. I didn't tell Sean that I knew. Instead, I looked for somewhere to live. I wanted to control my departure. A month ago, I found a lovely flat close to the hospital and packed my bags and left. I didn't have the strength to make a fuss. He's moved on. I'm glad for him. He deserves to find some happiness. It's silly. Faking ignorance allowed me to keep living in the house. But after Mathew's comments, I couldn't carry on."

"I sometimes worry about Oliver and his secretary." Kim confessed. "Have you seen her?"

"No, but Oliver never would."

"Sweet of you to say so. But he's behaving oddly at the moment. Something is up. I can't figure out what."

"Maybe he just needs a holiday."

"What about you? You helped plan it all. It must feel odd not to be coming. What are you going to do? We shall miss you."

"Thanks. Don't worry, I'll be fine. I'm going to use the time off to redecorate my flat."

CHAPTER 9

Nairobi - Sunday 22nd September

Martin hated leaving Enuto out there watching the mystery man while he had to dress up in his jacket and tie, and sit through dinner with Hank and Beverley. It was the price he had to pay to get access to the drive with his photos on.

When the meal finished, he excused himself and went to his room. He needed sleep, but scrolling through the mass of images came first. He had to find out where he'd seen that man.

If he'd photographed him, it had to have been somewhere in Africa. That limited him to folders of pictures taken in Egypt, Sudan, Ethiopia, Somalia, and Kenya. The man had distinctive Somali features, but Martin's time in Somalia had been brief, so it didn't take long to eliminate the Somali folder. Next, he checked the Kenya folder relating to trips up to the refugee camps on the northern border. It took him nearly an hour of scrutiny to find the image he wanted. Yes, the man was there, much younger, and not threatening.

Happy to have solved the mystery, he'd get a couple of hours' sleep before setting out again. He set his alarm clock and lay on the bed. His mind was racing through the range of emotions he had experienced since the first inkling of trouble in Nairobi. The initial surge of adrenaline that made him agree to cover the story had evaporated. Being unable to enter the mall spared him from the gory aspects of the siege, for which he was grateful.

Calls to Sandra and touching the everyday normality of life helped him face the assignment. Without her calm presence, he would never have come this far.

He woke in a sweat, long before the alarm. He fired up the computer and took another look at the photos.

He studied the picture more intently. His quarry might look innocent enough, but his companions worried him. They also looked familiar. Martin switched devices and replayed the news footage of the mall attack on his iPad.

One terrorist, captured on screen, and currently in the supermarket in the Mall was in the photo taken at the refugee camp. More alarming, the man next to him dredged up a distant memory of a man in Egypt, who supposedly beheaded a journalist.

He had to share this information. These were important links. He studied the refugee camp photo more carefully. Cropped the facial images and blew them up. After committing their faces to memory, he sent a copy to his phone. He would find Enuto and Barnard and show them the pictures he'd saved, then delete them. It was the least he could do to keep them alert and safe.

It bothered him he'd never made the connection when he took the photo at the refugee camp. How had he been so unobservant? He thought back to that trip. Hank insisted on the trip to the camps. He wanted an article about the best way to improve conditions for the refugees. At the first camp, the people, especially the children, seemed happy. At the second, everyone, including the children, had stayed aloof and avoided eye contact. The third camp was the worst. Hostile vibes, even from the children, shocked him. That feeling of wanting to escape had hit, a feeling he was sure he shared with the camp inmates. The man he'd seen outside the mall was in the pictures taken at the second camp.

Normally, seeing a refugee in the crowd wouldn't be a cause for concern, but the way he'd dodged the camera was suspicious. Was he in contact with the hostage takers inside the Mall? Did he pose a further threat?

Who should he inform? Who would take it seriously? The Kenyan armed forces and police were unlikely to make use of the information. The Brits were a better option. Or should he try the Americans, though they were possibly too gung-ho for his liking?

Martin needed to gather more evidence before the man got spooked. Find out where he went and who he met. Hank could figure out who should know what he'd found.

He had to warn Enuto and Barnard that they were tailing a dangerous man. It was unfair to involve them otherwise.

He emailed Hank, attached copies of the photos taken in Somalia along with the clearest picture of the suspect Enuto was following, asking him to decide which agencies to share the information with. He needed to travel light so selected a small camera, one that would validate his press pass, and left his room. The man on duty at the desk called for a taxi.

Even though it was still dark, the traffic was crawling. But at least it was moving. Police blocks stopped traffic heading to the mall. Diverting them away from the area. So, he paid off the driver and walked the rest of the way. Despite the effective cordon round the complex, there were a lot of onlookers. He used the tracking mode on his phone to locate Enuto as he didn't want to march up to him, in case the man they were following saw them talking. Once he spotted him, he kept well back, searching for Enuto's mark, assuming he would be within visual range.

The increase in the number of troops and policemen on the surrounding roads made him sure they'd be launching an assault on the building soon.

Tension was mounting. There were still a huge number of people unaccounted for, which was the excuse given for not going in. Sporadic gunshots were a reminder that the men inside were unlikely to give up without a fight.

Martin moved closer and made eye contact with Enuto. A slight hand gesture showed him where Barnard stood. A second gesture to a spot well beyond Barnard, to the man standing by a tea seller's stall.

Martin moved to stand beside Enuto. “Treat him like a wounded buffalo,” he said, without looking directly at him. “It's important to find out if he is working with anyone else.”

He found the photo on his phone and showed it to Enuto. “Look out for these men. If you see any of them, send me a text with the letter x in it.”

Enuto grinned, as if raising the stakes made the job more interesting. He signed that he'd swap places with Barnard so Martin could show him the pictures.

“I'll be close by, but not too close,” Martin added. Enuto nodded. No need to clarify that his white skin would make blending in difficult.

Martin waited for Barnard to come, risking a quick look at their quarry. He showed Barnard the photo on his phone and gave him the same instructions as he had given Enuto. He then backed away, but kept Barnard in sight.

The Somali man drank his tea, then moved again. Could he have been calculating the number of troops gathering to enter the building? Everyone was expecting the order to be given. There was a fresh flurry of activity as men in more formal uniforms arrived. These were the decision makers.

But their mystery man was heading away from the mall. Martin nodded to Enuto. Time to go. Enuto waved his fighting stick and set off. Barnard followed him.

Enuto had spent time in Nairobi, but Martin expected this man to go to areas neither tracker had ever been to. His initial route took them on familiar ground towards Parklands.

Dawn was breaking as they followed each other, keeping as far apart but maintaining visual contact.

Enuto stopped briefly under a magnificent old Jacaranda tree, the ground carpeted in mauve blossom. On another day, Martin would have stopped to take a photo. Today, his focus was on Enuto. Half a mile further on, Enuto gave the bush tracker signal to stop.

Martin leaned against a wall in the shadow of a tree trunk and waited. He knew he must contact Sandra to acknowledge her birthday. He longed to speak to her, but sent a text instead, keeping the message brief enough to show her he was thinking of her, then put his phone on mute.

Barnard took Enuto's place, and Enuto went ahead.

Martin ducked into the gateway of a temple. Sandra had taken him there once to see a Ragoli exhibition. The intricacy of the pictures created on the floor of the hall, using coloured sand, was astounding. There had been a raised platform to enable visitors to look down on the artwork.

Barnard set off again, and Martin followed. They were heading towards Ngara.

It wasn't long before Martin had attracted a group of begging children. Giving them something would only bring more, and with them, unwanted attention. He sent a blank text to Barnard, who slowed and looked back. Martin spotted an Indian sweetshop, which would be a good stopping place. He chased off the children and entered the premises, making sure Barnard saw him go in. He scanned the shop. There were chairs and tables on one side of the room, and a TV streaming the news in the corner. He ordered tea and a bun and asked if he could sit and watched the news.

The shop owner served him and talked about the terrible situation at Westgate. Martin listened, letting the man pour out how the community felt about the situation.

He was unstoppable, recounting how his neighbours got caught in the crossfire, with full details of their lucky escape and their treatment at the hospital.

Martin nodded and didn't respond. He didn't want to get too embroiled in conversation and was glad when some fresh customers arrived, and the man moved to serve them and repeated his conversation, leaving Martin alone to watch the news on the television. Martin ordered a second cup of tea and another of their rather sickly buns. This was the perfect place to wait for Enuto or Barnard to report back.

The shop probably rarely had European customers, but he was less out of place here than outside. The news on the screen showed troops ready to move into the mall. Reports of explosions and images of smoke billowing out of the building were no comfort.

Enuto sent a blank text. Martin quickly checked his phone to see what he had sent. Two pictures, one a house doorway, the second a shop which helped mark the location. Clever touch, to ensure visual context.

As Martin finished his tea, there was another message, a photo of an unknown man leaving the building.

They were on the move. Hank did well to connect the tracking devices. Martin could plot their movements on their phone. He wondered what to do. What action had Hank taken when he got the email and pictures?

His phone vibrated. The caller, Sandra. Unsure he could cope if she turned down his proposal, he ignored the call. He needed to be somewhere private to face that conversation.

CHAPTER 10

Ol Essakut - Monday 23rd September.

Sandra had another restless night. The baby was more active than ever. She tried sitting up and lying flat. Nothing helped. Eventually she got up, sat on the sofa with her feet up, and read. But concentration was missing. All she could think about was Martin.

He had been good about calling her often, but on his last call, she picked up more tension than had been there during his earlier calls. She put it down to exhaustion, certain he hadn't slept since he'd left, and had been relieved to hear he was staying at the club overnight.

Hank had been kind enough to keep her up to date on his activities. She was sure he was feeling guilty about dragging Martin away when she was close to giving birth.

At six, she received a text from Martin wishing her a happy birthday, along with an apology for not making it back in time.

Small consolation that he remembered; she'd rather hear his voice than get an impersonal text. She called him back, thinking he must have been worried about waking her. His phone went straight to message mode.

At seven, the children burst into the room and started singing. Sam and Emma never ceased to amaze her with their joyful approach to life. She had fallen in love with them the moment she met them. They arrived ahead of Juma and Wanjiru, who carried in a celebration breakfast for her to have in bed. Everyone was trying to make the day special because Martin was absent.

The children put presents on the bed beside her. There was an envelope addressed to her on the tray that Juma had put on a side table. The desire to snatch it up and open it had to be put aside. The children's gifts took priority. She took the two presents, shook them. No rattle. She smelt them. No smell. Choosing which to open first a dilemma. There was a solution.

"Eeny, meeny, miny mo, catch an elephant by his toe. If he trumpets, let him go. Eeny, meeny, miny, mo." As the rhyme ended, she had her hand on the most tightly wrapped of the two parcels. Which of the twins was most excited by her choice? Emma. She took her time; unsure how fragile the gift might be. Multiple layers of paper came off, then a layer of padding. A beautiful clay model of a mongoose emerged. She was speechless. All she could do was reach out and pull Emma close to kiss her to show her appreciation.

How had she missed knowing they were so talented? Sam was fidgeting beside her, desperate to see her reaction to his gift. She unwrapped it as fast as she could and found an amazing model of a bushbaby. They were both so artistic and had amazing teachers who encouraged them.

Finally, she picked up the bulging white envelope with her name written on it. She prised it open and saw the velvet-covered box. Stop. Read the letter first. She pushed the envelope with the box under the covers and distracted the children by suggesting they try one of Juma's banana muffins.

While they focused on food, she read the note.

Dear Sandra,

Please picture me on bended knee because that is how I planned this birthday surprise. I have taken the precaution of preparing this in case I get held up in Nairobi. I wish I was there with you.

I've taken a long time to find the courage to ask, but I'm asking now. Please, marry me on Saturday 12th October.

I love you. And I hope you'll understand that I don't have time to write more while Hank is stomping around waiting for me.

All my love

Martin

Her hand shook as she pushed the sheet of paper back into the envelope.

Jenny's arrival provided the distraction she needed. She slipped the letter under the covers, hoping that no one would notice.

Jenny hugged the children.

"Have you seen these gorgeous figures?" Sandra pointed to the two clay animals.

Jenny lavished praise on the children and begged them to make something for her. Jenny had adopted the role of grandmother to the twins, and it was a joy to have her share the occasion. General chit chat, and eating her breakfast gave Sandra a moment to let the message from Martin sink in.

She was struggling to decide whether she was pleased or terrified by his proposal.

Then Emma pointed out that she hadn't shown them her other present.

She smiled at the children. "Oh, it wasn't a present. It's a pair of earrings your father promised to get mended for me ages ago." Lying to the children didn't sit well with her, but she needed them to believe her.

"Can I see?" Emma begged.

"Not now." Sandra answered, putting her hand over the partially hidden envelope. "You can see them when you get home this evening. Hurry or you'll be late for school. Jacob is waiting for you."

After they'd gone, Jenny queried, "Earrings?"

Sandra sensed from her expression that she detected the lie.

Sandra prised open the lid. Inside, tucked safely in place, was a magnificent diamond ring. She snapped the box shut, wanting to jump for joy, but something made her hesitate. She'd turned him down years ago. And it made sense that he would want to marry her now she was having his child. But fear marred her joy. Would this assignment bring back all those terrible memories? And if it did, would he still want to marry her?

A week ago, or a year ago, she'd have said yes without hesitation.

Right now, she wasn't sure. Yesterday, when he called, he'd sounded distant. Had he regretted leaving this letter for her, or worse, was he falling apart again? Could she help him if he did? Did she have the strength?

Previously, when he'd proposed to her, she hadn't been ready to commit to anyone. Her brief marriage to Nick left her with serious trust issues. Martin understood and accepted that she needed time to adjust to the legacy Nick had entrusted to her.

It had taken a couple of years before she agreed to move into Martin's family home and bring his children to live there. She was glad that they had chosen early on to admit that Martin was Sam and Emma's father, rather than continue the lie that Nick was their father. Their mother had married Nick and later told him he wasn't their father. She died shortly afterwards, and he kept their paternity secret. He'd even set up a trust for the children and made Sandra the controlling trustee, to ensure the children would one day inherit the Ol Essakut estate, which included land that belonged to their mother's family. All of which was now a major share of the Ol Essakut Conservation project.

"He's proposed?" Jenny said, as she poured herself a cup of tea. "I thought he might."

Sandra managed a nod.

"Will you accept?"

Trust Jenny to be forthright.

"I don't know. I'm afraid. He sounded so odd on the phone yesterday. I'm not sure I can decide until this baby is born."

"You think this assignment will bring back the nightmares?"

"Maybe, and I don't think I could cope if it does."

"You could say you want to give your answer face to face. That will give you breathing space. Meanwhile, I'll find you a pair of earrings to put in that box. I have a pair that will fit."

Jenny always found solutions to problems. It was hard to work out when Jenny had not been there for them.

Sandra had been so happy when she agreed to move from her house in Nanyuki and live with them at Chui farm. Having Jenny close and involved with the family as they grew helped everyone. The children adored her, and so did everyone on the estate.

Jenny wasn't the sort to sit around doing nothing. She was marvellous at supervising the children's homework and took on training the housekeeping staff and the guides who worked at the various camps run by the conservation project. She was always willing to act as hostess, with the knack of making even the most travel weary guest, feel relaxed and at home with their new surroundings.

With the breakfast over, Sandra had time to reread the letter and let the proposal sink in. Of course, she wanted to marry him. But the fear that this assignment would mess with his head wouldn't go away.

Jenny was right. Delay things by saying she'd give him the answer in person.

She was contemplating getting up when Hank called.

“Have you heard from Martin today?”

“I had a text early this morning, but he has either run out of charge, or he's switched his phone off. When I tried to call him back, it went straight to message.”

Hank muttered, “Fool must have forgotten to switch it back on.” Something in his tone was unconvincing, and it scared her.

CHAPTER 11

Nairobi - Tuesday 25th September.

The sweetshop in Ngara became Martin's sanctuary. The owner Jaz had come over and sat with him and quizzed him. He could tell that Martin was trying to be unobtrusive, but told him that a white man in this area was too unusual for it to go unnoticed. “Tell me why you're here, and I'll see if I can help.”

Martin confessed he was a journalist and admitted he was trying to follow someone.

“Connected with the trouble at the mall?”

Martin shrugged. “Maybe.”

“In that case, you can sit upstairs. There's a window that looks out on the street. No one will bother you. I'll send a message to your friend and tell him where you are. Better not to go out there until after dark.”

Martin had wondered if the kind gesture was more about his local customers being put off by a white man in his shop, or because he suspected Martin would prefer to remain invisible in this predominantly African quarter of town.

He'd noticed the connection between Martin and the two Samburu men outside. And offered to have food and drink taken to them.

As it got closer to nightfall, he asked the shopkeeper to get him something dark to wear. A dark green hoodie and a pair of black trousers appeared along with some advice.

"If you pretend to be drunk and have a woman with you, you'll be less out of place. My employee, Ester, a hardworking woman who is struggling to survive, might go with you. She's not a prostitute. But she needs money for medicine for her sick child."

Martin couldn't fault his idea. "Can you ask her?"

The man shuffled off and came back smiling. "She's agreed, but says she needs to go home first to check on her family."

Martin agreed and suggested they leave as soon as it was dark.

Martin couldn't believe his luck in choosing this place as a haven. Jaz ushered him through a curtain that led to a room behind the shop and introduced him to Ester, who was obviously nervous about her role. Martin shook her hand, told her how grateful he was, and asked how much she needed for her child's medicine. The figure she mentioned humbled him. It showed how hard life was. He handed her four times the amount and told her he would pay her more for her help later.

She looked at the cash, and her eyes filled with tears. She gripped his hand between hers and muttered, "Asante sana."

The shopkeeper told her to get the medicine to take home when she finished work. He then took Martin upstairs to his family quarters, briefly introduced him to his wife, who was in the kitchen, cooking samosas to sell in the shop below, and led him on into their best room with a tv, sofa and armchairs and a brightly patterned rug.

"You look tired. Rest here and you can watch the news. No one will disturb you."

"You're very kind."

"I'm looking out for myself and the community. And because of what's happening down the road, I'm happy to do anything that might keep my family safe."

The hours of waiting gave Martin time to wonder what Sandra thought of his proposal. He considered calling her, but doubts about his ability to honour his proposal crept in. His mental state, triggered by the incident, and the fact the nightmare had resurfaced the night before, showed him he was still a long way from full recovery. Perhaps he should accept professional help. He prayed for Sandra's understanding. Would she be willing to wait?

He reported back to Hank. with details of where he was. And his plan to stay there until dark.

Before they set off, Martin spoke to the shopkeeper, and gave him cash to give to Ester the next day.

"Please give her what she needs. I don't want her to become prey to greedy neighbours."

"I will make sure she is okay." Jaz answered.

Wearing the baggy clothes the shopkeeper had got for him, he explained to Ester his plan. He didn't want to stand out, and would pretend to be drunk. And assured her he wasn't after sex.

She shrugged, puzzled, but not unhappy. Martin gave her the equivalent of a week's wages. "First, help me find my friend. Then buy some food to take home. Tomorrow," he pointed to the shopkeeper, "he will give you more money." Her eyes widened in disbelief at this news.

She put a clean, well-worn cardigan over her work clothes, and picked up a tatty, woven basket with string handles and waited. She had carried a message to Enuto earlier, so knew exactly where to go.

Enuto was hiding in a doorway near a little kiosk that sold a mix of goods, from soft drinks to cigarettes that one could purchase individually. Cash was tight in the slum. Martin halted beside Enuto and explained he was going with Ester to her house and that he'd be back shortly.

He moved on, letting Ester lead the way, trying to make it look as if he'd drunk too much. She stopped at another little kiosk shop and asked for some posho. The woman serving handed out a tiny bag.

Martin said, “No, give her a big one.” The woman did as he'd instructed and handed over a decent sized bag. Martin hadn't finished. “Tea, sugar, bread and milk. And a Tusker.” A drunk would want booze. Ester didn't complain, but carefully put the items in her basket and let him pay.

They moved on, and he saw Barnard tucked into another doorway. He made his way over to him and pretended to be asking for a light for a cigarette. Ester went to the fruit stall to get what she needed. While he waited for her, he got a quick update from Barnard.

Ester now led him down a tiny alley. They had to stick close to the wall. There was a stinking drain running down the middle. The nauseating stench of rotting food and excrement made him want to gag. Mangy mongrels roamed the paths, and there was a blast of music from a beer seller's stall. They turned into an even narrower passage. The only light came from kerosene lamps that shone from open doors. Some offered a glimpse of a family huddled round a food pot, some had prostitutes in the doorway, offering their services.

Most upsetting was a gang of glue sniffing kids, barely older than ten, who were in a dazed zombie like state. The abject poverty level of this hellhole was the worst he'd ever witnessed in all his years of reporting. What made it worse was that change was unlikely.

Ester took a few more turns to reach her home. It was a corrugated shack with an open drain running past the door. Martin was glad his brief employment would help keep a roof over the heads of her family. She pushed open the door and invited him in. Her three children sat on a low, string bed with a very lumpy looking mattress on it. There was one upright chair, occupied by Ester's cousin, who looked after the children while she worked. She was heavily pregnant herself. The children looked terrified by his presence. He declined her invitation. "Make sure they're okay. I'll wait out here." He heard a rasping cough. It didn't surprise him. In conditions like this, ill health was normal.

While he waited, he got a text from Enuto along with a photo of two unknown visitors entering the house. He tapped on the door. "Can we go?" She gave the children hugs and led him back to the bigger street. As he entered it, he saw Enuto had moved closer to the door that Barnard had been watching. They had obviously swapped roles. And now Martin saw the door opening. Three people emerged, all heading in different directions.

He signalled for Barnard to follow one. Enuto, the next, and pointed that he'd go after the man from the mall.

Martin took a quick shot on his phone camera, sent it to Hank, and quickly deleted it.

"Come," he said to Ester, knowing he needed her to make himself less conspicuous.

The man walked at a fast pace. It was a struggle to keep up. But Martin didn't have a choice. He needed to see where this man went. And hoped that Enuto and Barnard were keeping up with the men they were following.

When they reached a busy road, his quarry stopped and talked to a man in a battered old Peugeot. Martin slowed down and noted the registration number. He had to figure out how he could follow if the man got into it. Someone careered into him. He turned to check that

Ester was okay. Too late. Someone had his hands in his pocket. Pickpockets. He tried to push them away. Another person barged into him, spun him round and landed a punch to his midriff, winding him so badly he doubled up and then a second blow hit him in the face.

He caught a fleeting glimpse of Ester fleeing as his assailant pinned his arms to his sides and dragged him backwards. He struggled, but someone grabbed his legs, and a third person shoved a dusty, foul-smelling bag over his head. They bundled him into a vehicle and piled in to hold him down. He heard the door slide shut. The engine roared, and the vehicle lurched forward so violently he slid backwards, landing against something painfully hard, with his captors' weight pinning him down.

Soon their weight shifted, but not enough to give him freedom of movement, and they bound his hands and feet together with cable ties. The suffocating cover over his head made breathing hard, and he was terrified that if he made a noise, they would tape his mouth shut too. No one said a word throughout the entire episode. He went limp, hoping they would take the bag off his head, but he wasn't sure they noticed or cared.

Lying helpless, he figured he'd need an excuse for being in that neighbourhood, and for following his mystery man.

Stick to the truth. Admit he's a journalist. There was his press card to prove it. Say he recognized the man from a trip to a refugee camp years ago, and wanted to find out how life was treating him since then.

Had Ester got away? Would she tell the shopkeeper what happened to him? Had he put her in danger? What happened to Enuto and Barnard? What had he got them into?

CHAPTER 12

London - Tuesday 24th September

Sean snapped. Rosie, cut it out. I've had enough. I understand you hate getting up early and that you'd rather not be coming. But you are. Get used to the idea. And sorry about the unpacking and repacking. Better for it to happen now than at the airport in front of everyone. Security will be crazy at the moment."

She stared out of the window, her expression hostile.

"If you don't like my choice of radio station, then we will drive in silence." He reached over and hit the off button. Silence was preferable to the hiss and crackle on the station she had tuned into.

The traffic was almost at a standstill. They crawled along. Rosie probably hoped they would miss the flight. She didn't care that he had everyone's travel documents. No one could go anywhere if he didn't get to the airport.

Vanessa was the probable reason for Rosie's attitude. Would seeing her set Rosie off again? Too late, nothing he could do to stop her kicking off at the airport in front of everyone. He hoped for Vanessa's sake she wouldn't. They'd met several times over the last few years, but Rosie had avoided a meeting since Fay moved out.

He should have got them together sooner. Time had been against him. Convincing Vanessa she should come on the trip had taken longer than he expected. Sensing reluctance from Rosie, he'd not mentioned that she'd agreed to join them.

He had been upset at finding out Vanessa had signed the lease for a new studio flat before he'd asked her to move into his house. Was it her way of telling him she wasn't ready? They'd never discussed future arrangements while Fay was around. But since Fay moved out, he'd foolishly expected living together to follow. Was he deluded? Still, getting her coming on holiday with his friends was a step in the right direction. The perfect chance for everyone to get used to the situation.

The traffic stopped moving. Rosie had her earplugs in and was gazing out of the window, her head nodding gently to the rhythm of whatever was playing on her iPod. It seemed anything was preferable to talking to him.

There were moments when her likeness to her mother, Jean, caught him unawares. Rosie had her mother's fine cheekbones, dark wide eyes with sweeping lashes and well arched brows. Her recently dyed hair, black with a few red and deep blue highlights, intended to shock him, failed, as he made no comment. Maybe it was the wrong tactic.

Would Rosie be easier if her mother had been around to guide her? He was certain Jean would have been able to convince her that piercing her eyebrows was not a good idea. He shivered. Thinking about Jean wasn't helping. Her death had sunk him into a deep depression, and he couldn't go there again.

Fay had stepped in and made life easier for Matthew and Rosie. She never tried to replace their mother, but always treated them as if they were her own children.

If anyone was to blame for Rosie being so mixed up, it was himself. He hadn't handled the loss well, but

Fay had held them together and kept the family going. Eventually, he asked her to marry him. It seemed the right thing to do. Fay had put so much into the family. Effort he had taken for granted, so it was hardly surprising she had left. He'd given nothing in return for all her loving gestures to him and his family.

Someone hooted at him. The traffic was moving, and he hadn't noticed. Rosie glared at him, obviously annoyed that he'd drawn attention to them. He put the car in gear and slowly eased forward into the slow crawling mode that required concentration to avoid running into the car in front.

Sean checked his watch again. Twenty minutes delay so far. He was cutting it fine, and still had to abandon the car and get the bus to the terminal. He pulled his mobile out of his pocket and handed it to Rosie.

"Phone Oliver. Tell him we're nearly there."

Rosie reluctantly took the phone. Yanked one of her earpieces out of her ear, and scrolled through the list of numbers until she reached Oliver's.

"Dad said to tell you we are nearly there," she said, with no greeting or trace of concern. "Okay, I'll tell him." She snapped the phone shut. "He says everyone else is there. They'll hold our place in the queue."

Sean reached the motorway exit and was glad he knew his way round the airport. A bus was waiting, so he dropped Rosie and the luggage off and went to search for a parking space.

Rosie had boarded, still plugged in to her iPod. She didn't even look up when he reached his seat.

It didn't take him long to find his friends. They were all together, with a mountain of luggage. Vanessa stood slightly apart. She wasn't the shy type, and it never occurred to him how intimidating being thrust into a well-bonded group might be. She'd met them all before.

They'd attended her exhibitions, but as buyers, not as his partner. He hurried over and gave her a hug.

"Sorry, I never intended to introduce you to everyone like this."

She smiled. "Don't worry. It isn't as if they're total strangers." She pulled away, and said over his shoulder, "Nice to see you, Rosie."

Rosie gave her a withering look and turned away.

Sean knew then Rosie wouldn't play nice, and said a silent prayer, that she wouldn't create an atmosphere that would spoil the holiday.

"Hi. You all remember Vanessa from her exhibitions?"

The adults in the group nodded and smiled in her direction.

Sean opened his briefcase to produce all their tickets.

"I've had a call from Simeon, Martin's friend. He's worried. Martin hasn't proposed to Sandra yet. Please don't mention the wedding until we're sure it's on."

"What the hell's stopping him?" Oliver asked.

"Seems he went to Nairobi to cover the siege at the shopping mall, and has got himself involved in some sort of covert operation chasing after someone he spotted in the crowd."

"Typical Martin." Edward said.

"They've booked a through flight to Mombasa, and Simeon's girlfriend, Amina, will meet us at the coast and help us make plans for our time down there."

Sean handed out the tickets and followed everyone to the check-in desk.

Rosie chose that moment to announce that she needed to find the ladies.

Oliver overheard her and intervened. "Sorry, you'll have to wait for our bags to be checked and weighed. There'll be one in the departure lounge."

Rosie gave him a surly look and dumped her bag onto the scales and hovered by the counter, watching her rucksack disappear through the flaps into the baggage handling area. Sean was relieved to have got this far, put his and Vanessa's bags on the scales. The woman behind the desk scrutinized their documents, wrapped tags on the bags, and was just about to hand him back his passport and papers when Rosie stepped backwards onto his foot. She lost her balance and fell headfirst onto the bags on the scales, kicking Sean's shin on the way down. In the scramble to get herself upright, she used Vanessa's bag for support, squashing it flat. As she righted herself, she shoved the bag down the conveyor belt.

"I'm fine," she said, brushing off the attention that her fall generated, stuck her hands into her jacket pockets and walked away with a smug look. Sean hobbled away from the queue. Rosie stopped to talk to the Edwards sons, Nicholas and Timothy. She took her headphone off, and let them have a quick listen. Seeing her connecting with them was a relief. Maybe she would stop being a surly teen for the duration of their holiday.

With Rosie temporarily distracted, Sean grabbed Vanessa's hand and squeezed it. He needed to make amends for being late and putting her in an awkward situation. He had barely touched her when Oliver's voice, in his firm commanding tone, interrupted.

"Come on. Let's get through security."

Rosie grabbed Sean's free hand and pulled him towards the gate. Vanessa, with an understanding smile, stepped away. Sean loved her for being so undemanding.

Sean never understood why everyone moved when Oliver spoke. The man was a born organizer, being tall, with a deep voice helped. It enabled him to shepherd the group effortlessly, making Sean feel redundant.

Kim kept her children, David and Alice, close to her side, handing out treats so they never complained of being hungry or thirsty. Sean marvelled at her calm approach to motherhood. The children had lost their baby look and turned into mini people. Kim, a beautiful woman, was completely unaware of her effect on men. Oliver was a lucky man.

Penny, who usually helped organize everyone, stood to one side, letting Edward supervise their competitive boys, who were so close in age they were often mistaken for twins. The boys had grown nearly a foot since their last holiday. Now they were all arms and legs and looked set to top Edward's six-foot height. Sean thought Penny looked strained and gaunt. Could Edward be having an affair? He hoped not. He felt a stab of guilt over Fay finding out about Vanessa. But no time to dwell on that now.

Timothy had been born a year after Nicholas, who never let his brother forget he was older. Which created some intense rivalry. Penny seemed immune to their squabbles, while Edward often fed their competitive nature by suggesting challenges for them to compete over. Sean couldn't help thinking that he didn't want to be around when their hormones kicked in and they started dating. Things might get nasty.

Their progress through the airport went smoothly. Sean wished his son Matthew had joined them. His presence might have made Rosie less possessive and given him time to pay attention to Vanessa. Instead, every time he got within two feet of her, Rosie found an excuse to interrupt.

"Dad, can I have a drink?"

"Dad, can you hold this for me?"

"Dad, how much longer before we board?"

He knew he was being played. He had expected her to be difficult, but this was getting to be annoying. Still, ignoring her might create further tension. Pandering to her demands was safer. With luck, she'd get bored and give him a break. On the plus side, he'd noticed that with each of her demands, Vanessa got a sympathetic look from Kim and Penny. He hoped that loyalty to Fay wouldn't make it hard for them to welcome Vanessa to the group.

Finally, it was time to board the plane. Rosie pulled Sean along the aisle and insisted he took the window seat.

"I don't want to look out," she said, plonking herself down in the seat next to him. Sean saw Vanessa being ushered to the seat that Rosie should have taken a couple of rows back. He wanted to protest, but with a shake of her head, Vanessa stopped him. She seemed content to sit on her own. He promised himself to make it up to her when they landed.

Sean was captive in his inside seat, with Rosie's hand luggage on the floor against his feet, making it almost impossible to move. He was grateful when Rosie stuck her earphones in and switched on her music. At least this way they wouldn't argue.

He could hear the younger children being calmed by Kim. Oliver had a seat on the opposite aisle to the family and looked relaxed. Penny and Edward had sensibly separated the boys, who were playing electronic games.

Everyone seemed content, but the group's normal camaraderie was absent.

CHAPTER 13

Nairobi - Tuesday 24th September.

Martin lost track of how long they had been on the road. He could tell they were still close to the city, because of the noise of cars passing, the horns hooting, and the smell of exhaust fumes that penetrated his head covering.

The floor of the van was hard and uneven. Bumps in the road became more and more painful. His hip pressed against a fixing for seats on the floor. Being tightly wedged into the space, he couldn't move to avoid them.

His captors were remarkably quiet, he knew three were involved with bundling him into the van, and as he only heard one door close, and the engine had been running when they pushed him in, it meant there was at least one more person involved, the driver.

He picked up a strong smell of bhang. One of them had lit up. From the grunts the others made, he assumed a joint was being passed around. That's all he needed. A bunch of stoned captors. Maybe smoke would make them loosen up and talk. Possibly even let slip what they intended to do with him.

They hadn't emptied his pockets. Which surprised him. Maybe they only had instructions to pull him off the street. Nothing more. Still, having his phone didn't mean he could use it. Fortunately, it was in silent mode. A habit developed early in his career. A badly timed phone call or the buzz of the vibration could spell danger.

He was glad now that Hank had installed the tracking device. But it would only be useful if Hank was aware something had gone wrong. And what could he do?

They came to a halt. He felt something sharp touch his ribs, and a menacing voice said. "No noise or I kill you." His tone was convincing. Nothing apologetic about it.

The van door slid open. Boxes were being shuffled beside him, and then he heard a thud as something landed on the roadside, followed by angry muffled voices. Someone wasn't happy. He didn't dare move or make a sound.

Suddenly, there was action. The man who held the knife pressed against his rib pulled away to pat his body. He touched the pocket where Martin had his phone. With some shoving and pushing and pulling, he extracted it.

Goodbye to the tracking device, crossed Martin's mind. He was on his own unless they kept the phone in the van. After an argument. The door shut, and they drove on. The knife threat was over for now. He couldn't help but wonder what they had dropped off. Probably miraa, the leafy plant that had become a major trading commodity up and down the country. Miraa had one drawback: it had to be delivered while it was fresh. Chewing the leaves gave a high.

The sound of the wheels changed. They'd left the tarmac and were on a corrugated murram road. The driver slowed down. There was an optimum speed for going over the corrugations to give a smoother ride. This driver hadn't learned that. Then another turning, this time onto an even rougher track. The sort sculpted by rain that had to be taken slowly. The jostling took him close to screaming. After more twists and turns, the vehicle halted. The engine idled, the door slid open, and one man got out. He heard the clank of chain on metal, the squeak of a hinge, and then they moved again. But only for a short distance before the engine stopped.

They unceremoniously yanked him from his cramped position and made him stand up. Then, with a man on either side grasping his elbows, they shoved him forward. The ground was uneven. Tufts of grass and sharp stones made him stumble, but they held him upright.

The screech of a bolt being pulled, and the creak of rusty hinges, made him wonder if he had reached his destination. They led him on. The stench of goats penetrated the stinking bag and filled his nostrils.

The floor in the building was flat. Rough concrete, at a guess. They shoved him against an upright post and threaded a rope around his chest and tied him to it. He had enough clarity of mind to arch his back and breathe in deeply, expanding his chest fully, hoping for a bit of slack when they were done.

With his torso firmly attached to the pole, they emptied his pockets. They took his small camera, and his press pass, and his wallet with only one card in it. A card that had a daily limit set on it. And all the cash he carried. Once that was done, they cut the cable ties that held his hands behind his back. The sound of duct tape being unrolled had him fearing worse was to come. One man held his hands palms upwards with his wrists crossed. They wound tape around his wrist. The man with the tape noticed something under his sleeve. He shoved the sleeve up. Martin heard the sucking of air between the teeth as the man tugged the sleeve back down. They dismissed the silicon bands as worthless.

He continued to wind duct tape around Martin's crossed wrists in every direction to prevent his hands from touching each other. But in such a way that if he put his arm close to his chest, his hands would rest on his shoulders. Martin was grateful the tape was stuck on his sleeves and not on his skin. Next, they bound his ankles together and pushed him down to a sitting position, and anchored his feet to the pole with more rope, forcing his legs into a bent position.

Satisfied he couldn't go anywhere, they left. The door slammed behind them, and the bolt slid home.

What now? He had not fought them. He had stayed calm, but the bag over his head was torture. Not being able to see was bad, but the suffocating feeling was unbearable. Did they have a plan for him?

All he could do was listen. He thought he heard children playing when they'd arrived. But now they were silent. The stink of goats helped identify the bleats and muffled bell sounds. They were close by, probably in a pen near the door. A chicken squawked, followed by a chorus of clucking.

His mouth was dry. Would they bring him something to drink? Or wouldn't they care if he lived or died? A motor engine fired up. It sounded like the one he'd travelled in. But he couldn't be sure.

The noise of the bolt scraping back interrupted his dream. One that had haunted him for years. He was grateful to be pulled out of it before it turned him into a total gibbering wreck. And struggled to recollect where he was. Sweat poured down his face. The coarse material covering it made his skin itch, but he could do nothing about it. A glimmer of light penetrated the sacking over his head. He waited hopefully, praying they would remove the hood. Someone fumbled with the cord behind his neck and yanked the bag off. Temporarily blinded by the torch shining in his eyes, he blinked and tried to focus on his captors and his surroundings.

Someone pressed a cup into one hand. He got it to his lips and took a sip. Water. He drank more.

Who were they? He didn't dare ask. He wanted them to speak first. Maybe then he would get some idea of what they had planned for him. He shivered, as he remembered the man he from the refugee camp, had been with a man who was later involved with the beheading of a hostage. Was he part of this group? Was that going to be his fate? Those thoughts were not helpful. He had to survive. He had everything to live for, a woman he loved, a child on the way and a wedding to get to.

How long could he take sipping water before they'd lose patience? Over the rim of the cup, he watched as a frightened woman approached; she bent down and placed a plate of posho beside him. Would he be able to reach it? Had they considered that? The cup was empty, and the woman took it from his hand and scurried away. Someone was still standing behind him, holding a dim torch. He could hear his breathing. The torch gave enough light to see that the room had a concrete floor, breeze block walls, and a tin roof. He couldn't see any windows. But the mess on the floor, and the stench, was proof that goats had been here.

The woman returned with the cup and placed it beside him and hurried out. The men followed, leaving him in the dark to feed himself.

It took a lot of contorting, to reach the food, and to get it from plate to mouth. Harder was to find and pick up the cup without spilling the contents, to wash down the posho. He ate not because he was hungry, but from fear that he might not get any more, and he needed to maintain his strength. The fact they had brought him food was a good sign. They wanted him alive.

The next visit was at dawn. A minute chink of light told him that the sun was rising. When they opened the door, sunlight flooded in. The man held it open to allow the woman to enter. She brought another plate of posho and a fresh cup of water.

Martin thanked her, and she looked terrified and darted out. He looked at the man with her. He had covered part of his face. The whites of his eyes were yellow rather than white, which was not unusual. He also had that glazed look of a bhang user. Would he speak? Martin decided it was best not to push his luck.

CHAPTER 14

Mombasa - Wednesday 25th September.

During the lengthy delay in Nairobi waiting for their transfer flight to Mombasa, Vanessa sat alone on a hard seat, pretending to read her book while watching the others, trying to figure out the dynamics of the group. So far, they had welcomed her, but in a polite but slightly aloof way. They weren't total strangers. She'd met them before, but never as a substitute for the friend that they were expecting to join them. She didn't envy them. Travelling with children looked like hard work.

She had wondered how Sean's daughter would react to her presence. She hadn't expected her to be visibly hostile, or that she would monopolize her father's attention. The more Rosie succeeded, the harder it became for Vanessa to pretend she didn't mind. Sean barely managed to speak to her since the start of the journey. Her hopes of romance on this holiday were diminishing rapidly.

On the flight to the coast, Rosie won again and insisted Sean sat with her.

At Mombasa, Rosie continued to monopolize him, keeping him busy fighting to fit her bags onto a trolley with dodgy wheels, then rushing him through the customs area. Vanessa was stuck waiting for her bag to appear. Soon the carousel was empty, her bag was missing.

Edward, who was near the customs area, dumped his holdall on the floor at Penny's feet. Vanessa heard him say, “Mind this while I help Vanessa locate her bag.”

It was a kind thought, but she was used to fending for herself.

Edward reached her, put his hand on her back and propelled her towards the information desk.

“Don't worry Edward, I can sort out my own bags.” She'd always been able to fend for herself.

“I'm sure you can, but I wanted a chance to talk to you.”

She looked him in the eyes. “If you're worried I'm going to say something, don't be.” The statement didn't need an explanation. His affair was his business, not hers.

She saw his shoulder relax. “Thanks.”

Vanessa felt sorry for him. The man was a fool. Lauren was no match for Penny. It was tempting to warn him that trouble lay ahead. The transition from an affair to a full-on relationship had pitfalls. Something she was rapidly learning.

Sean had told her he and Fay were over and convinced her that Fay was waiting for the right moment to move out. The timing depended on his children and their exams. He'd forgotten to mention which exams, and one year rolled on into another. Not that she minded. She was comfortable with their relationship as it was.

Fay's departure had meant Sean pressured her to join this holiday with his best friends, their children, and Rosie. She had met his children, Matthew and Rosie, briefly long ago. Now she was feeling trapped, with Sean expecting more from her than she was ready to give.

Edward nudged her. “Are you alright?”

“Yes,” she said and focused on the missing luggage.

The assistant behind the counter listened to their story and passed them a form to fill out. A lazy fan swirled slowly overhead, trying to shift the moist hot air that engulfed them as they stepped off the plane.

Vanessa didn't have any hope of her possessions arriving soon, but the procedure had to be followed. She didn't care about the clothes. But the prospect of being stuck without her carefully selected tubes of paints and her brushes upset her.

By the time they rejoined the others, Oliver had all the bags stowed and everyone was sitting in the air-conditioned bus. It was a relief to get into the comparatively cool atmosphere.

Sean was beside Rosie in the front two seats. Rosie's bags occupied the nearest vacant seat. Vanessa had no intention of showing she noticed the obvious ploy, smiled sweetly at Rosie, and said, “Sorry about the delay. I'll sit at the back with the boys.”

Hardly the best start to the holiday. Getting Rosie onside was going to be a challenge.

The boys needed distracting. Penny looked worn out, and Edward needed a break from acting as referee to the competitive pair. Their current argument was over who had eaten the most biscuits on the flight. They turned everything into a contest. The adult challenge now was to find a suitable competitive sport to entertain them until they reached their destination.

She rummaged in her bag and pulled out a pad and pen.

“Okay, who wants to play?”

“What?” they asked in unison.

“My version of I spy.”

Both children nodded excitedly.

“Can I play too?” Edward chipped in.

“The more the merrier. The rules are simple. I tell you what to look for. The first one to spot it scores a point.”

“What's the prize?” They asked.

“I've not decided. It depends on how seriously you take the game.” That satisfied them. She drew lines down the page, wrote their names at the top and as the bus pulled out of the airport, said, “Okay, first challenge. A coconut on a tree.”

The boys peered out the windows, desperate to win. Edward gave her a kindly wink. Penny managed what looked like a grateful smile before closing her eyes.

Vanessa wondered how she could do that when there were so many exciting things to see. Vanessa didn't want to miss a moment. Maybe Penny wasn't well. She was rather pale. Still, helping with the boys could ease her way into the group.

Rosie had already made it clear she wanted to monopolize Sean, so it was unlikely they'd ever get a moment of privacy. She couldn't believe that less than a week ago, she contemplated asking Sean about having children. This holiday might cure that notion forever.

Rosie had her earphones back in place, her head nodding to one of her head-pounding rhythmic downloads on her iPod, leaving Sean to enjoy the scenery in silence.

The boys played fair. She kept items in mind, the donkey with cart, occupied them for all of two minutes. A Mercedes without tinted windows lasted for five, then she tried a bicycle with three passengers for only two minutes. A black cow proved harder, especially as she chose it just before they got onto the ferry to cross the harbour entrance.

Everyone had to get off the bus and walk onto the ferry. Edward bought lukewarm drinks from a vendor. Oliver herded them all to the front of the ferry, with instruction to get off the ferry as fast as possible so they could get back into the air-conditioned bus and get ahead of the other traffic, to arrive at the beach house faster.

The hordes of other foot passengers jostled for a suitable position, and it was hard keeping the group together. Rosie was taking her time. Sean's tight lips showed he was struggling not to lose his temper. Vanessa soaked up the visual feast the vibrant crowd presented, taking in the variety of dress that ranged from multi-coloured kikois to all-encompassing burkas and sparkling sequin covered saris. And thinking about the colours that she'd mix to capture the range of skin tones, from the darkest shades to the pale skin of Kim's children.

The ferry chugged over the stretch of dark green water. Its battered metal plates grated as they grounded on the concrete ramp before the whole thing shuddered to a standstill. The attendants lowered the chains, and in an instant, the flux of passengers and motors surged forward. Some locals sauntered off with huge material wrapped bundles balanced on their heads. Others balanced large cans, or big wide metal pans or sacks of charcoal. Some pushed bicycles, others had children tied to their backs.

Vendors of fruit, soft drinks, cheap watches, scarves, and sunglasses crowded round them as they hurried up the ramp to the relative safety of their transport.

Vanessa found it enthralling. She wanted to whip out a sketch pad and capture the scene. But it was time to move on. Everyone returned to the seats they had occupied before their short stint of rubbing shoulders with the locals.

Oliver and Kim got their toddlers, David and Alice, to sit quietly on their laps, and both children fell asleep as soon as the bus got going.

Vanessa had met both Oliver and Kim before, and had always found them charming. They hadn't ignored her, but being preoccupied with their children barely managed more than a nod and a friendly smile. The safari would be tough enough with one hostile teen in the mix.

The boys demanded to continue playing the game. The score was even, and there hadn't been arguments, so Vanessa kept it going.

At last, they reached the property. The driver hooted his horn, and the watchman came running to open the gates. Vanessa had spotted a small shopping complex not very far away, where, with luck, she'd be able to find what she needed to survive without her bags.

The drive, made of compacted coral, snaked down the grounds, weaving round vast silvery trunks of leafless baobab trees. Gradually, they entered a verdant coconut grove. Through gaps in the vegetation, they caught sight of sparkling sand and clear turquoise blue water. In the distance, a white line of waves marked the reef, beyond which the deeper sea disappeared into the skyline.

There was an enormous cheer from everyone on board.

Vanessa ended the game to keep her charges happy. “Even scores,” she declared. “That means you both get ice creams when we go to town.”

CHAPTER 15

Mombasa - Wednesday 25th September

It struck Kim as they arrived at the impressive house that was to be their home for a week, that no one talked about the shopping mall siege. The armed troops at the airport had been scary. And made her grateful for the change from their original destination. Nairobi looked like a place to avoid. That and the threat of Rosie kicking off dominated her thoughts.

Kim would not have let a terror attack put her off the trip, but it didn't mean she wasn't interested. It was no surprise to hear that Martin was covering the story. The last time she'd seen him was just before he returned to Kenya. Back then, she thought he looked haunted. So, the news that he was getting married pleased her. He needed a soulmate. She couldn't wait to meet Sandra when they got to Ol Essakut.

Martin's best friend, Simeon Mugo, had arranged for his girlfriend, Amina, to meet them at the coast. Sean was the only person who had met Amina. He'd met her in London at the launch of the botanical guidebook she had written, which Sandra, Martin's wife to be, had illustrated. Kim had seen Amina's photo on the book cover, but in real life, she was more striking.

Amina ushered them into the cool shade of the house, and introduced them to Moses, the headman of the household, Josphat, the cook, and the two girls, Perpetua and Wanjiku who she said would help with the children along with their cleaning and laundry duties.

Once introductions were over, Sean waded in with the question that was on everyone's mind. "What's happening in Nairobi?"

Amina, after a tiny hesitation, said, "As far as I know, the army has taken control and sent troops in. It isn't going well. A fire is burning out of control, and there's been looting of the shops."

"Is Martin still there?" Sean asked.

Amina shook her head. "Not at the Mall. He went chasing after someone he saw in the crowd. He's disappeared. No one knows where he is."

"Martin can look out for himself," Sean said, perhaps trying to reassure her. "He's certainly had enough practice."

"True, but this is different. We're all anxious." She turned her attention to the children and quietly added, "Simeon wants to help look for him. But is stuck at Ol Essakut. Please, get yourselves settled in."

Kim sensed that Simeon's desire to get involved was the reason she closed the topic. Maybe she'd speak more freely later, when she'd got to know them.

Kim was happy to go along with her suggestion about getting settled in, as it was too hot to hit the beach.

The families scattered to their respective accommodation, with a plan to meet up later in the airy, makuti roofed dining room. Amina had promised to outline the excursion options on offer over lunch.

Oliver, Kim, and their two little ones were on one side of the house. Edward, Penny, and the boys had rooms on the other side. Sean, Vanessa, and Rosie would be upstairs. To Kim's delight, their vast bedrooms had a little private shaded veranda, air conditioning, and, to her relief, excellent mosquito screening on the windows, as well as huge canopy nets around the beds. Amina was in a separate cottage, to one side of the property.

Kim couldn't wait to peel off her travel clothes and put on something cooler. The humidity was intense.

As she slipped into a very loose sun dress, she wondered how Rosie would hide the scars that Fay had warned her about.

Then she realized that without luggage, Vanessa had nothing to change into. She rummaged through her case, picked out a new swimsuit she had been looking forward to wearing and a beach wrap. She'd offer it as a gesture of friendship.

CHAPTER 16

Mombasa Wednesday 25th Sept

Having nothing to unpack, Vanessa strolled across the lawn to survey the beach. It was everything the brochure had promised. The tide was out, leaving miles of glorious blinding white sand stretching as far as she could see. A couple of camels were being led into the distance. The gentle flop of waves, and the rustle of the palms, made Vanessa glad she'd agreed to come with Sean. At least, if the situation with Rosie deteriorated, she could sit and sketch.

She turned to face the house, which was a lovely mixture of new and old. The wings on either side were modern. All the rooms had air-conditioning. The hub of the house was a traditional construction, with huge beams supporting a makuti roof, complete with vents to let the hot air out and keep air flowing. Decorative wrought iron work added security to the inner veranda and the windows.

She was pleased her bedroom was upstairs, as it would help to let the breeze in. They wouldn't have to rely on the air-conditioning unit.

Vanessa wondered what to do next. Moses approached her and asked if she would like a drink before lunch. When she asked for a soft drink, he seemed pleased.

"I hear you have no luggage," he said. "Come. I help you."

Vanessa followed him and he unlocked what she thought was a cupboard. But this was no ordinary cupboard. It was a veritable Aladin's cave full of goodies. There were shelves all along one side, piled high with towels and beach wraps in every colour imaginable. There was a stack of hats, a big locally made basket full of shoes, flip-flops, daps, flippers. A mountain of goggles, and a clothes rail with about thirty swimsuits, and an assortment of shirts, shorts and skirts hanging on it. On one wall was a set of shelves with a vast selection of toiletries that put her local chemist at home to shame.

"Who do they belong to?"

"People leave things behind. We keep them for anyone who needs them."

"Are you sure?"

"Yes, you look. I'll get your drink."

Vanessa couldn't believe that her wardrobe problems could be so easily solved. She selected a couple of swimsuits and three kikois. Enough to keep her going for a few days. She found a bikini that would be great for a tan. Would she have the confidence to wear it? Maybe. Beach wraps to match were next, and as she wasn't sure if she was going to get to raid this treasure house again she picked out a couple of t-shirts, a pair of shorts, and a long multi-coloured cotton skirt to cover any eventuality. Finally, she added sunscreen and a pair of flip-flops to her bundle.

As she was leaving, she spotted a bookshelf full of board games, crafting tools, and in amongst them all was a brand-new paint box, and a cellophane wrapped watercolour pad. She rummaged deeper and found pencils and rubbers and paintbrushes. Now, no matter how difficult Rosie became, she could survive.

As she emerged, Moses reappeared with her drink. A pint glass filled with ice fruit and a mixture of fruit juices. It surprised her that there wasn't a little umbrella in it. Seeing she had her hands full, he put the drink on the table, and then turned and inspected her haul. He shook his head, and went back and pulled out two colourful beach bags for her to carry her bundle of belongings, his beaming smile a sign he approved of the choices she'd made.

"If you need more, you tell me," he said as he firmly locked the door and pocketed the key.

Vanessa was torn between the desire to quench her thirst, and the need to get out of her travel-stained clothes. The drink won. She sank onto a Swahili day bed, picked up her glass and made a silent toast to the staff in the house who might be her only allies for the next week. After changing, she'd head to the beach and break open the pad and paintbox and start sketching.

She had barely taken more than a sip when Kim appeared. She clutched a swimsuit and a wrap, which still had a price tag attached.

"I thought you might need these." She held them out.

Vanessa was touched. At least Kim didn't bear a grudge.

"Kim, that's so sweet of you, but they've sorted me out." She pointed to the two beach bags by her side. "Moses let me loose on the emergency supply of clothes. It seems I am not the first guest to arrive with no luggage."

Kim seemed relieved not to relinquish her new purchases. She pushed them into her bag and sat down.

"You will let me know if you need anything."

"Thank you. If Moses asks you what you want to drink, I'd recommend this. It's delicious. Fruity, lots of orange and limes, I think."

"Alcoholic?"

"No. I can't handle booze at lunchtime and get through the day. Where is everyone?"

"Perpetua whisked my two off to the sandpit. Oliver's either in the shower or asleep. The humidity hit him. Thank God, our room has air-conditioning. I expect Penny and Edward have collapsed in a heap too. Nicholas has started collecting insects already. The staff have supplied jam jars. And Timothy is in the lounge, his nose stuck into a book. What about Sean and Rosie?"

Vanessa shrugged. "Trying to get the internet connection up and running. Rosie wanted Sean to set up his laptop, so she could email her friend and download new tracks onto her iPod."

"You mean finding excuses to have Sean's undivided attention?"

Vanessa nodded, glad someone else had spotted Rosie's behaviour. How long would it take for Sean to notice? It was obvious Sean wasn't used to this level of attention from his daughter, which made Vanessa determined to avoid fighting for his time.

"The beach looks amazing. I wish I could go for a long walk. Unfortunately, I can never go far with the kids in tow," Kim said. "And I wouldn't dare take them down there in this heat. Never mind the risk of sunburn. They both have such fair skin."

"If you can get away. I'd love the company. Sean doesn't share my enthusiasm for walking." Vanessa hoped Kim would agree. "He'll only walk under duress and if the destination is a pub."

"Maybe I can get Oliver to watch the children this afternoon."

"We could head off after lunch."

"Sounds like a brilliant plan."

Lunch was a sumptuous cold buffet; the table laid out informally with a garland of frangipani and bougainvillea blossoms along the length of the table.

Vanessa was first in the queue. She filled her plate with salads and prawns and selected a seat at the end of the table. Rosie put herself at the other end. She waited, wondering if Sean would join her or Rosie. Sean, armed with his plateful, looked to be heading towards her when Rosie called him and pointed to the seat next to her. He caught Vanessa's eye. She smiled and shrugged. Then turned to see who would take the seat she had hoped would be Sean's.

The food was delicious, and the atmosphere relaxed. Vanessa listened rather than joined in, trying to work out the group dynamics. She'd only met them briefly at her exhibitions and never spent time with them individually, and never as Sean's significant other. It might take time for them to become comfortable with her new status.

Amina sat at the other end of the table near Sean, talking quietly about Martin and Simeon. Rosie ate without interrupting. So different to her behaviour when she and Sean tried to have a conversation.

Oliver and Edward were planning sporting challenges. Cricket on the beach, and a swim when the tide was right for the twins to catch waves on body boards.

Vanessa hoped Penny would find peace while the boys indulged in competitive activities. She looked in need of a rest. Kim's toddlers had already taken to Perpetua, who had introduced them to the shady sandpit. They wolfed down their food and begged to leave the table so they could play in the sandpit again.

Kim grinned at Vanessa when she gave her permission. She spoke to Oliver, who nodded.

"Looks like I'll be free for that walk," Kim announced. She turned to Rosie and asked. "Rosie, do you fancy coming? Vanessa and I are going to walk on the beach."

Rosie's eyes widened in horror and shook her head. Was it the thought of the walk or her presence that made the idea so unappealing? She hoped no one picked up on her delight when Rosie rejected the idea.

"How about you, Amina?"

Amina shook her head. "Sorry, I have calls to make. Maybe another time."

Did her refusal had anything to do with Martin and Simeon?

Nicholas and Timothy bickered. The jars of bugs causing discontent. The cruelty aspect of keeping them captive brought Timothy's animal rights instincts to the fore. Condemning the fanatical entomologist's behaviour as unacceptable. Vanessa, who struggled to tell the two boys apart, had the bug collector sitting beside her, with his prize finds climbing the walls of their glass prisons on the table. The other had a book on his lap. She could tell the bugs fascinated him, but she understood his desire to free them.

Before the war between the boys reached full pitch screams, Sean interrupted.

"I have a solution." He moved down to her end of the table and pulled up a chair. "No one wants anyone to suffer. Agreed."

They nodded.

"Especially not these bugs." He picked up the jar and inspected the contents.

His enthralled audience waited. "They look quite happy, but Timothy is right, they need to be released. Here's what we will do."

Vanessa loved he had them totally under his spell. She had never witnessed this side of him.

"Nicholas, I'll take photographs of all the bugs you find." He nodded to the boy. "Timothy, your task it to identify them before we release them. Are you both okay with that?"

Neither child looked too sure about it. Sean realized they needed convincing.

"There are too many bugs to look after them all before they eat each other. This way, you'll have a record of them. Nicholas, you find them. Timothy will record them. I'll find a website to help name them."

A mistake. Sean had set a challenge. Never mind Rosie demanding his attention, Sean could end up photographing bugs all day. Still, photography was his hobby, so a pleasurable task. The bugs in the jars were beautiful. She might paint a few to test the art supplies extracted from the supply cupboard.

Both boys mulled over the plan and agreed. He shook hands with them. "Deal?"

They smiled as if winning points over adults was a private plot of their own.

He gave her a look with a hint of apology. She smiled back. "You don't mind if I go off with Kim, do you?"

He shook his head. "I know your idea of heaven is a long walk on the beach. I'll come if you want me to."

She touched his hand. "No, stay and keep this lot in order."

"As long as you don't mind."

"Not at all. Anyone else like to come?"

The rapid head shaking round the table made her happy as she and Kim got up to leave.

CHAPTER 17

Wednesday 25th September

Vanessa slapped on a fresh layer of sunscreen, grabbed a kikoi and a sun-visor and went to wait for Kim at the gate that led onto the beach. Everyone else was settling down for a post lunch laze.

Kim's two little ones were happily playing in the shady sandpit. Vanessa was impressed with how confident Kim's children were. They were a credit to their mother. Oliver's role was less obvious. He had been good with them on the plane, paying enough attention without letting them dominate his time. Sean could learn a trick or two from him.

Kim bounced down the path with a huge smile on her face.

"Think we can make it to the rocks at the end?" she asked.

Vanessa peered up the beach and wondered if she'd have set the target so high on her own. The rocks were far away.

"We can try," Vanessa answered.

"Let's find a band of smooth sand along the water's edge. Less painful on the soles of our feet while they harden up," Kim suggested.

"Sounds good. I hate walking in soft sand. Let's go."

They sped across the soft sand to the tide line.

"Phew, thank heaven, this is cooler. That was blistering hot." Vanessa paddled in the water to cool down. “I love walking in bare feet, but seldom get the chance.”

“Me too. I'm a fast walker.”

“Don't worry, I'll tell you if the pace gets too tough. I haven't had a decent walk for ages.”

It didn't take long for beach vendors to pester them. Each time they showed their empty hands, said thank you but no thank you politely, using a few Swahili words drilled into them by Amina. And kept moving at a brisk pace. Soon the tactic worked, and they were left in peace.

The nearly deserted beach filled as the afternoon progressed.

A few children paddled in the rock pools. Fishermen mended nets under the shelter of the palm fronds at the top of the beach. In front of one hotel, the seaweed had been cleared. Sunburnt, overweight tourists played volleyball against a team of fit young locals. Couples hand in hand, joggers, even jugglers, watched the game. A few people lay on towels, soaking up the sun, turning a dangerous shade of red.

There was no need for conversation. The pair of them occasionally stopped to catch their breath, and soak up the scenery, stare out to sea, focus on a distant sail, or glance inland to pick out the thatched roof of a house, or an upturned fishing boat.

Kim was right about the smooth stretch of sand at the water's edge. In some places where the water had ebbed, sand crabs had disturbed the smoothness digging their way out, leaving little piles of sand which were easily flattened as they trod on them.

There were tiny salmon pink shells the size of a baby's fingernail along this line of the beach. A few yards up, the shells were fractionally larger, and more mixed in colour. Pale purples, oranges, scraps of red coral all mixed up with cowrie shells and scraps of green bubble seaweed and dark clumps of the more common seaweed.

Sights set on the clump of rocks jutting out at the end of the beach. They walked purposefully. Vanessa matched Kim's pace with ease. She'd be happy to keep her company whenever she wanted. She hoped Kim and the others would be more open with her as the weeks went by. It wouldn't be a problem if they didn't because Vanessa actually enjoyed silence. But she'd also love to break down any barriers caused by her replacing Fay. She needed a break. Rosie certainly wouldn't give her one.

Kim kept striding on until she touched the rock. Then she turned to Vanessa and laughed. “Wow, we made it. I've longed to do this since hearing we would come to Diani. I was worried that without Fay here, I'd have no one to walk with. Sorry, I shouldn't have said that.”

“You were good friends. There is nothing wrong with missing her. Please don't be embarrassed to mention her.”

“It's not just that. I feared the children would be unsettled and that the beach wouldn't be as beautiful.”

“How far have we come?”

“No idea. This is a vast improvement on the last holiday Sean organized.”

“Tell me more.”

“It wasn't totally his fault. He booked us into a place in Greece. It looked fantastic, but the brochure they sent was for the hotel next door. Ours was still under construction. We arrived on a special feast day. And found all the decent accommodation was full. The only place available on the island was a cramped, rundown place.” Kim sat on the sand, facing back in the direction they had covered. “This is heavenly.”

"Do you enjoy going on holiday with the same crowd every year?"

"I didn't think I would, but you get used to it. Having people around allows you to do things that would otherwise be impossible. Like taking off for a long walk."

Vanessa wasn't sure of the logic.

"If Oliver and I were on our own with the children, I wouldn't have left him alone with them. Not because I don't trust him, but he'd be bored. He'd have offered to come with the kids. We'd have been lucky to get to the water's edge."

"I get the picture. I've never had children to consider."

"And now you have Rosie. That child can really wind people up. She sure is doing her best with you. I admire your patience so far."

"Nice of you to call it patience. Cowering in a corner is what it feels like. I'm worried she thinks she's winning."

"Oh no, you're doing fine. My guess is she'll give up soon. Trouble is, then she might start making everyone else's life a misery. Fay asked me to watch her. She's worried that Rosie's depressed. Personally, sulky is more like it."

"What's her brother like?"

"Matthew? He could be quite moody. I thought he was supposed to be coming."

"He cried off a while back."

"Let's stop and have a drink on the way."

"I didn't bring any money."

"I did." Kim patted her hip. "I've stitched a little pocket into my bikini. I've learned that it pays to carry a card with you. You never know when you'll need it."

They walked back at a more leisurely pace. Kim seemed ready to chat, and Vanessa's fears of a lonely holiday disappeared.

Kim had stayed at home to bring up their children. And Vanessa got the impression of a quiet, organized woman.

"I'm worried about Penny." Kim frowned.

"Why? She's quieter than expected. I assumed missing Fay had something to do with it." Vanessa answered.

"I don't think so. She's different, somewhat disconnected."

Vanessa said nothing. Maybe Penny knew about Edward's affair. Or had something else going on. One thing was certain: Vanessa would not tell her about Lauren.

"What did you give up for your children?" Vanessa asked to get away from Edward and Penny's potential marital problems.

"I'm a midwife. Unfortunately, babies don't work to a decent timetable. Oliver was relieved when I quit."

"I'll bet he was."

"I'd also had a miscarriage. Stress of the job wasn't to blame, but Oliver thought it was. When I fell pregnant again, I agreed to quit. Thankfully, David and Alice arrived with no problem, and with only eighteen months between them, I had my hands full. We didn't need the money, so it made sense to stay home with them. But I really miss the work. I haven't told Oliver yet, but I've just completed another course to bring my qualifications up to date. The exam results come out this week. With both children going to school, I'm keen to start again."

"Wow, that's great. I hope he's impressed."

"I think he will be. What about you?"

"Being an artist was always my big dream. I've had moderate success with exhibitions, but art doesn't pay the bills, so I have extra jobs. That's how I got involved with dressing flats and houses for sellers. It turned out to be fun, stimulating, certainly varied, and financially rewarding."

"Is that what brought you and Sean together?"

Vanessa was uncomfortable with the direction the conversation was heading.

"Fay introduced us. And yes, I guess work brought us closer."

"Sorry, I didn't mean to sound nosy or disapproving. I didn't know until Fay told me the day before we left."

Vanessa wished she knew what Fay had said, but it was too soon to ask.

"I'm worried Oliver is seeing someone else," Kim blurted out. A tear trickled down her cheek. "He's been behaving oddly for weeks. But I'm afraid to ask." She brushed her cheek with the back of her hand. "Ignore me. I'm probably imagining things."

This sudden intimate insight surprised Vanessa. "I'm sure he isn't. You seem so right together."

"Do you think so?"

Vanessa nodded. Yes, she did. She liked the way Oliver watched out for Kim in a subtle, effortless way.

"Maybe something else is worrying him. He works in the city, hardly a stress-free environment. Could he have problems at work?" she suggested.

"Has Sean said something?"

Vanessa shook her head. If Sean had, she would never break a confidence.

Kim put her hand on Vanessa's arm and stopped walking. "I'm sorry. I shouldn't have asked. Forgive me."

"Nothing to forgive. You're worried and I'm touched that you trusted me enough to ask. He probably needs a break from work. This holiday will do him good."

“Wow, we've been so busy talking we missed our stop for a drink. I hope they'll give us a cup of tea when we get back to the house.”

“I am sure they will. It looks as if they can provide whatever we want whenever we want it. Don't you find it odd, enjoying a holiday in the sun while Martin is missing?” Vanessa said.

“Yes, very unsettling. But we all agreed not to let the terrorist attack cancel our trip. Doing so would be an extra win for them. But Martin's disappearance has thrown us all. Oliver and I decided that the only thing we can do is to accept the plans put in place. They don't need to be worrying about us.”

“That makes sense. Let's hope he turns up soon. What's he like?”

“He was always such fun. But the last time I saw him, he was stressed. He looked haggard, suffering from exhaustion from being on the front line too long. He went home to Kenya and stayed here. I hoped he'd find peace. The fact he has asked Sandra to marry him is a good sign.”

“Have you ever met her?”

“No. But she sounds lovely.”

Oliver was waiting for them on the veranda. He gave Kim a hug, and within seconds, her children dragged her over to the sandpit.

Sean was nowhere in sight.

CHAPTER 18

Ol Essakut - Thursday 27th September.

Sandra was struggling with lethargy and a nagging pain in her back. How long could she pretend she was fine before Jenny noticed? She sat on the veranda watching stormy clouds obscure the mountain.

"This heat's exhausting. Let's hope there's rain on the way." She hoped Jenny would blame the weather for her listlessness.

"They forecast thunderstorms. We need a soaking. The top dam is rather low."

Sandra had learned early on, after taking on control of Ol Essakut, that maintaining a steady water supply was essential for the running of the estate. Martin had helped create a series of dams to hold water on the land for the dry periods. It helped to keep the wildlife on the ranch and stop them from going to areas where they were less welcome.

"I take it you still haven't heard from Martin?" Jenny continued. "I presume the children don't know he's missing."

Sandra picked up the glass of ice-cold water Juma had brought out earlier. "No point in alarming them. I'm sure he'll turn up in good time, pretending he's fine."

"You don't have to hide your concerns from me."

"Sadly, I do. The alternative is too depressing."

Juma provided a distraction as he delivered coffee for Jenny and another jug of water and glasses. He was on a mission to ensure she kept well hydrated.

"Why won't you let me run you into Nanyuki to get the doctor to check you over?"

"I'm fine, just hot. I hate it when thunder is brewing."

"Did you get much sleep?"

"No. The baby was doing cartwheels all night." She ran her hand over her bump. "I haven't heard from Hank, which is nearly more stressful than Martin not calling."

"I'm sure he'll have a good reason."

Sandra appreciated Jenny's effort to be reassuring. She'd be equally concerned by the absence of news.

"Simeon's found someone to look after his new recruits." Jenny stirred her coffee. "He's visiting the camps to check the guests are not worried. Then he'll join us. He's keen to go to Nairobi to help find Martin."

Sandra had to keep calm. She didn't have a choice about resting. Her energy levels had plummeted, and it was an effort to stay awake, let alone tackle the tasks she would normally do. The news that Simeon wanted to help made Martin's disappearance more unsettling. How would Amina react if Simeon became embroiled in something dangerous?

Hank's initial call broke the news that Martin had followed a man seen in the crowd, hadn't raised alarms. His next call saying that three men had grabbed Martin and bundled him into a van caused panic. Especially as they didn't know what direction they'd gone.

Sandra, too shocked, didn't ask the million things that she now needed to know. Most of which Hank wouldn't have an answer for.

Simeon bounded up the steps sooner than she expected. Reassured her that all their guests were happy, and the camps running smoothly. She relayed everything Hank had told her.

"I'll call him and get an update." Simeon got through to Hank and fired a load of questions at him. His expression getting more concerned with every reply that Hank gave. "Yes, everything is fine here. I'll do what I can."

When he disconnected, he looked over at Sandra and said, "Sorry. It sounds as if Martin's got himself into serious trouble. Hank had a tracking device on this phone. They've taken him out of town, but it isn't working anymore. He assumes that whoever grabbed Martin switched it off. So, he's no idea where he is."

"What about Enuto and Barnard? Weren't they supposed to be watching out for him?"

"They'd split up, to follow men seen with the man Martin was chasing. They're fine and insist on staying there to see if the man returns to the area."

"I knew when Hank persuaded Martin to go, there would be trouble. Hank was so blasé about the whole affair. Handing out phones and laptops as if it was a kids' party rather than a bloody siege."

"I imagine he's in his element." Simeon shook his head. "Putting tracking devices on the phones shows he was worried. Not that it helps now."

Jenny got up to go, "I have some chores to do. Best I do them while you're here with Sandra."

Simeon smiled at Sandra and when Jenny was out of hearing said, "Mother hen?"

She nodded. "Big time."

The pair of them sat silently on the veranda, mulling over the news about the loss of contact. Then she remembered something and reached out to touch Simeon's arm.

"The fitness tracker you gave him for his birthday. Could that still be working?"

She didn't know how it worked, only that the children had found the grey plastic band, and decided it was too boring, and had decorated it with permanent felt-tip pens. Their efforts had transformed it into something you'd find on a cheap market stall rather than a sophisticated tracking device.

"Yes, but no use without his phone. And unlikely to work at this distance. If they've taken his phone, they'll have taken the tracker as well."

"Maybe not. Remember how the kids decorated it? It doesn't look like something worth stealing. The phone they took was the one Hank gave him. His is here with me, because all the Ol Essakut stuff is on it."

She grabbed the phone off the table beside her and handed it over.

Simeon took it, tapped the screen, entered the password, which he knew because he and Martin shared everything. He clicked on the tracking app.

Sandra was confident that if anyone could get it to work, Simeon would succeed.

"It's working," he said, a beaming smile on his face. The smile faded, and he added. "I suppose I ought to let Hank know."

"You look doubtful."

"I am. Hank has great connections and influence. But I doubt his spending power will be useful in the area shown on here. I have friends trained for this sort of job. I'd rather ask them to sneak in and find out if he is actually where the tracker shows he is. There's no guarantee. For all we know, they might have attached it to a goat and set it roaming."

"Don't say that. I'd rather you checked it out. Stealth is not Hank's forté. I trust you to do what's best. Though I am not sure Amina will be happy about your getting involved."

"Is there anything on the phone you need?"

"Nothing. I can check everything on mine. Take it."

It was the first time she appreciated modern technology and was grateful that they had embraced it.

"Where do you think he is now?"

"According to this, he's somewhere near Machakos. And has been in the same place for a while. Two of our rangers are from that area. Is it okay if I take them with me?"

"Of course you can."

"Good, but don't tell anyone about the tracker."

"What shall I tell Amina?"

"Don't worry. I'll speak to her. I will ask her to come back here to help Jenny."

"Thanks, I'd appreciate that. I'm not much use to anyone, and Jenny is already doing too much."

They heard Jenny's footsteps on the steps to the veranda.

"Who says I'm doing too much?" She flopped into a chair. "Come on, spill."

Sandra glimpsed panic on Simeon's face and knew she would have to respond. "Simeon. He's arranging for Amina to fly home. With everyone in Nairobi, and me out of action, the workload is too much for you."

"Trying to make me feel old?" Jenny said.

"No, of course not. But I need you here with m. What have you done with the children?"

"I sent them to clean up. They've been doing pottery and are filthy."

"I'd better be off," Simeon said, "I'll call when I get there."

"If you're going to Nairobi," Jenny said, "please tell Enuto that I gave his wife a lift from town. She's going to stay here with Barnard's wife until her baby is born. He needs to come back."

CHAPTER 19

Thursday 26th September

Sean thought they were mad to get up so early to catch a decent wave while the tide was full in. The children could swim when the tide was low.

On the way to the beach, the men talked about the trip to Fort Jesus in Mombasa.

"I'm hoping going out will break the ice between Rosie and Vanessa," Sean said.

"Vanessa's been amazing. I haven't heard her complain about Rosie monopolizing you." Oliver said, flicking him with a towel.

"I foolishly hoped Rosie would get bored and entertain herself. She's driving me mad. I feel guilty because Fay suggested she needed professional help, and I was too pig-headed to listen."

"Tough call," Edward said.

"Yes, but I can't call Fay for advice after the way I let her down."

The conversation ended when they plunged into the water. The waves rolled in fast and thick. All of them were experienced surfers and strong swimmers. They ducked under incoming waves and fought their way out to the furthest point where they could catch the biggest breakers. Riding in on wave after wave left them exhilarated and hungry. Sean led the way back for breakfast.

Vanessa had already left the table. He struggled to convince Rosie to eat something before they headed into Mombasa, which was not a great start to the day.

Amina suggested they leave before the temperature soared, because there was no shade at the Fort, except in the museum.

On hearing this, Kim opted to skip the trip and stay behind to mind all the children.

"If you want to wander round the Old Town," Amina said, "you should do it before noon, so you can get back to the house for lunch, and spend the afternoon on the beach or by the pool."

Sean, ignoring her reluctance, pressured Amina to be their guide. Her presence would ensure Vanessa wouldn't feel totally abandoned if Rosie was her usual demanding self. Apart from that, Amina knew the history of the fort.

Everyone had paid attention, including Rosie, and they left the beach house in good time. Not far down the road, they encountered a police roadblock.

Amina stiffened. The police ignored everyone except her, demanding to see her ID papers. She handed over what they asked for. They talked among themselves, surveyed the group, and handed her papers back and let them through. Her reluctance to join them now made sense. But there was nothing to fear with the group to vouch for her.

True to form, the minute they reached the gates of the fort, Rosie became demanding. She didn't want to listen to the guide give his welcome introduction on the history of the fort.

Amina nudged Sean and suggested he get Rosie potato crisps from the vendor who had set up his stall across the street. He took her advice and pulled Rosie away from the group so they could concentrate on the guide.

They found a patch of shade, and watched as the man held a potato in one hand, and with a sharp knife shaved wafer-thin slices straight into the oil filled wok on his charcoal stove. Within minutes, the crisps turned from cream to a perfect golden colour. He scooped them up into a wire mesh basket and shook them to drain the excess oil off them. He put that to one side and selected a polythene bag. Pulled the edges open, and with a quick movement, tipped the drained crisps in, added a sprinkle of salt, and offered them a taste.

They were delicious. Sean didn't think he had ever tasted a better crisp. Even Rosie was impressed. Before they could speak, the crisp seller pulled the sides of the bag together and, with a delft movement, touched the edge of the plastic onto the rim of his pan. Sealed. He repeated the procedure with the same precision. They were so fascinated; they watched as he prepared four bags. Sean paid him and they went back to catch up with the others.

Sean sensed the history of the place as he walked up the steep slope into the fort. Rosie moaned about the uneven surface underfoot. She was totally unimpressed by the age of the place, which the Portuguese built in the late fifteen hundreds. Or that the fort had been taken over by the Sultan of Oman, and then by the British. She sat on a ledge and picked at her fingernail, not caring that hundreds of slaves had been housed here prior to being shipped out. Or more recently used as a prison, before becoming a world heritage site.

Sean caught up with the others as they were leaving the museum.

Despite the heat, Edward was keen to photograph carved Arab doors in the old town and see if there were any dhows in the port.

Amina looked cornered. The police check and the looks she got from the locals had unsettled her. He was wondering how to solve the problem when Vanessa announced she had a splitting headache.

Penny was the first to react. “I have some aspirin tablets in my bag. Would they help?”

“No thanks. They're the last thing I need. I'm allergic to aspirin and carry an EpiPen with me. All I need is a glass of water and somewhere cool to sit.”

Amina was quick with a solution. “You and I could wait at the club. I can't sign you in because I'm only a reciprocal member, but I'm sure we can wait in the reception area, which will be cool.”

Sean understood Amina's enthusiastic solution solved more than Vanessa's headache. “That's very kind. And much appreciated. I doubt we'll be long in this heat.”

As they walked out of the Fort, Sean noted the hostile looks from passers-by fired in Amina's direction. Their behaviour made him glad that Amina had offered Vanessa refuge at the club rather than heading across the road to the old town. He watched them make their way through the club's gates with a twinge of envy. He'd prefer to be with them rather than chasing down hot alleys with his moody daughter.

CHAPTER 20

Mombasa - Thursday 26th September

Vanessa was grateful for Amina's suggestion to find shade at the club. They didn't go beyond the reception area, which had comfortable chairs. Amina ordered freshly squeezed orange juice and a jug of iced water.

Amina had described the club earlier. It was built below the imposing fort surrounded by well-maintained grounds filled with exotic palms, oleanders and frangipani trees. It was a bastion of the colonial era: carefully positioned to catch the breeze and monitor the old harbour.

"You're a lifesaver," Vanessa said as she sipped the iced water, hoping it would help ease her pounding head.

"Not at all. You saved me. I dreaded going into the old town. You must have seen the looks I was getting. Simeon warned me the trouble in Nairobi could stir up aggression towards anyone of Somali origin. I thought he was exaggerating. Now I believe him."

"You've been together for a while? Not tempted to get married?"

"Oh, he's asked. But our families will never approve. Cultural differences make it impossible. They want him to marry someone from his tribe. And this terror attack will make them even less likely to come round."

"That's not fair."

"True, but we can live with that."

Amina's phone rang. Vanessa heard enough to know Simeon was the caller. She walked out of earshot, up the driveway to stand in the shade of a palm tree.

Her stance betrayed her emotions. The conversation wasn't going well. Vanessa watched as the minutes ticked by. Her headache was easing. The cool air and the drink had helped. She must take care not to get dehydrated again.

Amina returned and sat down. Vanessa stayed silent, waiting to see if Amina would share any fresh information.

"That was Simeon," she said. "With a change in plans. He wants me to go back to Ol Essakut, and has arranged for a friend to fly down tomorrow to pick me up. Sandra needs people round her."

"Why? What's happened?"

"Martin's in trouble. He'd been following a Somali refugee who he'd spotted acting suspiciously in the crowd outside the mall. Turns out it was a man he'd photographed at a refugee camp a couple of years ago. Martin ended up in one of the slum areas. And was last seen being bundled into a van and driven off at speed."

"How terrifying." Vanessa said. "What can we do to help?"

"He's been asked to change your plans, too. It means leaving the coast a day early, and flying to the tented camp in Tsavo tomorrow for a couple of days before flying to Ol Essakut. I hope that with the humidity as it is, the others will be happy to leave the coast."

"I'm sure they'll agree to whatever you suggest. If possible, I'd love to skip Tsavo and come straight to Ol Essakut with you. To be honest, I'm struggling, not with the temperature, but Rosie is getting the better of me."

Amina's nod confirmed she understood.

"Will it be less stressful for you at Ol Essakut than here?" Vanessa asked.

"Yes. Everyone there knows me."

Vanessa looked at her watch and up at the gate. "I hope they hurry back." She didn't have to wait long before Sean appeared at the gate and signalled for them to join him.

He gave Vanessa a kiss. "You look better." He turned to Amina. "Thanks for rescuing her. This heat is unbearable. The others are in the vehicle, with the air conditioning on full blast."

The drive back was quiet. It was too hot to make conversation.

After a dip in the pool, Amina told them about the changed plans.

Moses set out a selection of drinks and had put a large bucket of ice on the table. Rosie appointed herself as waitress, pouring and handing drinks around. She presented Vanessa with a glass of fruit juice.

Vanessa was not a great fan of passion fruit, which appeared to be the dominant flavour. She couldn't complain, as that would appear churlish after Rosie's friendly gesture.

"Thank you," she said as she took a sip.

Rosie hovered over her. "I put extra ice in it."

Vanessa took a few more sips. Pretended to enjoy it, while struggling not to pull a face. It was too sweet and had an odd flavour. She forced a smile, and because she feared dehydration, drank more. Half a glass was her limit. She set the glass aside, hoping she could dispose of the rest without hurting Rosie's feelings.

Amina chatted with the others about the trip to the tented camp. Everyone accepted her need to go to Ol Essakut.

Kim surprised them by asking, "Would it be possible for me to go straight to Ol Essakut with you?

Both children have heat rashes, and I don't think they're old enough to appreciate a safari."

Oliver's face fell, but said, "You're probably right. It sounds like a good plan for our family."

"No. Oliver, you must go to Tsavo. I can manage the children for a couple of days."

"Are you sure?"

"Of course I can. And more important, my midwife knowledge might be helpful, as it sounds as if Sandra is having a tough pregnancy."

Amina gave Vanessa a questioning look, possibly wondering if she had been serious about skipping the safari. Caught in a tight spot, Vanessa had to decide if she was ready to admit Rosie had beaten her. How could she tell Sean? Was heat a plausible excuse to stop Rosie from feeling she had won?

"I'll go along with whatever works." Vanessa said, thinking there wouldn't be room on the plane for her and Kim and the children. She hoped Amina would realize that she hadn't told Sean she wanted to leave just yet.

The heat was making her head spin. She slipped away from the group to go to her room. She hadn't even made it to her bed when a tingling sensation started down her arm. A horrifying memory came back to her. This had happened once before. She needed her EpiPen. Where was her bag? Downstairs.

The bag became her focus. She spun round to fetch it and stumbled down the stairs. By the time she reached the bottom, she could barely stand. She knocked a picture off the wall and slumped to the floor. The crash brought Moses running and shouting for help.

Could she make someone understand? "Bag... EpiPen..." They hadn't understood, so she tried again. "Bag... EpiPen... "

Penny shouted. "She's having an allergic reaction. Find her bag?"

Someone brought it to her, and Penny rummaged through the contents, found the pen, and held it up.

"I think this is it. Does anyone know how to use it?"

Kim took it, and without hesitation bared Vanessa's thigh, removed the cap and place the end on the skin, then pushed the plunge button. That done, she massaged the spot.

Vanessa reacted with a bout of shivering. Kim reassured the others, "It is a normal reaction while the medication works. Can someone call a doctor?"

Amina made the call. The panic in the room eased. Oliver shooed the others away, including Sean, then knelt beside her, and together with Kim, promised they'd get the help she needed.

She squeezed Kim's hand to show she understood what they were saying. But it was hard to talk, with her throat swollen.

What had triggered this? She did a mental walk through of everything eaten and drunk that day. Nothing unusual apart from the drink Rosie brought to her earlier. The drink had tasted odd. She pulled at Kim's hand and gasped. "Rosie."

"She's alright." Kim answered.

"No, she did this... Aspirin." Vanessa croaked, her throat tight from the effect of the aspirin. She caught the unguarded disbelief on Kim's face, which changed to shock as the possibility that Vanessa was speaking the truth registered.

Kim had warned her to watch her step with Rosie. And Vanessa could tell she was thinking back over the subtle methods Rosie used to monopolize Sean.

Did they know Rosie was to blame for Sean arriving late at the airport? Had they registered the fuss she made about sitting next to him? Seen her spill Coke all over the white t-shirt found in the house store, or spotted when Rosie dropped ice-cream on a painting she'd done, and knocked Vanessa's camera off the table, damaging the battery case. Thankfully, despite Rosie's best efforts, the camera still worked. They wouldn't know she'd found the airline baggage label from her missing bag on the floor of Rosie's room.

Vanessa couldn't keep the charade going any longer. This was a stunt too far. Sean's inability to see what was happening under his nose, or ignoring it, hurt. The damage was irreversible. She didn't think that even if Rosie became the sweetest kid on the block that she could forgive her or him. All trust was well and truly blown.

Her head was spinning. The rash on her arms was turning into giant blotches. Why the hell wasn't she beginning to feel any better?

"This pen is out of date." Kim said, with panic in her voice. "God, I hope that using it hasn't done more harm than good. Never mind calling a doctor. We need to get to a hospital. Her breathing has been compromised. If this doesn't work soon, she could die."

Vanessa lay there wondering, why here, of all places? Africa was no place for a medical crisis. And her being ill would disrupt everyone's plans.

Amina told them the doctor had agreed to meet them at the local hospital, which was close by. Moses would drive them over. Kim and Oliver helped Vanessa to her feet and between them, almost carried her to the car.

Oliver tried to get Sean to stay with Rosie and the kids. But he insisted on coming.

Penny and Edward agreed to stay behind to mind all the children.

Vanessa couldn't help wondering what sort of hospital it would be. Her image of a Kenyan hospital was a long way from one in England. What she didn't expect was the small, brightly painted building with an efficient nurse waiting with a wheelchair to take her inside.

"What happened?" the doctor asked.

Amina answered for her. "We know she's allergic to aspirin. We think she took an accidental dose. But maybe she's allergic to something else."

Vanessa wanted to shout that there was nothing accidental about it. She'd been poisoned. But her throat constriction stopped her from repeating the accusation.

Amina was playing it down as an accident. Kim was going along with her. Was she trying to protect Rosie? Of course she was. Fay had asked her to look out for the girl.

Vanessa's struggle to breathe made it impossible to say anything. They helped her on to a bed in an airy room. The nurse took her pulse and temperature while the doctor studied her rash and listened to Kim's explanation and details of the out-of-date EpiPen.

"From your description, I don't think the date issue is a problem. But it looks as if she will need more than one dose. He gave instructions to the nurse, who returned with the medicine requested. He checked it and injected it and arranged for a drip. "We'll monitor her overnight to make sure she's responding."

Vanessa closed her eyes. At least here she'd be safe.

While Oliver and Kim discussed with Sean their plans to go back to their children. Amina leaned in and whispered. "Vanessa, please don't mention Rosie. You can't risk the police being involved. Justice here is harsh. If she did this, I promise she'll be punished."

Vanessa was grateful. Someone believed her. And whispered back. "Don't tell Sean. He might flip." Amina squeezed her hand and nodded. Vanessa watched them leave, wishing one of them had stayed.

Sean sat by her bed and Vanessa feigned sleep. Even in her half-dazed state, she got satisfaction from knowing Rosie's actions had brought Sean to her side.

The medication kicked in and she felt better, but was afraid to admit it. Staying overnight in the hospital was safer than at the house near Rosie.

Later Edward appeared. He had been sent to persuade Sean to go to have something to eat, saying he'd stay until Sean came back.

"There's no need," Vanessa croaked. "Penny needs your help more than I do. She's struggling."

"What do you mean?"

"Pay attention and figure it out."

Sean interrupted, "I'll tell the nurse that I'll be back later."

The moment he left; Edward whispered. "Do you really think Rosie is responsible?"

"Yes, and I understand everyone's trying to protect her by saying this was an accident. But no one puts aspirin into a drink by accident. She was there when I told Penny I was allergic to them. She heard, even if she pretends not to hear anything."

"Have you told Sean?"

"No. I don't know how he'll react. All I know is that it will create a horrible atmosphere in the house."

"What do you want to do?"

"I don't know. Amina warned me not to get the police involved. Have you any bright ideas?"

"She's right, you can't make your accusation public. We are in a strange country. The police are notoriously corrupt, and who knows how they would respond. At worst, they would lock her up. Kenya jails are no place for a hardened criminal, let alone a troubled teenager. At home I might give different advice."

"I get the picture. I'll keep quiet for now. But she has to face up to what she's done."

"I promise I'll make sure she understands the gravity of her actions."

"Will you tell Sean?"

"I will, but it might be best to wait until we reach Ol Essakut. We can deal with it without the danger of the staff here or at the house getting involved."

"Fine. But promise you won't leave me alone with her? And please persuade Sean not to come back. I don't need him here beside me."

"Not even if it annoys Rosie," he said with a smile.

"No, not even for that. I need to sleep and prefer to be alone."

CHAPTER 21

Machakos - Thursday 26th September

Simeon, and the two trackers with connections to Machakos, set off to Nairobi. Excited at the prospect, they'd collected what they needed for the trip, city clothes and their rungus.

Four of his ex-army friends, who'd left the army for reasons similar to his own, had without hesitation agreed to help. The Blue Posts Hotel was their rendezvous. They would bring maps and everything necessary for a nighttime rescue.

He did not intend to include Hank in his plans at this stage. If they could pinpoint Martin's whereabouts, a quick in and out to rescue Martin was his focus. Hank and his contacts could then deal with the kidnappers.

He reached the hotel ahead of the others. The trackers went to get themselves something to eat at the stalls by the gate. He booked a room and ordered sandwiches and tea and coffee to have while planning their moves.

On arrival, they spent a few minutes swapping updates of their personal lives and mulled over how differently they would have handled the situation at the mall.

"It's a disgrace."

"They should have gone in on the first day."

"Lives could have been saved."

Simeon listened, but made no comment. The mall situation was out of his control. Finding Martin wasn't.

They unfurled the maps and started making suggestions for the safest way to launch the rescue.

They'd take three vehicles. One pair would go north of the compound and one to the south. Using Google maps, they picked what looked like shady, isolated places away from the roads to park and wait. Simeon chose a spot close to the stream that bordered the property. The pair to the south were close to the road that led to it. Near enough to approach quickly to provide a distraction if needed, so the others could get in unseen. They all had cover stories planned in case anyone approached them. Everyone would wait for Simeon to text instructions. They also discussed bird calls they could use when close to the compound.

Planning the rescue gave Simeon a rush of excitement, not felt in a long while. But he wished it wasn't for real. If Martin got hurt by incompetence, he'd never forgive himself.

Having studied the Google earth maps, paper maps, and walked through the plan numerous times in his head, Simeon was sure he had the terrain memorized.

He reached his chosen spot, under a cluster of fever trees, east of the compound. He let the trackers make the first foray, and dozed in the vehicle until they returned.

They told him there were no vehicles on the plot and drew a picture of the layout of the compound on the ground. Marked where two men sat in front of the house, facing the door of the second building. A woman with a baby and two small children had come out to feed the chickens. And then she'd carried food to the other building. One man had opened the door and locked it when she came out without the plate. He'd then gone back to his seat.

Simeon relayed this information to the others. He would go himself before it got too dark.

He left the trackers to eat and rest and headed downstream. All was as described. There was a fenced off patch of maize, a full goat pen, and half a dozen chickens scratching the bare red earth surrounding the house. The two men still lounged on old car seats, drinking from tin mugs, looking very settled.

Lantana hedging surrounded the plot. Simeon was grateful it wasn't a prickly cactus, which was a popular hedging choice. The growth was thick enough to give cover to get close to the smaller of the two buildings, certain that Martin was in it.

Unlike the house, which was a typical mud and wattle building with a corrugated iron roof, this had walls made of concrete blocks. The lack of windows meant secure storage. His concern was that the door would be sturdy and well secured. And it faced the house, where the two men sat drinking.

He hunkered down and studied the men. Should he risk trying to contact Martin? An owl hoot might work. It was nearly late enough for them to be active. Owl hoots had been a signalling method they had used in childhood. Would Martin remember? It was worth a try. He cupped his hands and hooted. All the time watching the men drinking outside. The call hadn't registered with them. Good. He'd try again in a moment and make it louder.

He called again and listened for a response. Nothing. Only the sound of the goats moving round their pen, and the jangle of their bells.

He'd try once more. Perhaps Martin was asleep or unconscious, or worse still, dead. He checked the tracker signal. If Martin was still wearing it he had to be in there.

He waited for a cloud to block the last of the sun's dying rays to make it safer to move. Then he heard a muffled hoot.

His hopes soared. Was it him or his imagination? Simeon responded with a pigeon's coo, to signal that he'd heard.

It felt like forever before he heard a feeble return coo.

How long should he wait? Would the men go inside? Would the others return? Another hour would ensure darkness, which would make it easier to work. He moved away from the compound, keen to talk through the plan with his comrades, when he got a text.

Three vehicles were heading towards them. All travelling at speed, and likely to be there within minutes.

Simeon cursed under his breath. They'd missed their chance. Now there wasn't enough time to get Martin out, and far too dangerous to try. They'd never get away without being caught.

He hurried back to the trackers and called his friends.

Hold back, let's see how many there are, and then we can decide what to do. They all agreed that waiting was the best option.

Simeon hid close by to count how many people had arrived. Three in the first vehicle, four in the second, and two in the third. He couldn't be sure, but it looked as if three carried guns.

With that many men present, all hopes of rescuing Martin vanished. Simeon knew he had to get Hank involved. Time to make new plans. He would stay where he was. He would get the others to position themselves on the roads away from the compound, so that if anyone left, they could keep track of them.

CHAPTER 22

Mombasa -Thursday 26th September

Once the children had settled down for the night, Oliver joined Kim on their private veranda. He pulled her towards him and hugged her.

"You were amazing today. I've never seen you working in a crisis."

"Thanks, but that's what I trained to do." Perhaps it was time to tell him about her plan to go back to work.

"I'm glad Edward knows," Oliver said. "I hope he can convince Vanessa to keep quiet about Rosie's part in this debacle. And that she understands the need to stay silent, even though we all believe Rosie is to blame."

"Rosie's in a bad way. And I feel so helpless. I promised Fay I'd look out for her."

"I'm more worried about what happens when Vanessa returns. If Rosie can do that, what else is she capable of? And I don't want to witness Sean's reaction when he finds out. He's been struggling to control his temper with her. He told me Fay wanted her to get help. Which is why he's put up with her being so demanding."

"So, he is aware. Shame he hasn't told Vanessa. She's feeling ignored."

"Have you seen the scars on Rosie's arms? She keeps them well hidden, but her sleeve rode up and I caught a glimpse before she covered up. I pretended I hadn't noticed."

"That was kind."

"Not kind, cowardly. And not the only thing I've been cowardly about."

Kim sensed a change in mood. And prayed he wasn't about to announce he was having an affair. Suspecting an affair was bad enough. Facing the truth was her worst nightmare.

"I was going to wait until we got home," he said.

She took a deep breath and willed him to get on with his confession. Dragging it out wouldn't make it easier.

"They've made me redundant."

"What?" The word came out as a squeak rather than a question. She wanted to cheer. Losing his job she could deal with. In fact, she'd celebrate. It was always the wrong job, no matter how well it paid. "When?"

"Two weeks ago. I didn't want to spoil our holiday by telling you before."

"You fool. I thought you were having an affair."

"What?"

"You were behaving oddly, and jumped every time your phone pinged. You came home earlier. Your gym clothes were constantly in the wash. And you wore your best suit to work. I assumed that the new love of your life was a gym bunny, running on the treadmill next to you day after day."

He roared with laughter and leaned over to kiss her.

"No such luck. I was in the city, trawling all the job agencies, and going to the gym to vent my frustration. Sean let me use his flat as my contact address so you wouldn't find out. I had an interview on Tuesday. And I turned the job down. I can't face working in the city again."

"Is that what you've been applying for?"

"Old habits die hard."

"What would you want to do? Work with animals? Live in the country? Travel? What will make you happy?"

"Giving my family the best."

"Did it ever occur to you to ask us what we'd like?"

He stared at her, shook his head. "I've given you the home you deserve, the car, the holidays. What more do you want?"

"If you'd stopped to ask, you'd know I didn't marry you for a big house in suburbia. Nor do I need a fancy car parked on an immaculate brick drive. I'd rather live in a council flat and take the bus than carry on letting you get consumed by a job that devours your soul. Honestly, I had almost reached the point when I wanted out."

"Ouch." His crestfallen expression made her reach out to touch him.

"We want you to spend time with us. To be happy when you're at home, paddle with the kids, play cricket in the garden, and most of all, to laugh. I want the man I fell in love with back."

"Why didn't you say so sooner?"

"How could I? You were proud of your achievements. And enjoyed having your parents cheering you on."

"Don't bring them into this."

"Why? Do you think it will make them vanish?"

"No, I just think it's unfair."

"What? To remind you how your father only praises you if you have beaten a goal he set. That neither of them seem to care about you as a person. Sorry, you're right. Let's leave them out of this. Instead, let's talk about your colleagues, who were forever setting higher challenges for you to beat. How could I undermine that?"

"But you're happy to trash it now."

"It's the first time I've found the strength to say how much I resented it and them. I didn't want an expensive kitchen makeover, and I certainly don't want a new double garage."

"What do you want?"

"I want to be me. To have a career. To be a person in my own right, not just Oliver's wife, or David and Alice's mother. I've lost my identity, and I intend to get it back."

"I didn't know."

"That's the point. You only had time to pop in and reassure yourself all was well in the perfect world you created for us."

He was quiet as he digested her comments. Had she been too hard on him? Should she have kept quiet a little longer? No. She had to say what she felt. He put his head in his hands. She panicked. Had she tipped him over the edge? Should she have been upset by his news? No. No. No. His being fired was cause for celebration. So why not celebrate?

She went inside and raided the fridge, found a bottle of champagne, picked up two glasses. and rejoined him on the long Swahili Sofa. "Can you open this?"

Oliver looked confused by the proffered bottle.

"We should celebrate your freedom. Freedom to choose a new career. Freedom to become human again." Had she gone too far? Maybe she had.

Oliver's expression changed. A smile appeared.

"You mean that?"

She nodded. "Yes."

He popped the cork, and carefully poured two glasses without spilling a drop. "To new beginnings."

Kim raised her glass and touched his. "To finding ourselves. And I have news too. I passed my midwifery exam, and am qualified to start work again."

He reached out to hug her. "Wow. Congratulations. You kept that quiet. I'm thrilled for you."

The rustle of the breeze in the trees, and the slapping of the waves on the shore, made the moment magical.

They sat quietly sipping their champagne until Moses came and announced that the others were back, and dinner was ready.

They joined them. Edward, Penny, Amina, and Sean were standing by the table.

"Rosie not joining us?" Kim asked, having counted the places laid on the table.

"No," Penny said. "She ate with the boys and has gone to her room. Because Sean wasn't here, she kindly photographed today's haul of bugs so Timothy could release them."

Sean looked surprised, but didn't comment. Instead, said, "Vanessa's feeling better, but is staying in overnight and should be fit to travel tomorrow."

While Sean was distracted pulling out a chair for Amina, Edward said quietly to Kim and Oliver. "He doesn't know. Vanessa has agreed to stay silent."

Sean then asked, "What are you lot scheming?"

Oliver turned to Kim with a questioning look. "Time to share our news?"

"Yes."

"Kim's passed her midwife exams, and I lost my job."

There were gasps of surprise. Concern about what he would do next, and congratulations for Kim.

Moses had made the table look festive. The candles were lit; their places laid close to each other at one end of the long table. Frangipani flowers floated in glass bowls, and sprays of bougainvillea surrounded the base of the candlesticks. Everyone raised their glasses with a toast to new beginnings.

Oliver pulled out her chair. Kim couldn't remember the last time he had made such a gentlemanly gesture.

A dainty plate of smoked sailfish, with a salad garnish and wedges of lemon, served as their starter. The freshly baked bread rolls were piping hot.

"We should dine like this more often." Oliver said as he spread butter on his hot roll.

"I'd be overweight in a month, and you'd leave me," she answered as she did the same.

"When will you start work?" Penny asked. Kim had been concerned by her lack of engagement with the group. And was glad that she had at last joined the conversation. She had been too quiet all day, but she was a private person, so Kim didn't like to probe.

"When the children start school and are settled. Part time to start with." She felt cross with herself that she had added the last bit. Part time made it sound less important than it was. None of them understood how much the job meant to her.

"A good way to get back into work." Penny said with an encouraging smile.

Kim was pleased. At least one person understood.

Moses cleared away the first course and came back with a dish that made Oliver's eyes light up. A fish pie with prawns and fresh fish bought from the fisherman, who called daily, with baskets of fresh fish hanging from the handlebars of his bicycle.

The food was perfect. This fish pie would linger in her memory. A dish to remind her of the joy of being married to Oliver.

Mango sorbet completed the perfect dinner and then everyone moved to the veranda for coffee.

Amina took the role of pouring for everyone, and Sean handed the cups round. Then asked for an update on the situation with Martin.

Amina shook her head and said, “Nothing new. Simeon has gone after him. He thinks he knows where he is, but hasn't called to tell me more. He says Sandra is putting on a brave face, trying to pretend everything is okay. But she refuses to go to town for a checkup.”

Kim touched Oliver's hand; her happiness slightly dampened by knowing Martin was still missing.

“When's the baby due?”

“Not for two weeks.”

“At least my going back with you means she will have a midwife handy.”

Amina smiled. “That will put Jenny's mind at rest.”

“Who is Jenny?” Oliver asked.

“A lovely lady and old family friend who lives on Chui Farm, and keeps us all in order. She treats us all like her children and Sam and Emma like her grandchildren.”

Jenny sounded like a down to earth practical woman, and Kim looked forward to meeting her.

The only thing that took a shine off the evening was the unanswered questions about Martin, and the Rosie and Vanessa situation.

CHAPTER 23

Mombasa - Thursday 26th September

Vanessa was relieved that Sean agreed to leave the hospital, as she needed time alone. She dosed off and woke with a clear plan, to contact Fay. She couldn't call in the middle of the night, but she could text. And do it without Sean hovering over her.

She scrolled through the contacts on her phone, found the number, and keyed in her message.

'Hi Fay.

Sorry to have to beg for help. The situation here is not good.

Rosie has done her best to make my life difficult. Which I expected. Sean is unaware of what she's done. And even if he knew, I doubt he'd have the courage to call you for advice. But Rosie's out of control. And I'm terrified of what she might do next.

I'll understand if you feel you can't help. I know you love Rosie. Kim is doing her best, but she might be afraid to tell you.

Can you come? If so, make it a surprise. Let Sandra work out the logistics.

I'm going to Ol Essakut with Kim and her children tomorrow. The rest will head to Tsavo for a few days.

I wouldn't ask if it wasn't important.

Vanessa.'

She reread the message before hitting the send button. Had she done the right thing?

Less than fifteen minutes later, her phone rang.

“I've booked my flight. What's she done?” The resigned tone told Vanessa that Fay expected trouble.

“It is too serious to go into detail. But trust me. Your help is vital for her safety and wellbeing.”

“That bad?”

“Yes, and we're afraid to tell Sean in case he kicks off. Which would be a disaster. You might be the only person who can make her understand the dire consequences of her actions.”

“She hasn't tried to hurt herself?”

“No. Not yet. But come and judge for yourself.”

“How's Sean?”

“Struggling and unaware of her actions.”

“And your relationship?” Trust Fay to be forthright.

“Under pressure, but that's not why I'm asking.”

“I'll let Sandra know my flight details. You can fill me in when I get there.”

“Thank you. Turning up unannounced would be best.”

“I don't know why I'm agreeing,” Fay said, “But for Rosie's sake, I'll come.”

As the call ended, Vanessa wondered what had gone wrong between Sean and Fay. He certainly hadn't considered the impact on his children.

She slept again and woke dreaming about painting Rosie's portrait. An omen, or could it be a fitting punishment? The idea of making Rosie sit for her took root. Maybe the resulting portrait could be her parting gift to Sean. Because she was certain their relationship was doomed.

The staff, and the facilities at the little hospital, were a far cry from the horrors she'd envisaged when they brought her in. It was a well-appointed modern building with a private room that was up to the standard of the nearby hotels. The staff pampered her and made her feel safe.

The temptation to flee to the safety of her new studio flat had gone. Making Rosie understand the enormity of what she had done had to be addressed.

The logistics would be tricky. But with Fay coming, the decision to stay was easier.

Kim and Amina came to pick her up from the hospital.

"Where's Sean?" she asked.

"Edward and Oliver persuaded him the waves were perfect for a final surf. And we pushed him to go. We wanted a chance to find out what you intend to do about Rosie."

"Nothing at the moment. Just keep us apart."

"We guessed that's what you'd say," Amina said. "You can fly to Ol Essakut today with Kim and the children. Sandra offered to let you stay at Chui Ranch rather than with the others at the Ol Essakut house."

"How will I explain my decision to Sean?"

"Simple," Kim said. "Say you can't face the heat."

"That should work," Vanessa agreed. "I've spoken to Fay. I've asked for her help with Rosie, but please don't tell Rosie or Sean or the others. It's best that they don't know."

"Thank you. I nearly called her myself." Kim said. "None of us feel qualified to help."

"I didn't tell her what Rosie did. Rosie needs to own up to her actions."

When they reached the house, Rosie hurried towards them. As if she wanted to talk.

Vanessa turned to Kim and said, "Keep her away from me."

Kim nodded, stepped forward and caught Rosie by the arm and pulled her to the side. Rosie looked pleadingly at Vanessa, who ignored her, and walked into the house and out onto the veranda.

Sean had obviously been watching for their return, and came bounding up from the beach. He left a trail of wet sandy footprints on the flagstones as he reached to hug her. Vanessa held him at arm's length. "Don't make me wet. I'm fine."

He gave her a peck on the cheek. "Great. I guess I should rinse the salt water off." After showering under the outside shower, he came and sat on the wall near her. "You're okay, aren't you?"

"Yes, but I don't think I can cope with the heat and dust of a safari. Amina says I can fly with her to Ol Essakut."

His face fell. "I'll come with you." He reached for her hand.

"No. You can't let the others down. Besides, there isn't a seat on the flight for you." She didn't dare mention Rosie. Her wishes didn't matter. "I need a couple of quiet days, and I can paint if I feel strong enough."

Her reasoning satisfied him. "Okay. Any more news about Martin? I wish there was something we could do."

"Sticking to the plans they've made for us as a group will give them less to worry about."

"What time will you go?"

"Fairly soon, but you're booked for later this afternoon. You can have another swim before you leave."

"I'll change so I can come and see you off."

"No. Stay with Rosie and the others."

He looked unsure, but to her relief, agreed without argument.

CHAPTER 24

Machakos - Thursday 26th September

Martin's spirits were raised by the owl call, and was certain Simeon was close by. Simeon was cautious, and unlikely to make a move without a plan, or before it was completely dark. But his hopes of rescue were dashed when he heard a convoy of vehicles arrive. Doors slammed, voices carried. Someone was being shouted at for being a fool. Was this part of Simeon's plan? No. The anger was genuine. That much he gathered; the rest was unclear. The thump of approaching footsteps prepared him for the worst.

The door flung open; four men entered. Their faces covered. Was this a good sign? They didn't want him to identify them. Was he to be released? What price would they demand for his freedom? He sensed from their arrogant stance that these men were higher up the scale than the men who captured him. Which made them more dangerous.

He took a deep breath. Stay calm. Don't show fear.

A powerful torch shone into his eyes, blinding him.

"Who are you?" One demanded in flawless English.

"Martin Owen, a photojournalist." No point in trying to pretend to be someone else. They would have seen his press pass.

"Why were you following this man?" He pointed the torch away from Martin and shone it on a fifth man, who was standing in the doorway. It was the man from the refugee camp, his face uncovered. His swagger gone as he cowered in the beam of light.

"I had seen him before at one of the refugee camps." Martin had to make his answer plausible. "I wanted to ask him how he was, and if he'd found work. People like a follow-up story And I thought it would be a good one."

The man pulled out a knife and waved it at Martin. "I don't believe you."

Martin forced himself not to flinch. The man stepped back and began cleaning dirt from under his nails with the knife. "Wouldn't the trouble at the mall be a better story?"

"Maybe, but I got there too late. All the papers already have pictures."

"Why didn't you approach him when you first saw him?"

"I wasn't sure it was the same person. But when I was certain that it was. I chased after him and found myself here."

"Do you expect me to believe that?" He kicked Martin's shins. "When did you see him at the camp?"

"A couple of years ago."

Another kick, this time harder. Martin clamped his jaw shut. He didn't want to scream. His legs were hurting enough.

His tormenter turned his attention and light on the cowering man. "Is this true?" The man nodded. Martin was grateful. Maybe now they would talk to him rather than beat him up. But his gratitude was short-lived. A kick knocked him sideways.

"Who knows what you were doing?"

Was it safer to say no one? No, he had to let them know others would look for him. "I left a message at the news desk. They'll wonder why I haven't called in." That avoided naming Hank.

“What number do you call?”

“The one on autodial on my phone.”

The answer wasn't what his inquisitor wanted to hear. He broke into a tirade at the man in the doorway. Then he launched another kick, spun round, and marched out. The rest scurried after him. The door slammed shut, and the bolt rammed home and the lock clicked shut.

Martin struggled to straighten up to find a less painful position against the post. The kicks had twisted him awkwardly. But slowly, inch by inch, he wriggled until he could no longer feel the notch that had caused him so much discomfort, and could rest his head against the post. The kicks had hurt, but done little more than add bruises to his already battered body.

He couldn't work out why the man was so angry about his phone. Maybe he was asking if they still had it. Martin didn't think they did. And wondered if they'd ditched it for fear of it being tracked, or just to make money from it. Had they checked it for a tracking device?

He ran over the excuses he could use if they had. Company phone, always tracked to help stop them from being stolen. Yes, but would they believe him?

Had wishful thinking led him to believe that Simeon was out there? Had the owl hoots, and the cooing, been his imagination going wild?

He strained to pick up any sound to confirm his presence. There was nothing other than the angry voices of his captors. Then they returned. They put the bag over his head and untied the ropes attached to the post. Then, hauled him to his feet and, with a man on either side, and dragged him outside and pushed him against a vehicle. They spun him round and shoved him backwards so violently his head crashed against the floor. His legs were lifted and pushed inside. His captors clambered over him. No care taken as they settled themselves using his body as a footrest. He lay there, afraid to move, afraid of further kicks.

CHAPTER 25

Ol Essakut - Friday 27th September

Sandra's stress levels were up and down like a Yo-Yo.

Simeon told her he was sure he had located Martin, but couldn't attempt a rescue before it got dark. She had heard nothing more. What was holding things up? Had they tried and failed? Why wouldn't anyone tell her what happened?

She felt like a beached whale, barely able to move. The nagging backache wouldn't go away. But she didn't dare tell Jenny. She was already fussing too much.

Thankfully, Amina was coming back to shoulder some of Jenny's workload and be a calming influence.

What puzzled her was that Amina was not coming alone. Some of the Martin's friends were coming with her. Why they wanted to skip the Tsavo part of the itinerary was unclear. What had gone wrong? Whatever it was, it had prompted Sean's wife Fay to come out to deal with a problem with Rosie. She specifically asked for her arrival to be a surprise. All Sandra had to do was arrange for her to get to Tsavo. When the call ended, Sandra was left with questions. Who was the woman Sean had come with? What was up with his daughter? Would the wife turning up send sparks flying?

Sandra wished she knew more about Martin's friends. Martin was always invited to join them, but hadn't for the last seven years. Why did people assume that because she was pregnant, she didn't need to understand what was going on?

When Sean chose to come to Kenya to celebrate twenty years of their joint holidays and booked for them all to stay at Ol Essakut. Martin was delighted, but also apprehensive. But as plans developed, he looked forward to the event. In all the time she had known Martin, he hadn't seemed to have or need friends around him other than Simeon. Not that he was anti-social, but that he held back from developing close bonds with anyone. Bonds that she felt he had with these old school friends. Why else would he have called them about changing their plans before he had gone off to Nairobi?

Now he was missing. And she hadn't been able to accept his proposal. The baby kicked, as usual, when she thought of Martin.

Jenny fussed all morning, freaking out about her going into labour. She spent ages on the phone arranging for a delivery pack to be sent to the Aero Club in Nairobi. And instructing Amina to pick it up on her return flight.

Sandra hated the fuss. Yes, she was tired and had swollen legs and a nagging backache. She'd go to the hospital when Martin got back, and not before.

After lunch, the plane buzzed over the house and set Jenny off again. She jumped up to tell Juma to send someone to the airstrip to pick up the arrivals. There was no need. The staff knew the routine well enough for it to happen without instruction.

A little later, Amina, accompanied by two women and two children, joined them on the veranda. Jenny welcomed them and wasted no time in taking charge of the children, suggesting they go with her to meet Sam and Emma. The cute pair were whisked away, leaving Amina to introduce her fellow travellers.

She touched Sandra's shoulder and pulled Kim forward. “This is Kim.” She waved toward the other guest, who was standing apart from them. “And this is Vanessa.”

“Welcome. Excuse me for not getting up. Take a seat.”

“And you'll be pleased to hear,” Amina grinned. “Kim's a fully qualified midwife, which might come in handy if you decide to give birth in a hurry.”

“No chance. This little one is waiting for Martin to get back.” Sandra stroked her bump.

The women smiled at the gesture.

“Any news?” Kim asked.

“Only that Simeon thinks he's located him. He has a few of his old army friends to help, and two trackers from here are on their way to see if they can rescue him. Has he spoken to you again?” She looked at Amina, who shook her head. “Well, come on spill. What made you all change your plans?”

“I skipped the safari because the kids can't cope with the heat.” Kim brushed a strand of hair out of her eyes. “And I thought you might like to have a midwife on hand.”

Jenny reappeared in time to hear this last sentence and wasted no time in insisting that Kim check Sandra over.

Resisting Jenny's demands would be useless, so Sandra said, “Fine. Fine. I agree. But let her have a cup of tea first.”

Vanessa looked at the others before she spoke. “I had an allergy problem and also thought the heat might be too much. And I've been struggling with Sean's teenage daughter and felt it would be safer for both of us to remove myself.”

“Safer?” Sandra queried.

“Yes, long story. I'll explain later.” Amina said, shutting down the topic.

Jenny's eyebrows raised, but she fired her next question at Amina. "You picked up that parcel?"

"Yes. That's what delayed us. Fortunately, it gave the children a chance for a run about at the Aero Club while we waited."

Sandra could feel Kim's concentrated stare at her swollen ankles. Her doctor said that she must rest, which was all Jenny had allowed her to do. Having a midwife here was perfect.

"Have you been a midwife for long?" She wanted to prove she was not averse to help.

"Ten years before the children were born. I've just retrained so I can go back to work. When are you due?"

"Two weeks." Kim frowned, so she added, "I'm happy for you to look at my notes as soon as we've finished tea. Maybe you can put Jenny's mind at rest."

Kim smiled. "It will be a pleasure. I've missed working, and am longing to get back to it."

Sandra turned to Vanessa. "Amina said you lost your bags and you're an artist."

"Yes."

"I am sure I have things in my wardrobe to help, and you're welcome to use my studio. I haven't used it for weeks."

"That's kind of you. I guess I ought to explain the full reason I'm here." She took a deep breath and began telling Sandra what had happened leading up to the aspirin in the drink. "It could have killed me. I've been asked not to tell anyone, including her father, for fear of repercussions. Amina gave a graphic warning of what might happen if the police got involved. Angry as I am, I wouldn't wish that on her."

Sandra liked her honesty. "I'm not sure I'd have been so kind under similar circumstances. Do you know why she did it?"

“She probably blames me for Sean and Fay's breakup. Which I'm partly responsible for. And the reason I asked Fay to come.”

“You asked her?”

Vanessa nodded. “Yes. Awkward, but felt like the right thing to do.”

“Tricky for you all.”

Tea arrived, complete with scones and biscuits. Jenny took control and poured them all a cup, and handed round the plates. When they finished, she asked if they wanted to listen to the news.

Sandra shook her head. “No. Sorry, I find it too depressing. The fact Martin isn't there is no help. I'll go for a rest. Kim, come with me, and I'll give you my notes.”

She lumbered to her feet. Kim was close enough to help her up, but held back. It was bad enough to struggle without people making her feel totally incapable.

Sandra made it up the stairs, but her back pain was worse than it had been earlier.

There must have been a telltale sign in the way she moved to make Kim ask. “How long have you had back pain?”

A gripping twinge took her breath away, making it hard to answer. “A couple of days.” She regretted the admission as she sensed that now serious fussing would begin.

Kim suggested she lie down while she read the notes. She moved to the window seat and opened the file. “When was your last scan?” she asked.

“About halfway through. There was a power cut when I was due to have another one. But everything seemed to be okay, so I didn't bother to go back. Why? Have you spotted something?”

“How active is the baby?”

"Very. I am constantly being elbowed in the ribs. Can you tell the sex? Not that I want to know. We decided we'd rather have a surprise."

"No. That's not clear." Something about her tone had Sandra second guessing. "What is it?"

Kim ignored the question and headed toward the door. "I'm just going to fetch that pack that we picked up. I'd like to listen to the baby's heartbeat if that's okay with you."

Was this routine, or something more frightening? Could there be a problem? Should she admit the nagging pain in her lower back had gone on for over twenty-four hours? And own up to all the other aches and pains?

Kim returned, bringing the pack with her. She was smiling. "It has just what I need." She pulled out a trumpet shaped device. "Far better than a toilet roll."

Kim asked her to expose her bump. After running her hand gently over Sandra's extended belly, she picked up the trumpet, place the wide end to Sandra's skin and leaned in and put her ear against it. She moved the trumpet gently to another spot. Sandra held her breath. Kim looked at her between movements. "It's okay for you to breathe."

She tried a few more spots, then put the instrument to one side and had another feel.

She stepped back a pace. "Has anyone suggested you might be having twins?"

"No. We talked about it. Martin had already fathered twins. And the doctor said it was unlikely that I would, as there aren't any in my family." Sandra stared at her, the question sinking in. "Twins? No. It's just a big baby."

"I'm not so sure. Look," Kim held out the scan. "Can you see a faint shadow? That could be a second baby hiding behind the first. I think I picked up a second heartbeat. They're in so in sync with each other, it's hard to be sure. It's a pity you didn't have a second scan."

"I didn't think it was important, and kept finding excuses not to go."

"It might have given a clearer picture. And they are right, you having twins because of Martin's history, is unlikely, the odds against it happening."

Sandra stared at the image and had difficulty spotting the shadow child. Kim pointed out another spot. "This could be a foot and this shadow a hand." Soon Sandra saw what Kim was seeing. There was something there.

"I could make them move, but I don't want to. They seem to be in the perfect position right now. The back ache is your pelvis preparing for birth."

"But they can't come until Martin gets here. He wasn't around when his first two children were born. It's really important for him to be present."

"Don't fret. You're a long way from ready. Amina says Simeon is on the case, and the others are confident he'll bring him home."

CHAPTER 26

Tsavo - Friday 27th September

Edward had been watching Penny carefully since Vanessa's comment. And he couldn't work out what was wrong. She was her usual efficient self, making sure the boys had the right clothing, applied sunscreen, and eaten, but there was something different about her.

Had someone told her about Lauren? If so, why hadn't she said anything? No. It couldn't be that. Or she'd be angry with him, and he didn't pick up any animosity.

While they were checking into the camp, Penny went to find the ladies, leaving her bags on the table. Her phone buzzed, and without thinking, he picked it up. There was a message from her mother. Only part was visible, but enough to panic him.

Penny returned, and the boys dragged her off to see some marvel. He wanted to know what else her mother had said, but it would have to wait until they were alone. He dropped the phone into her bag and went to complete the check in forms.

He followed Penny as she walked slowly towards their tent. She said the heat was getting to her, but since seeing that message, he knew that heat was just an excuse. There was more going on. Kim's parting comment should have been warning enough to ask questions. Did he dare probe? The children rushed ahead and were busy unpacking and inspecting every inch of their canvas accommodation. Then they rushed over to report their findings before he could broach the subject of her mother's message.

The camp was run in an old-fashioned way. There were three solidly constructed buildings that provided a social and eating area, a store and the generator house. Spread out on each side were the canvas tents. Each had a wooden frame to support a thatched roof, which helped keep the tents cooler. All the tents stood on solid concrete plinths, giving a clean, flat surface for the bed bases. Their tent was one of the larger ones with a dividing canvas wall down the middle. One half for the boys and the other for them. Behind the tent was a surprisingly spacious bathroom with conventional plumbing.

"Thank heavens. I won't have to wander round the camp at night in the dark to find a toilet," she said. "I was worried. My stomach is playing up, and I dreaded that."

Outside the front was a deck with four folding canvas chairs and a table. A Kerosene lamp hung from a hook on the branch of the overhanging tree. It was too early for it to be lit, but it was comforting to know it was there. Their guide had told them that the camp electricity went off at ten o'clock.

The boys were in their element. Their staff had discovered that the boys were fascinated by any creature that moved. They added a couple of bugs to the growing collection. Among them was an enormous dung beetle, along with its pile of dung, which went into one of the many plastic containers that Nicholas carried with him to house his latest acquisitions.

Sean might regret coming if they were going to keep him fully occupied taking photos. Rosie had surprised them by helping when Sean had been at the hospital with Vanessa. Edward noticed she was more subdued than before, and would respond when spoken to, but never instigated a conversation.

He was sure Penny was sorry that Vanessa had gone to Ol Essakut with Kim and Amina. Their initial hesitancy over Fay's replacement had turned to respect. How Vanessa had not lost her temper with Rosie during the week was a miracle. Maybe it would have been better if she had kicked back. Some sort of reaction might have stopped Rosie from carrying her vendetta so far that Vanessa wound up in the hospital.

It had been difficult to witness the whole thing and not be able to take any action. Had they been back in England, then the whole situation might have had a completely different slant on it. Rosie could have found herself under arrest for attempted murder. Sean had no idea how fortunate they were that Vanessa had agreed to go along with the plan to say that the aspirin taking was an accident. The nightmare of the local police being involved was beyond anyone's imagination. If Vanessa hadn't recovered so quickly, Rosie could have found herself in a tricky situation.

Their camp escort offered to let them have tea in front of their tent and told them that the evening game run would be leaving in an hour's time. Penny sank gratefully into a chair under the dappled shade of an acacia tree.

Yellow weaver birds flitted about in the treetop. Hanging precariously upside down on the underside of their nests that dangled precariously from the branch above. A few superb starlings flashed their brilliant blue plumage as they darted back and forth, skimming the water in the shallow pool about ten yards in front of their tent.

He could hear the excited voices of the children. What gems had they found now? He hoped they wouldn't come running back yet. Penny needed a few moments on her own to soak up the warmth of the sun and let the tension in her neck ease. The strain of the journey had really knocked her sideways.

"Are you sure you'll be okay for the game drive?"

She shook her head. "I'd rather lie down. Can you manage on you own with the boys?"

"Of course I can. But I'm happy to skip it if you want me around."

"No. You should go with them. I'll be fine."

"Are you sure?"

"Yes, stop fussing. Go. Have fun."

He was reluctant to leave her. There was more to her staying behind than just the heat and the bumpy ride to the camp. But the boys were tugging at his sleeve, eager to go.

She sipped her tea and watched a couple of warthogs running along in the dry grass just outside the perimeter of the camp and laughed at the way their tails stuck up in the air as they ran. A group of vultures circled the sky in the distance. He wondered what they had found to scavenge.

"Come on Mummy," Timothy said.

"Sorry, I'm not coming on the game drive. I'm going to have a rest before dinner." Timothy stroked her hand, and she added, "You can tell me all about it when you get back." This made his face light up.

Edward loved her for not spoiling the day for the children because she was tired.

"Have a good rest," Edward said. "Come on boys, we don't want to miss anything." He got up, bent, and gave her a kiss on the forehead and said, "Love you."

As he walked away, he knew he had to make a complete break with Lauren. The problem was how. He had tried to call her several times, but she wasn't picking up. He had sent texts telling her not to do anything about property. Still nothing from her. Finally, he'd sent a text saying that he couldn't leave his family.

That got a text in reply.

'You'll regret it.'

Edward stared at the message. Was it a threat, or a prediction?

CHAPTER 27

Machakos - Friday 27th September

With his head covered, all Martin could do was concentrate on breathing. He didn't know how far they had travelled. All he could tell was that most of the journey was on murram roads. Then they hit a smooth surface. Not long after which, the vehicle came to a halt. It was only a temporary respite. A warning not to make a noise and more pressure of the feet on his body added to his tension. A door opened and shut. There was the rattle of a petrol nozzle and the buzz of the pump. When it stopped, there was a last rattle and then silence. No one in the vehicle spoke or moved. The door opened and closed, and the engine started again. The smooth ride didn't last long. They were soon back on rough tracks.

His head ached and his muscles tensed with every bump on the road. Exhaustion won, and he woke part way through his recurring nightmare. He was back in the war zone, taking risks in search of that elusive shot that would show the world the brutality of the situation.

His skin was clammy, and he was shaking. He couldn't bear that the dream was back. The dreams nearly broke him, and he'd fought to get over them.

He had to focus on the present situation. Showing weakness could be fatal.

The silence in the vehicle surprised him. Maybe they were sleeping, or maybe they were too frightened to speak.

When they stopped again, he sensed this was their destination. The door opened, and the men who had been resting their feet on him got out, and dragged his feet to the edge and manhandled him into a sitting position. Moments later, with a man on either side holding his elbows, he was half lifted, half dragged up a slope into a building and lowered onto what felt like a plastic stacking chair.

He stayed silent, praying for the suffocating bag to be removed.

When it was, it took a moment for his eyes to adjust to the bright light. His captors had their faces covered. They were in some sort of garage, with worn tyres stacked on one side and rusting car parts on the other. He faced sliding doors that were partly open.

Someone placed a sugary bread roll in his hand. He muttered thanks and took a bite. Better eat while he could. It was so dry he choked so badly he dropped the roll. Water was offered instead. When the coughing eased a fraction, he took a sip. He drank as much as he could, afraid that he might not get more. He had barely got halfway through the bottle when someone snatched it out of his hand.

He saw a man climb down a ladder into the inspection pit. Two others lifted him and dragged him over to the side of it. They kicked his legs, and his feet went over the edge and they lowered him part way and let go. The man in the pit broke his fall and kept him from crashing face first. He shoved him against the end of the pit and ordered him to sit.

Once Martin was where he wanted him. He pointed to a bag in the corner and said, "Food. Water." He climbed out and removed the ladder. Someone dropped a blanket into the pit and said, "Stay quiet, or we'll gag you."

Martin nodded. All the while assessing his new prison. The pit was about six feet deep and just over two feet wide. Even without his hands being tied, he doubted he'd be able to haul himself out of it. The greasy floor was dry. There were scraps of rag and a few nuts and bolts, and in amongst the debris he spotted a screw. A sheet of corrugated iron was dragged over the top, cutting out the light, apart from tiny gaps between the bumpy ridges, which also let air into the pit.

He sat still for a while, stretching his legs out. Listening in case his captors said anything that would give a clue where he was or what they intended to do with him.

But all he could gather was that they left two men to guard him. The others left, and the sliding door rattled as they closed.

Being able to move his legs was good after being tied with them bent for so long. Had he really seen a screw? Could he find it? Could he pick it up? Would he be able to use it to cut the tape that bound his hands and feet?

If he shuffled forward enough, he could get to it. But first he would try to stand up. He succeeded. Being able to change his position was a bonus, but he had to keep quiet and not alert his captors. He sank down again and moved a little way down the pit, feeling all the time for the screw. It took ages, but at last he found it and picked it up. But how could he get it to break the bindings?

If he gripped the screw between his teeth, he could try to pierce the tape to weaken it. But first, he needed to get into a comfortable position. With more bottom shuffling, he lay down with the coarse blanket as a pillow and got the screw head in his mouth. Now, if he moved his hands closer with luck, he could puncture the binding, and if he kept doing that, he might break through to release his hands. Again and again, he pushed his wrist against the point of the screw. Holding it tight between his lips was a strain, and twice he relaxed his lips and the screw fell out. Retrieving it was difficult. The third time he dropped it, exhaustion kicked in, he was too tired to continue.

There was movement in the space above him. Chairs scraped on the ground. Mumbled conversations. The smell of cheap tobacco seeped into the pit. And then shuffling of feet. The little light that had filtered through the edge of the corrugated lid of the pit went out. A while later, he heard the rhythmic sound of snoring.

The last thing Martin wanted to do was sleep and risk the nightmare returning. To keep himself awake, he tried to visualize himself lying on the beach at Diani, with Sandra lying beside him and the children playing in the sand nearby. These happy memories filled him with joy and resolve to keep his cool and to survive this ordeal. He had to get back to her. He had to tell her how he loved her and how much joy she brought into his life.

With fresh resolve, he fumbled to find the screw he had dropped earlier to continue his task of breaking through the tape binding his hands.

It was tiring work, but he persevered until his lips could no longer hold the screw in place.

And then he was running.

A bullet whizzed past his nose, and another slammed into his arm as he ducked for cover. He dived into a doorway, hoping for shelter from the sniper. Only a fool would risk entering the danger zone. Getting this far had been easy, but getting out alive was another thing.

With his back to the wall, he sank down to catch his breath and assess the damage. Luck was on his side. It was only a flesh wound. He pulled a dressing out of a pocket in his trousers and pressed it into place. He closed his eyes, thinking how close he had been to death. An inch higher and he'd be out there in the street, riddled with bullets. But it wasn't over. The sniper knew he was here. He'd watch like a hawk for even the slightest movement so he could notch up a kill.

When his heart stopped pounding, habit made him raise his camera and record the destruction that surrounded him. The dust laden furniture and the trapping of daily life of a family home surrounded him. Amongst the splintered furniture lay toys. As he panned the room with his lens, he heard a whimper and froze. His lens fixed on the terrified eyes of a child sitting on a pile of rubble. Tears and blood had streaked the dust on her cheeks. Her hair was partly covered by a green sequined scarf that hid the lower half of her face. She hugged a doll to her chest. There was no way to tell her age. Probably about four years old, maybe older, poor nutrition made it hard to tell.

There was a bundle of cloth beside her. Feet stuck out from under a fold of fabric. Further back was another body. Instinct made him want to grab the child and comfort her. But he couldn't. The sniper was waiting.

If she moved, she'd be in equal danger. Did she understand she had to stay where she was? Hopefully, fear would stop her from moving. He had nothing to offer her. No water, no food. She edged off the pile of rubble she was sitting on. He put up his hand and hoped she'd understand it meant stop. He pointed towards the doorway and made a gesture of a gunman. Her eyes widened, and she inched her way back.

Outside, distant sporadic gunfire kept them pinned where they were. Then a vehicle roared up the street. An explosion followed, and the building shook. A cascade of dust from the half-collapsed ceiling fell on Martin. The firing outside intensified.

The fear was too much for the child. She set out across the room towards him. The little figure was in full flight in his direction. A burst of bullets made Martin duck.

He screamed, "No."

Too late. Bullets ricocheted around the room. One hit his shoulder. Momentum propelled the child towards him. She landed on top of him, pinning him to the ground. He held her tight. When the firing stopped and the dust settled, he realized that the warm, sticky blood on his hand wasn't his own. He adjusted his position and felt her breath on his neck and heard a faint sigh. They lay there for a while; the breathing getting slower and slower. He touched her head. Her hair was thick with blood. A bullet had hit her head, and another her chest. All he could do was hold her as she took her last gasp, and keep her close as her blood soaked through his clothes and hardened.

He didn't remember who found them. He woke in the hospital. The child was gone. He never found out her name. Who took her? Or where they buried her. That hellhole had broken him. All he wanted was to get out of there and wipe the memory.

He sobbed. He hadn't cried for her then, but now that he remembered those final moments, he couldn't stop.

The clatter of tin penetrated his thoughts. A torch shone onto his face, bringing him back to reality and the current danger he faced. He was captive, with no idea of his future.

There was a shout. "Get him out." The ladder was put back, and a man came into the pit. Martin had to bend his legs to avoid being trodden on. A second man joined him and somehow pulled him upright. More hands reached down, and they manhandled him over the edge, leaving him lying on his side.

"We told you no noise." The man with the perfect English accent said.

"A nightmare," Martin said, trying to stop his sobbing. Sandra had told him that sometimes he screamed, but mainly that he moaned. The screams only happened if he reached the part where the child ran towards him. He had never reached the moment of her death before.

"Your phone. Who was tracking it?" The man demanded, not caring about his excuse.

Martin squinted because a beam of light was focused on him. "I don't know."

The man kicked him in the ribs. "I don't believe you."

"It's a work phone. Maybe the newspaper set it up," Martin said, as he caught his breath.

"And why would they do that?"

"Protecting their property. Stop it being stolen," he stammered as another kick landed.

"Lucky for you, my men got rid of it. The man who bought it has been arrested. And that makes me angry."

More kicks hit their mark, leaving Martin gasping for air as they shoved him over the edge. Luckily, his feet hit the ground first. His legs gave way, and he fell forward. He stretched his arms out as best he could to stop his head from hitting the concrete floor. Some of the tape holding his hands, weakened by his action with the screw, tore with the momentum. Moments later, the iron lid slid into place, plunging him into darkness.

CHAPTER 28

Tsavo - Friday 27th September

Penny watched Edward walk away. There was something different in his behaviour. He was more considerate, and saying he loved her, a complete surprise. She couldn't remember the last time he'd uttered those words.

It was odd being the only woman to have come to Tsavo. She missed Kim and Vanessa and missed Fay even more. Fay would have loved the flight and views of the spectacular expanse of the open plains, with the pilot pointing out what to look for. Fay would have competed with the boys at spotting animals. And maybe even got Rosie to join in, instead of sitting at the back with her headphones on sulking, while Sean sat up front with the pilot.

She waited until they were out of sight before lying down and closing her eyes.

It was dark when she woke, and it took a few minutes to work out where she was. There were voices in the distance. Louder than the voices were cicadas, hyrax and nightjars. She closed her eyes again, trying to guess what other creatures might be out there making the unfamiliar sounds.

Then reality kicked in. How long had she slept? Why had no one called her? Where were Edward and the boys? They should be back by now. She forced herself to sit up, and nervously put her feet on the sisal bedside mat, and tipped up her shoes before putting them on.

Outside, the solar lit path guided her to where people were sitting round a big fire near the dining area.

She scanned the crowd, searching for Edward and the children, expecting them to be near the fire. They weren't there. Nor were the others. The camp light made it hard to check the time. She had to find someone who might have information about the rest of the group. But who? Disorientated, and scared, she hurried to reception. When she got there, she saw Fay standing by the desk. She gasped. The doctor hadn't warned her the drugs might cause hallucinations. Next, she'd find out she wasn't in Africa at all.

She looked again. Fay was hurrying towards her.

"Thank God I've found you," Fay said as she flung her arms round Penny's neck. "I thought they'd brought me to the wrong camp."

Penny stammered, "Why are you here?"

"Vanessa called. Said there was a problem with Rosie. Said she needed me."

"She said that?"

"Yes. So, I came to see if I can fix things. Tell me what happened?"

Penny saw the manager walking towards her. She pushed Fay's hand off her arm and moved towards him.

"Excuse me. I can't find my husband or my children. Where are they?"

"They're fine. They came across a baby elephant in trouble, and have been helping to save it. We've sent another vehicle out to bring them back."

"Is anyone hurt?"

"No. They should be back within an hour."

Fay stood beside her. "Are Sean and Rosie out there too?"

"I think so. They all went together."

"Are you all right?" Fay asked.

"Sorry, just jumpy. This all feels like a bad dream."

"I can assure you, I'm real." Fay squeezed her hand.

"I hate not knowing what they're doing."

"I know what you mean. I thought life would be peaceful without having to deal with Rosie and her tantrums. Instead, I missed them and wish I could wind back to how things were."

"Well, I can assure you tantrums would have been pleasant compared to how she's behaved."

"She can't have been that bad?"

"She made Vanessa's life a misery. And nearly killed her by giving her aspirin, even though she knew Vanessa had an allergy to it." Penny shouldn't have blurted that out, but too late to retract the words.

"Seriously?" Fay said. "Vanessa gave no hint she had done anything like that."

"Vanessa was lucky. She'd mentioned her allergy to aspirin, and that she carried an EpiPen. Kim used it before the situation was irreversible."

"My God, poor kid."

"Lucky is more like it, because we persuaded Vanessa to say it was an accident. Only we all know it was deliberate. Except for Sean. No one dares tell him. No one wanted Rosie to be arrested and face a charge of attempted murder."

Fay blinked with shock. She obviously didn't know how to respond. So, Penny gave her time to digest the information by asking. "When did you arrive?"

"First thing, then I had to wait to get a seat on the late plane coming here." She stared at Penny, and added, "Are you all right?"

Penny knew her mind had wandered. Dark thoughts were taking over. She must snap out of it.

Fay asked, "What's wrong?"

"Everything. My family is in the bush somewhere. I can't find my phone. And I have cancer." The words tumbled out, and she couldn't pull them back.

Fay enveloped her in a hug.

Penny pushed her away. “Don't be nice to me. I can't handle that.”

“Would you rather I became professional and asked about the symptoms and the treatment?”

“Not really. They'll operate when I get back, and I don't know what other treatment will be necessary.”

Fay made her sit down. The information had, as she feared, made a difference, changing how Fay treated her. She was glad the others didn't know. But also found it a relief to have told someone. Someone she trusted, with whom she wouldn't have to pretend to be fine.

“How have Edward and the boys taken the news?”

“I haven't told them. You're the only person who knows.”

“What?” The shock in her voice was undisguised. “That must have been hard on you?”

“I didn't want to spoil the holiday. That news would have been a complete mood killer. Though with the way Rosie behaved, it might have been an excellent distraction.”

“That bad?”

Penny nodded.

A waiter came up to ask if they were ready to eat as dinner was being served.

Penny nearly declined, but felt that being surrounded by others might make her fears for the family less overwhelming. She expected Fay could probably do with a meal. Airline food was never very satisfying. As she stood up, she saw lights of an approaching vehicle. She waited where she was, hoping that Edward and the twins were back. The passengers disgorged. An elderly couple and a pregnant woman with a toddler emerged.

Penny hurried over to quiz the driver.

“Everybody fine,” he said. “I'm going back now for the others.”

He closed the door and departed. Leaving her feeling frustrated. The elderly couple were wending their way to the dining area. She hurried after them, desperate for information.

"Excuse me, can you tell me what happened? My husband and my two boys are missing. Were they with you?"

The old lady gripped her wrist. "Nicholas and Timothy, are they your boys? They're a delight. Don't worry. They're having the time of their lives."

"Why didn't they come back with you?"

"We needed to get back. My wife needs regular medication, and she didn't have it with her. Your boys didn't want to leave. They're quite safe. In fact, they were busy making friends with the Masai herdsmen who turned up. And they won't starve. The driver who fetched us delivered a huge hamper of food and drinks, enough to keep everyone happy all night."

"Thank you."

She hurried back to Fay. "Seems they're okay. Let's eat?"

Fay linked her arm through hers." Fill me in with what's happening with Martin?"

"We've been told he's missing, but don't think that's the full story. We're all struggling with enjoying ourselves, knowing Sandra must be going out of her mind with worry. Amina too, because Simeon has gone to find him. We all wish there was something useful to do to help."

The food comprised a sumptuous hot and cold buffet. Penny opted for chicken and mushrooms in a rich creamy sauce. "Not very 'African', but it's what I fancy," she said to Fay.

"Sounds delicious. I'll have the same."

The waiter carried their plates to the table. Fussed over them, took a drink order, and then left them to it.

Fay tucked in as if she hadn't eaten for days, which she probably hadn't. Penny tasted hers. It was better than expected and soon she had a nearly empty plate. She hadn't eaten much for weeks.

At last Fay wiped her mouth on the starched linen napkin, leaving a faint smear of lipstick on it. Penny marvelled at how in the middle of nowhere, crisp, starched linen was the norm. The last time she'd seen a linen napkin was at a ridiculously expensive restaurant with access to professional laundry services. But here, with a limited supply of water, they achieved old colonial standards. How they kept this pristine linen white was a mystery. All the rivers were muddy from the bright red soil. She made a mental note to ask and smiled.

It was crazy. She had a life-threatening disease and her curiosity about silly things showed how mad she really was. Edward was always teasing her because she needed to know everything. Maybe she should have been a writer so she could use all the useless facts she had stored in her memory bank.

Nicholas had inherited her natural curiosity. His current passion for bugs was all-consuming. Was it a bad thing? Not if she ensured he tuned into other things, and people. Timothy was more rounded. He took an interest in people and had his own passions. She imagined he'd become an eco-warrior, wanting to save everyone and everything from destruction. Nicholas would get bogged down on the finer details. The smaller habitats, the mini eco systems of his current interest. And prayed that they wouldn't fall out over their differences.

It was something she should discuss with Edward. He needed to be aware, as she was sure he would otherwise not notice. Maybe it was a man thing, maybe it was just Edward, but he sometimes was so unobservant of the subtle mood changes that occurred between the boys. There were distinct signs in their body language, and their speech, which came before a fight. If she heard a voice pitch hit a certain level, she would offer a biscuit, or suggest taking the dog for a walk, or simply interrupt what they were doing. It was usually enough to dispel the tension that was building.

Fay gazed at her intently. “Dare I ask what you are thinking about?”

“What will happen to the boys if my cancer is too advanced?”

Fay, God bless her, didn't tell her she was being a drama queen. Or suggest the cancer might be treatable. She listened, letting Penny pour out things that she had never, ever told anyone.

“I don't know how my parents will cope. This could break them.”

“They may surprise you. That generation is stronger than you'd expect. But that's not what's bothering you, is it?”

Penny looked round the room. A lot of the other guests had finished their meals and were vacating their tables. Some had drifted towards the chairs round the fire outside, others heading to their tents. The waiter cleared their plates, brought them some fruit salad for dessert, and left them to carry on with their meal.

“I was going to leave Edward.”

Fay nearly choked on her mouthful of fruit. “Why?”

“He's having an affair. I want to do what you did. Get out with my pride intact.”

“I'm not sure that's quite how it worked for me.” Fay said with a wistful look in her eyes.

“No?”

“I've known about Sean's affair for years. I left because we should never have married.”

“But you were so good together.” In all the years of annual holidays, they had seemed perfectly matched. Sharing a house tested cracks in a relationship, and none had been visible. Penny had always considered them to be a forever couple, and Fay was the perfect stepmother to Rosie and Matthew.

“I married him for his children.” Fay put her spoon down. There were tears in her eyes. “I've never admitted it before. But it's the truth. When Vanessa rang to say Rosie was in trouble. That's when it really hit me.”

“But I don't understand. Didn't you love him?”

“Oh, yes, I loved him, but not as much as I loved his children. Vanessa filled a need that I didn't. He married me because he wanted a mother for Rosie and Matthew. He never said so in as many words, and I never asked.”

“What made you walk away?”

“The children were growing up and would leave soon, and I couldn't face being left in a loveless marriage. And like you, I had a health scare. Which turned out to be a scare and nothing more. It made me think about my future. I had to take control of my destiny. It was that, or sink into deep depression.”

“What did you tell the children?”

“That's the problem. I didn't. They assumed it was because of Vanessa. It didn't occur to me it would cause problems, for them and for her. I didn't know she'd come on holiday with him. I expected him to let them get used to me being out of the way before making her part of the family. They knew her. She's been around for years, as his colleague. The funny thing is, I don't think Vanessa was ready for the whole ready-made family syndrome, and certainly didn't expect hostility. What an introduction to family life. I'd have run long before being hospitalized.”

“It was horrible to watch. And to be honest, we all thought Vanessa was the reason you'd left. But had to admire her patience. She never lost her temper. Even though Rosie got to her in so many ways. Rosie constantly demanded Sean's attention, so he never got a moment alone with Vanessa.”

“I should say it serves him right, but believe it or not, he has my sympathy.”

“No need for that. He couldn't see what was happening. None of us felt it was our place to interfere.”

CHAPTER 29

Tsavo - Friday 27th September

Sean watched the two excited boys run to their mother. They didn't stop to breathe. Words tumbled out. The Masai. The elephant. The bugs and all the things they saw. Stopping briefly to say something to the person with her.

That's when Sean registered it was Fay. What was she doing here?

He didn't think the boys had realized she hadn't been there earlier. For them, Fay being around was perfectly normal, and he doubted anyone had explained why she hadn't been with them all along.

Sean turned to see if anyone else had spotted her. Rosie stopped by his side. Blinked and froze. Unsure how she should react. He didn't know either. She checked to see what he'd do. He looked over at Fay.

Fay made the first move. She got up and gave Rosie a hug. Then she leaned over and gave Sean a peck on the cheek.

"What are you doing here?" he stammered once the shock wore off.

"Vanessa said that Rosie and I needed to talk."

"Vanessa?" he gulped and looked over at Rosie.

"Yes. She said it was urgent. I had time off and thought I should come. Do you mind?"

"I... no...," he stammered, "but..." He broke off, unsure what to say,

“Are you glad to see me?” Fay asked, looking at Rosie, who nodded. “Good.” Fay turned back to Edward and Oliver. “You all look as if you've been busy.”

The children and adults, Rosie included, were covered with streaks of bright orange-red mud. Their shorts, and shirts, legs, arms, and faces were coated with the stuff, and there were lumps of it stuck in their hair. All had satisfied expressions of a job well done. Exhaustion forgotten by the excitement.

“Slow down, and tell us what you've been up to.” Penny said.

Nicholas and Timothy barely stopped for breath as they answered.

“We saved a baby elephant.”

“It was in the mud.”

“Some Masai stopped us and asked for help.”

“They had spears.”

“They didn't have any pants on.”

“They wore blankets and had mud in their hair.”

“It was a big elephant.”

“No, it wasn't, it was only this big.” Timothy put his hand up to about a foot above his head.

“No, it was this big.” Nicholas stretched his arm higher.

Penny and Fay turned from one to the other as they spoke. It was like watching a tennis match as the words came from one side then the other. Rosie said nothing.

The conversation continued.

“Our truck had to pull a tree out of the way.”

“We had sausages and boiled eggs.”

“And cake.”

“And lemonade.”

“And crisps.”

Penny's chance of getting the boys to bed was out of the question. With their level of excitement, it was probably better to let them talk it out first before anyone suggested sleep.

Which suited Sean fine, as he wasn't ready to be left alone with Fay and Rosie. The babble of conversation gave him time to get over his initial shock.

A waiter came and asked if they wanted a drink or some coffee.

“Great idea. What's everyone going to have?” Sean asked. They needed to come down off their high before anyone would settle. “Can you do a hot chocolate for the boys?”

The waiter smiled and called over another member of staff and issued instructions, then took the order for a round of drinks. The men ordered beers. Fay, a glass of wine. Rosie mumbled her order for a coke. And Penny stuck with water. The hot chocolate arrived, along with a plate of biscuits. The chocolate served in enormous mugs, topped with a dollop of thick frothy cream, with a liberal sprinkling of hundreds and thousands and powdered chocolate all over. And to add to the sugar rush, there were two individual bowls filled to the brim with mini marshmallows.

Sean saw Penny's horror. So much for a soporific drink. With that much sugar, the boys would be buzzing for hours. Penny shrugged, but said nothing. They looked so happy. Their faces glowing with mud and excitement, and sheer joy at the size and luxury of their nighttime drink.

Edward sat beside her, while the boys were oohing and aahing over their treat.

“Good rest?”

“Yes, but sorry I missed all the excitement. But probably good that I wasn't there. Because I'd have insisted the boys come back sooner, and they'd have missed out on all the fun.”

When they all sat down, Sean noted Rosie left a seat for him next to Fay. Quite a contrast to her efforts to make sure Vanessa never got near him. Was she hoping that they would make up and life would go back to the way it used to be? Would finding out it would never happen set her off on a destructive cycle? He hoped not. She had been behaving better since Vanessa became ill, and he hoped that would continue for the rest of the holiday.

The boys were so engrossed in their drinks, dunking marshmallows, and catching them as they floated to the top. That their report dried up.

"Did the elephant get back with its mother?" Penny asked.

"No. Something must have spooked the herd." Sean answered. "They're going to fly it to the orphanage in Nairobi tomorrow."

"That can't be a straightforward task."

"No, but the team from the elephant sanctuary is pretty good at it. They'll tranquilize it, and then put it on the plane, and fly back to Nairobi. The airport is only a short distance away from the nursery, so the last bit of journey is not so hard. Then they get it settled and eating, before introducing it to the other orphaned elephants."

Rosie uttered for the first time. "The warden said that it might be too weak to survive." There were tears in her eyes.

Edward shook his head. "Oliver said they thought this one has a good chance of survival. Sometimes they are much weaker."

"Daddy, can we adopt her?" Rosie asked.

"I am sure we can. From what they were saying, the babies they rescue stay in Nairobi until they are about two years old, then they ship them back out to a special area in Tsavo to join a growing herd of orphan survivors."

"What an amazing scheme." Fay said.

"It all started about twenty years ago," Sean continued, "when Daphne Sheldrick, a game warden's wife, saved one baby. Ever since then, every time they find another, she gets a call. She has a base on the edge of the Nairobi game park. Part of the plan is not to tame the elephants, but to get them to have as normal a life as possible. As soon as they're fit enough, they join the others and learn to forage for food. To start with, they get fed enormous bottles of specially formulated milk, and have a keeper to mind them twenty-four hours a day. He will even sleep in their stable. If the elephants are really young, they put sunscreen on them, especially on their ears, because in the wild they would find shade under their mother's legs."

The boys were making loud gurgling noises with their straws as they sucked the last few drops of chocolate drink out from under the remaining foamy topping. They had cream moustaches and crumbs from the biscuits down their fronts. Penny said it was time for them to go.

"Edward, we need to get these two to bed if they want to get up in time to see the elephant being shipped out."

Sean flashed a look that said thanks. Fay smiled across the table at her. Rosie looked alarmed.

"Do you want to walk back to your tent with us, Rosie, or do you want to stay with your dad and Fay?" Penny asked.

He wondered if she'd made the offer because she felt he and Fay could do with a few moments alone, or because Fay had asked her to.

Rosie looked undecided.

Fay solved the dilemma. "Rosie, I'd like to talk to your dad for a few minutes. You and I can talk lots and lots tomorrow when I'm not so tired. I promise I won't keep him here for long."

Rosie seemed happy with that. She got up, gave Fay a quick kiss, and stood patiently waiting as the boys spooned out the last spoonful of cream from their mugs.

Penny asked Rosie, "Did you enjoy the adventure?"

"It was wonderful."

Sean noted that her response was relaxed. The pout had gone. The surly sneer was missing. Was there a chance that her moodiness was over? Sean hoped so. But having both Fay and Vanessa here could create a whole new set of problems.

CHAPTER 30

Tsavo - Saturday 28th September

Edward woke and found that Penny was no longer beside him. He crept out of the tent to find her. She sat, with a rug around her shoulders, staring out at the distant skyline, which was slowly becoming visible as the inky black of night turned purple and pink as daylight took over.

He pulled the second chair closer to hers, and took her hand and whispered, “Morning.” He brushed her cheek with a kiss.

Her cheek was wet. He knew he had to get her to talk. Whatever she was hiding from him needed to be aired. “I know about the hospital appointment,” he whispered. The last thing they needed was the boys waking up.

She stiffened in her chair. “Who told you?”

“I saw a text your mother sent. Why didn't you tell me?”

“I didn't want to spoil everyone's holiday.”

“Why would it spoil anything?”

She didn't answer. It was light enough to see her expression. Not a routine trip to the hospital. This was serious.

“How bad is it?” She shook her head. He touched her hand. “I need to know.”

“Cancer, and it could have spread.”

“Those pills? Not vitamins? What's the plan?”

"Operate as soon as I get back, then chemo, maybe radiotherapy. I don't really know."

"Why didn't you tell me?"

She shook her head. "Telling you would make it real. And I wanted this time together to be special, not filled with fear."

"Who else knows, apart from you mother?"

"Mum only knows I'm having an operation. She doesn't know what for. The only other person I've told is Fay. I broke down yesterday, and told her, but she's promised not to say anything."

They sat in silence, watching the sun peek over the horizon. A glorious golden orb. A few giraffes came down to the water hole, and a family of warthogs with their tails up in the air, in single file, made their way across the flat ground to wallow in the muddy fringe of the pool.

After a while, she looked at him. "Promise you won't tell the others. Or treat me differently. I don't want to spoil everyone's holiday, especially the boys. This trip has been messed up enough with Martin going missing, and Rosie's diabolical behaviour. Do you think you can do that?"

He lifted her hand to his lips. "Your wish is my command."

"Thanks. We'd better get dressed, or we'll miss seeing that baby elephant being moved."

"Are you sure you want to come?"

"Wouldn't miss it for the world. Don't worry, I'm fine. I slept well last night."

"Good, it would be a shame to miss it," he said, though deep down, he was struggling to process what she had told him. Could he really pretend that everything was fine? He had to. He owed her that. Thank God he had come to his senses and already ended things with Lauren. This news changed everything.

The sky was getting brighter by the minute. The birds started chattering and not long after that, there was a rattle of a tea tray being delivered to their tent.

"Hodi. Hodi," the room boy called. As he deposited a tray on the table outside their tent. "Game run leaves in thirty minutes."

The air was fresh. Little clouds dotted the sky like balls of cotton wool. And in the distance, clear of cloud, stood the snowcapped pudding shaped Mount Kilimanjaro.

Pictures in the dining room showed the mountain looking as if someone had emptied a pot of custard on the top, which was dripping down the sides. Now all they could see was a narrow topping, with snow barely slipping down the sides, probably a consequence of global warming.

The tea was strong, and the heat-treated milk that was used so much of the time out here tasted odd. He remembered now why Penny preferred coffee in places like this.

The boys rushed out and gobbled up the biscuits and the bananas that had come on the tray.

Armed with cameras, sun cream, sunglasses, and the usual assortment of bug collecting pots, they headed towards the main building to wait for their driver to go on the game viewing trip.

Rosie and Sean were talking to Fay when they got there. They looked relaxed, which was a good sign. He hoped it would stay that way. He really didn't feel up to dramas today. Not while he processed what Penny had told him. It changed everything. No, that's not true. The holiday had changed everything. His crazy infatuation with Lauren no longer meant anything to him. He'd been stupid to think he could leave Penny and the boys. What madness had come over him? Would Lauren accept that it was over? Or would she be difficult and make things messy? Maybe he should confess to Penny, to prepare her for potential flack.

The boys ran off and talked to the driver, who had befriended them the day before. He promised that after the game viewing drive, he would take them to the airstrip to see the baby elephant being loaded up to make its journey to Nairobi.

The driver told them a leopard had been spotted, and he wanted to get there before anyone disturbed them.

The boys piled into the front seat next to their new friend. Rosie went to the back to sit next to Fay. With everyone settled, the driver set off.

Sean turned to him and Oliver and said, "I had a call from Amina. Martin's been located, but they haven't rescued him yet. And Sandra is happy to have Kim on hand."

"Thank God they know where he is, but it hasn't stopped them worrying that they haven't got him out." Edward said,

"The situation sounds dangerous if they haven't dared to extract him." Oliver said. "But maybe it's safer to be cautious."

The conversation came to a halt when their driver slowed down to point out things in the distance. A buzzard. A secretary bird. A warthog family. Ostriches. Zebra. Thompson's Gazelles. The list was endless. As soon as the boys said they had seen it, he'd move on. There was a feeling of excitement. Leopards were notoriously difficult to find and the chance of catching one in daylight was very special.

He veered off on an almost invisible track. Penny seemed nervous. It was her first ever visit to Africa. The scale of the landscape was almost overwhelming. The plains stretched for miles and miles. How anyone knew which way to go puzzled Edward. There were no road signs on the dirt tracks. The vegetation varied from scrubby bush to more stately green stemmed ones with flat tops. Or great fat round baobabs with scars that showed where elephant tusks had gouged chunks out of them over the years.

Edward swapped notes about cameras with Sean, giving Penny the chance to close her eyes.

The engine noise changed. The driver slowed to a crawl on a barely visible track. Grass brushed against the doors; wait-a-minute thorn bushes scratched the paintwork. No one spoke. Everyone's eyes were fixed ahead.

Sean had his camera ready. He and Edward positioned themselves so they could stick their heads out of the raised top to get a clear shot of whatever their driver headed toward.

They inched on, the grass thinned, and there were fewer bushes. They reached a bare, rocky area. Ahead were three fallen trees.

The driver stopped and switched off the engine. He put his finger to his lips.

The boys looked at him, waiting to see where he would point. He bent his head and said something to them.

They peered through the windscreen. It took a moment for them to focus on the target. But simultaneously, gasped and pointed at a branch stretching out to the left. Draped along the limb, perfectly disguised by the dappled shade from overhanging leaves, was a sleeping leopard.

Edward thought of Vanessa. She should have been with them, sketch pad at the ready. It was such a beautiful pose. Maybe Sean's photos would come out well. Edward would take some, but his camera and his skill would never match Sean's. The boys took turns at leaning out of the window to snap them with their own cameras.

Once everyone had the pictures they needed, the driver described the habits of leopards. The boys listened intently, enthralled by every word. Edward marvelled at how he'd fathered such budding animal lovers when he couldn't even look after a dog. Nicholas's love of bugs made him was grateful that Timothy's demands to release things had kept his brother's bug farm at a minimum. Otherwise, it could have become out of control. Hopefully, the photographing and identifying and releasing system would continue when they got home. Edward wasn't much of a zoologist; his preferred passions were for history and literature.

The driver asked everyone to put their seat belts back on. He wanted them to see the hippopotamus.

Just the mention of hippos got the children singing "Mud, mud, glorious mud", a song Edward had taught them years ago when they were suffering from chicken pox when they were on holiday in France. He smiled at the memory and turned to Penny and said, "France?"

She replied. "Chicken pox."

The memory made him feel so much closer to her. How had he allowed anything to threaten what they had? How was he ever going to make amends?

It took a few careful turns to get the vehicle safely facing away from the leopard. It didn't seem bothered by their presence, having slept through their entire visit.

The drive back to the bigger track was easier because they had their own flattened grass tracks to follow. Penny looked better. The halt had helped. He was glad to see her take a sip of water, as she'd told him she had to be careful not to get dehydrated.

The boys had a checklist of animals they needed to see. The driver was helping them to tick off more and more. Giraffe. Hartebeast. Eland. Silver backed jackal.

Rock hyrax. Marabou storks. Hyena. They rejoined the main track for a few miles. This time, they headed down into a little valley with a river running through it, marked by a weaving line of trees. The driver once more turned off the main track and followed another faint pair of tyre marks until he came to a spit of land above a pool of water. He stopped. Signalled for everyone to be quiet and to stay where they were. He got out and walked to the edge of the buff. He wandered a little way off, first to the left, then to the right.

Sean muttered something about him looking for a bush to use as a screen for a loo.

Everyone giggled, but the driver came back with an armed ranger. "Stay quiet. Follow me."

They clambered out. Stretched themselves. The heat came as a shock after the air-conditioning of the vehicle. The air was dry, and he could taste dust in it.

Strange grunting noise came from the direction of the water. The driver waved for them to follow him. He held the boys by their shoulders. Slowly, they all moved forward. They could see the bank on the far side of the pool. There were six zebra drinking. Sean raised his camera and snapped a photo. They inched forward some more. And soon realized that in the pool below were at least fifty hippos. All you could see of them were two ears, two lumpy eyes and a nose and a hump of their backsides.

Occasionally, one would yawn and expose the huge top and bottom incisors that made them such dangerous animals. One chomp from those jaws with those teeth gripping onto anyone they felt was a danger to them was most likely to be fatal. The driver explained they were nocturnal grazers, spending most of the day wallowing in pools like this, seemingly harmless. Something disturbed them. The water swirled as they bumped and hustled beneath the surface, making it look like a pot of boiling liquid. Then, as quickly as it erupted, the noise ceased, and the water went still.

The guide pointed to what looked like a log lying in the water. A crocodile. It didn't seem interested in either the hippos or the zebra at the water's edge. Was it sleeping, or just waiting for the perfect moment to attack?

Penny took a sip of water. The driver noticed.

"Are you all right?" he asked.

"A little hot. I forgot my hat."

"We'll go back now. I'll shut the roof and put the air-conditioning on high."

Edward saw her catch Fay's arm. The look Fay gave him was enough to show Penny had told her he knew about the cancer.

CHAPTER 31

Tsavo - Saturday 28th September

Oliver stared out of the window as they drove back to the camp for breakfast. He wished Kim was with him to share the experience. But she was right. Having the kids around would have changed it.

Maybe one day he could come again with her.

He looked round to check the others. Penny looked very pale. She hadn't been on top form during the trip. And Edward was quieter than usual. Something was up. What had he missed?

Sean had been helping the twins with photography hints all day, now that Rosie was no longer welded to his side, the way she had been when Vanessa was around. Instead, she chatted to Fay, occasionally laughing. Quite a transformation.

He spotted a small plane in the distance.

“Is that the one coming to collect the elephant?” he asked.

The driver checked on his radio.

“Yes. If everyone is happy, we can go to the airstrip first, to watch the loading.”

There was general consent.

The driver took a cross-country route to a wider track. They jostled along with no one complaining about the bumpy ride.

When he pulled up at the strip, the driver had a word with the boys.

"Now, it's important that you don't get in the way. Do you understand?"

They nodded. "Good. First, we have something to eat. I have bananas, and muffins, and bottles of water for everyone."

Oliver loved the way the staff anticipated their needs.

The driver got out and opened the back and pulled out the cool box and handed out the water, and let them help themselves to the food.

The plane circled overhead, and then came into land, bumping along the cleared stretch of red soil. It turned and taxied back, close to where they had parked.

Oliver saw a trail of dust approaching and assumed it was the team with the elephant. The pilot and two others got out and came over to introduce themselves.

One was a vet, and the second was a member of the orphanage staff.

The children latched onto the orphanage man, bombarding him with questions about caring for the baby elephants.

Oliver was more interested in chatting with the vet, Malcolm Scott.

"Hi, I'm a qualified vet, too, but got into the pharmacy side of the business rather than hands on. Now, I wish I'd stuck to working with animals."

"It's a pretty amazing job out here. No two days are the same. I'm based at a research project near Nanyuki, but help the trust as a sideline. We mainly work with wildlife, but also help with the local pets and farm animals."

"Sounds interesting."

"Yes, but what I really love is days like this," Malcolm said. "Working with wildlife is special. But you need to work fast in unusual locations."

"I'd love to do something like that."

“Why not? We could do with more vets.”

“I'm only here on holiday.” Oliver said.

“Yes, but what's stopping you from trying it? Come and visit me. I'll give you a taster of my work.”

“I might just take you up on that offer. We're heading to Ol Essakut, near Nanyuki, soon.”

Malcolm laughed. “That's where I'm based. On the estate. Follow me. I'll talk you through this.”

Oliver went with him. The others had been told to wait at a distance.

The little elephant was in the back of a truck. The keeper had a large bottle of feed with him. And while he coaxed the baby to drink, Malcolm assessed the animal for weight and condition.

“He's not in great shape. I'm going to have to go easy on the sedative. I'll give the minimum, and if necessary, give more on the flight.”

There was a flurry of activity as the team tried to get a tarpaulin in place under the elephant. Which was a tricky task, getting the baby to lift its feet before they could unfold it under him.

“We need that in place to move him when the sedative works. We use it to slide him in and out of the plane,” Malcolm explained.

Over the next half hour, Oliver watched and listened as Malcolm went through all the checks he would make, and detailed why each was important. Then, with the team in place, injected the sedative.

As the drug worked, the rangers gently coaxed the animal to lie down in the centre of the tarpaulin. And as soon as Malcolm gave the signal, they reversed the truck as close to the plane as they could get and slid the elephant out of the back of the truck and up a ramp into the open side of the plane.

They had done this before. It was a well-practiced move, done with precision.

Malcolm shook Oliver's hand. "Get in touch before you leave. There's a lot I can show you, and maybe I can tempt you to stay."

Oliver didn't dare respond. Tempted, he might be, but he had Kim and the children to think of. Before he could reply, Malcolm boarded the plane, and it taxied to the far end of the strip to prepare for take-off.

They got back to the lodge closer to lunch time than breakfast, and all agreed that an early lunch was called for.

Oliver noticed Fay and Edward talking to each other. Both looked very serious, and occasionally glanced towards Penny, who had found a seat in the shade, away from everyone else.

He went over and sat beside her. "Is Edward all right? He seems rather tense."

"I think he's worried about Rosie and what she did. And we can't put Martin's disappearance out of our minds."

Oliver wasn't convinced. But if Penny wasn't prepared to admit it, he wouldn't push. "The boys are having a great time."

Penny smiled. "Yes. Loving every second."

They were called for lunch, so he followed her to the buffet.

While they queued, his phone buzzed with a text from Kim.

'Sandra's very stressed about Martin. Kids are missing you. Wish you were here. Love.'

Oliver filled his plate and joined the others at the table, and told them what Kim had said, adding, "I'd love to go to Ol Essakut today."

The mood changed.

"Do you think it would help to have friends around?" Edward asked.

“I'll text Kim and ask what she thinks.” Oliver tapped out a message.

Her reply came back swiftly. 'Amina thinks it might.'

He told the others and added. “I'm keen to get back to Kim and my kids. What about you, stay here or see if we can get up to Ol Essakut?”

Penny was the first to answer. “I'm happy to go. I'm finding it too hot here.”

Edward nodded, “Yes, good idea.”

Rosie chipped in. “I need to see Vanessa to say sorry.”

Sean looked puzzled. “What for?”

Tears filled her eyes, and she looked down. “Fay, can you tell him? I can't.”

Everyone waited for Sean's reaction. Fay touched his hand and said, “Not here.” And got up to leave the table. Sean followed.

Penny reached out and held Rosie's hand. Rosie glanced towards her and said. “Sorry, I've been such an idiot.”

All eyes were on Sean and Fay. They all knew what Rosie had done, and were concerned about how Sean would react when he found out. The only good thing was that Rosie wanted to confess, even if she couldn't find the words to tell him herself.

Oliver wondered if Sean would lose it. But Fay made him sit on a bench, and they talked.

Rosie whispered. “Do you think he'll ever forgive me?”

Penny wisely didn't give a glib answer. Instead, said, “He'll need time, don't expect too much too soon.”

They had all finished their coffee when Sean and Fay rejoined them.

Sean sat opposite Rosie and asked calmly, "Are you willing to accept whatever punishment Vanessa chooses?"

Rosie nodded.

"Good. But we need to have a conversation about what made you do that. There are things you don't seem to understand."

She nodded again.

He looked at Oliver and said, "I'm happy to head to Ol Essakut to put things right with Vanessa. And see if there is any way we can help Martin."

"All agreed?" Oliver checked for their reactions. "Okay, I'll ask if it's possible."

CHAPTER 32

Ol Essakut Saturday 28th September

Vanessa hadn't expected Sandra to welcome her with open arms. But she did. Amina had told her what Rosie had done.

"Calling Fay, and removing yourself, was the right thing to do."

"Ol Essakut ranch is far more beautiful than I ever imagined. And the view from this veranda her at Chui farm breathtaking. Is the mountain often hidden by cloud? I glimpsed the peak earlier, and thought it magical." Vanessa took another look, hoping to see the snow-capped peak again..

"It's often clear in the early morning." Sandra said and suggested that it might suit her better to stay on at Chui Farm rather than the Ol Essakut house. "When the others arrive, you can decide if you want to join them or not. I'm happy for you to stay on for as long as you want."

As if that wasn't generous enough, she gave Vanessa access to her studio and art supplies. And provided a bundle of clothing and shoes to cover her needs as it was cooler at Chui Farm than at the coast because of the altitude.

Vanessa, wanting to be as unobtrusive as possible, spent time with the children. Sandra's pair had taken charge of Kim's little ones, and Vanessa sketched them as they played. She'd never tried painting children before, and was loving the opportunity.

Ideas were forming for a series of bigger paintings based on her sketches. A different direction to her usual subjects, but one that excited her and made her keen to get into the studio.

Kim was busy with Sandra, making sure everything was ready for the unexpected extra baby. While Jenny pretended she wasn't anxious, Vanessa knew she was far from happy with the idea of a home birth, especially as it seemed Sandra was expecting twins.

Vanessa saw Amina hurry into the house. Something was up. The children had been playing with mud, and were ready to move onto something else. Vanessa supervised them as they washed the red mud off their hands. The pigment in the soil left them with orange skin, but there was nothing she could do about that. Sensing that there was something happening at the house, she suggested they draw pictures for their parents. A task they enthusiastically set to.

Wanjiru appeared and asked Vanessa if she could go up to the house, and said that she'd watch the children.

Vanessa reached the veranda in time to hear Amina talking to Kim.

"I've had a message from Oliver. They want to come here today. Have you any idea want made them want to change their plans?"

Kim shrugged and called Oliver, who answered immediately. She asked a few questions and ended the call with, "Okay, I'll tell them."

She looked at Amina. "They're willing to go along with whatever you can arrange. It seems coming back suits them all. Penny's not coping with the heat, but he thinks there's more to it." She turned to Vanessa and added, "He said to tell you that Rosie has asked Fay to tell Sean what she did."

Amina picked up her phone and made a call to confirm the flight details. And then said to Kim, "That's all sorted, but now I need your help. The wife of one of our rangers is having a difficult birth. Would you be willing to come and see if you can help?"

Kim looked concerned. "I don't have my bag. I'm not sure what I can do."

"Take that pack. It is supposed to have everything you need in it." Sandra said.

"I'll get it." Amina rushed inside.

Kim was in no position to argue, and simply checked that it was all right to leave the children in Vanessa's care, and left with Amina.

All this gave Vanessa time to take in the last snippet of information Oliver had passed on, and wondered how had Sean reacted to hearing his daughter nearly killed her? She was glad she hadn't been the one telling him.

Fay had suggested she think of a suitable punishment. But at that point, Fay hadn't known what Rosie had done. What would Fay consider adequate?

Vanessa had never handed out a punishment. It wasn't in her nature. Memories of that crazy dream of painting Rosie's portrait came back to her. Making Rosie sit for it would certainly punish Rosie. She wasn't sure she was ready for a close encounter. And it didn't solve the bigger issue. That of Sean. This trip had made it clear her independence was too valuable to give up.

Sandra interrupted her thoughts. "Worried about facing Rosie?"

Her accurate guess surprised Vanessa. "A bit. I wish I knew how Sean reacted?"

"He's probably mortified that his child would try to kill you. Let's hope Fay will break it gently."

Sandra reached out and touched Vanessa's sketch pad. “May I?” Vanessa pushed it towards her, glad that talk about Sean had ceased, and waited for a reaction.

Sandra smiled as she turned the pages of sketches of her children playing. “These are wonderful.” She kept on until she found the drawings of Rosie on the beach before she really kicked off. “Is this Rosie? She's beautiful.”

“I asked her if she'd sit for me. But she refused. Now, I'm considering making her sit for a portrait as a punishment.”

“That's an interesting idea. She's bound to agree. Now she needs to make amends to get Sean to forgive her.”

“I hadn't thought of that. All she wanted was his attention and was afraid that I would dilute it.”

“And her project backfired.”

“Not completely. She got me out of the house.”

“Yes, but I doubt he's been the adoring parent since you left.”

“I hope I did the right thing by asking Fay to come out. I thought she'd be able to talk sense to Rosie. It seems she's helped her through bad patches in the past.”

“How well do you know Fay?” Sandra asked.

“We were good friends while at college. I always felt guilty about my affair with Sean because of it. But in the end, she was the one who left. I never tried to take him away from her, though I guess we'd never have got together if their relationship had been strong.”

Vanessa knew she shouldn't let a fifteen-year-old rule her life. But the relationship had been so badly damaged, she could never take on his family. Telling him would be hard, but it had to be done.

“If she agrees, I'm worried I'll might be tempted to add horns to the picture.”

“You know you wouldn't.”

"No, I guess not."

"She'll sit for you if she wants your forgiveness."

"I don't think she knows the meaning of the word forgive."

"She's only a kid. She deserves a chance."

"What makes you so sure?"

"Kim said she had been completely different since the incident. I used to do a lot of work with troubled teenagers. Most just needed someone to hear their side of the story. It is amazing how seldom they're encouraged to open up about their thoughts and fears."

"And you reckon I should do this?"

"It can't hurt."

"What if I open up some deep, emotional issue that I can't handle?"

"There's plenty of us around to deal with her if she's in a vulnerable state."

"I guess that's decided. Now all I have to find out is whether she's up for it."

CHAPTER 33

Ol Essakut. Saturday 28th September.

When Kim was asked if she could help with a difficult birth for one of the staff, her first reaction was panic. She had no equipment, but that was promptly solved.

Sandra said, "Take the pack you picked up in Nairobi. And don't worry about the children, they will be fine here."

Amina wasted no grabbing the pack and, and ushering her down to her vehicle, and heading over to the staff quarters.

"Enuto's wife usually lives in her tribal village, but she's come to Ol Essakut so she could be near her husband. She doesn't speak English. But Enuto does. We can use him as a translator."

Kim wasn't sure what to expect, but the neat rows of houses impressed her. Especially how clean everything seemed compared to housing she had seen on the way to the ranch.

A tall man wearing a shuka, with shoes made from car tyres, took Amina's hand to show his gratitude that she had brought help. Amina introduced her to Enuto, who ushered them to a house and in to a bright, sparsely furnished room where his wife lay on a bed. Another woman sat on a chair beside her. Kim noticed he didn't step past the threshold.

Kim took the woman's hand. It was clammy. She held her hands over the woman's stomach, to indicate she wanted to feel. The woman nodded.

"How long has she been like this?" Kim asked. Amina said something to the woman on the chair and relayed her answer.

"Since yesterday, when her waters started."

"Tell her I need to see if the baby is coming."

Once she had a nod of approval, she uncovered the woman's legs and looked. She gasped. Panic set in. She had seen nothing like this except in textbooks and never expected to have to deal with it. The woman had been circumcised. On close inspection, the situation looked more botched than any of the grainy images she had seen in the course material on her refresher course. She stepped back.

Amina asked, "Is there a problem?"

"Yes, can we go outside for a minute?" Amina followed her out. "It looks as if she had a massive infection caused by circumcision. Scar tissue surrounds her birth canal. I've never dealt with anything like this, and not sure I have the skills needed. Can you find someone who has?"

"I thought you were qualified."

"I am, but not in this country. This problem is not one I've ever faced before. And I can't do this without pain relief. What if the baby dies? What if it all goes wrong? Where will I stand?"

"Honestly, I don't know, and I understand your fear. But she's been in labour for too long already. You're here. You must be able to do something. If you don't, she'll probably die."

"True."

"What's in the pack?" Amina opened the back of her vehicle.

While Kim looked through the contents. The only thing she had used from it had been the trumpet to listen to Sandra's baby's heartbeat. There was a scalpel, stitching needles, already threaded. Antiseptic wipes. And numbing gel.

"Okay, I'll do my best, but I want you to take photos. I need evidence so that if there's a problem later, I have proof that I did what I could."

"Amina nodded. "I'll use my phone."

"I am going to have to cut her. A rip could cause catastrophic damage."

Amina understood and explained to Enuto what was happening.

A scream from inside galvanized Kim into action. Without waiting for an answer, she grabbed the pack and ran inside, and checked the baby's heart rate. The beat was getting weaker. No time to dither.

The baby was in the right place. She got the mother to move to a position where she could work and applied the numbing gel. It would take a few minutes to take effect. But a moan warned her another contraction was about to hit. She couldn't delay. She had to make a cut to prepare the way for the baby.

But she couldn't cut without letting the mother know what she was going to do. How? She clenched one fist, and using a finger, tried to show that it wouldn't go through the tight clench. Then she picked up the knife and made a pretend cut to the fist, and poked her finger through.

The terrified woman nodded. She understood. A powerful contraction hit. She stifled a moan, but the beads of sweat on her brow showed how bad the pain was.

Cutting couldn't wait. She had to do it now. Kim prayed the numbing gel had worked. All the time trying to recall the lecture they had on the subject, and all the things that could go wrong. What had they said needed to be avoided? Could she do this? Could she get it right? Her hand was shaking as she positioned the scalpel.

"Amina, photo please."

She said a silent prayer as she made the incision. How far was enough? She put the knife aside to wait to see.

Kim's refresher course included lectures on the problems of female circumcision because the issue was becoming more common with the influx of migrants from around the world. But she'd never expected to have to deal with one so soon. And in a less than perfect setting. The house was clean, but a long way from hospital standards. Amina was standing behind her, camera in hand.

She heard a vehicle arrive. She recognized Sandra's voice. Then a tap on the door. Sandra called softly. "Kim, tell me what's happening?"

"You should be resting."

"I know," she said, coming into the room. "But birth in their world is women's business. I've been talking to Enuto. He told me his wife's sister and another girl from her age group had died in childbirth. Their babies couldn't come out. They were all circumcised by the same woman, and he's afraid. That's why she came here to have the baby. He is happy for you to do whatever is necessary to save her and his baby. I promise there won't be any repercussions."

"No wonder she's terrified." Kim said.

"I'll reassure her."

"No pressure then," Kim said. She heard a moan and checked to make sure everything was as it should be. Another contraction. The baby had moved further down. The heartbeat was weaker. How would she know if she had cut enough? The mum was tiring. She needed to get the baby out.

Kim felt the mother's tension ease when Sandra took her hand and spoke gently in her language. This was someone she could trust.

Kim lengthened the cut. The remaining waters gushed out.

"How's she doing?" Sandra asked.

"Getting close, but I'm worried that she hasn't the strength to push hard enough. The baby is stressed, but the head is presenting. I need her to give all she has with the next contraction."

Three contractions later, the head emerged. She checked the cord was not round the neck and told Sandra to make sure that the next push was a big one. Are you ready? Come on, one, two, three, and the baby slipped out into her hands. She laid it down on the cloth she had put on the bed, and tied and cut the cord. The baby looked fine. Now all she wanted was for him to breathe on his own. She rubbed gently, then more firmly until he let out a wail. She passed the baby to Sandra. Her work wasn't done. There was the afterbirth to deal with, and then she'd have to repair the cuts she had made. As far as she could tell, her incisions had prevented a tear. She delivered the afterbirth. It was intact. She set it aside, wondering if there was a ritual for it. Her next task was to repair the cut. She needed to do it while the numbing gel was still working.

She stepped away. The sight of the mother and child wiped her exhaustion away and replaced it with elation, reminding her why she loved her work.

"What happens with the afterbirth?"

Sandra said something to the woman in her own language. She smiled and pointed to her friend by her side, who had been silent throughout. She got up and took the bundle that Kim had wrapped up. Sandra explained about the stitches and that Kim would return to make sure everything was all right.

Sandra passed on this information in a way that seemed to be understood.

The translation produced a huge smile.

"Time to go, I think," Sandra said.

Kim gathered the remains of the pack that the mother had no use for and touched her hand before she stepped outside.

On hearing that he had a son, Enuto's face broke into the widest smile Kim had ever seen. Without thinking, he stepped forward and hugged Kim. Then froze and stepped away as if he'd received an electric shock, and put his hands together and bowed an apology.

Sandra took his hand, which he shook for ages. When she finally pulled it away, she said. "Time for me to head home. Will you come now?"

"No, I want to make sure mother and baby settle, then change before I come back to the house. As long as Amina doesn't mind waiting."

She returned to the room, and was delighted to see that the baby had latched onto her mother's breast. When he was full, and nodding off, she checked the stitches she had put in, and asked if she could take the baby to show to his father. Amina had explained that usually men were barred from the birthing place.

She carried the child to the door and called Enuto over to see his son. The man's reaction was the reason she did the job. Happy that all was as it should be, she handed the baby back to his mother, and let Amina drive her back to the main house to change before going back to Sandra's house. As they drove there, the plane bringing the rest of the party back from Tsavo flew over.

CHAPTER 34

Ol Essakut–Saturday 28th September

Sandra had joined Vanessa and Jenny with the news of Kim's success. The children were playing ludo. The plane bringing the others flew overhead, signalling it was about to land. Amina and Kim hadn't returned.

She understood enough to work out Fay's presence would be awkward for Vanessa, and braved the question. "Will it be difficult facing Fay?"

Vanessa thought for a moment. "I don't think so. Fay and I were close friends in the past. Sean and Rosie will be tricky. Asking Rosie to sit for a portrait will be a challenge. She seems to hate her body, and trying to shock us with goth hair and makeup. Hopefully, I can show her something she hasn't seen in herself," Vanessa said as she put her sketch pad and pencil down.

"Do you want to move down to the Ol Essakut house to be with the others?" Jenny asked.

"If it's okay, I'd rather stay where I am. The whole situation rocked my relationship with Sean. The portrait might be my parting gift."

Sandra thought it best to change the subject, so asked to see the latest drawings Vanessa had been working on. "I'm envious. I seem to have lost the urge to sketch since I got pregnant. They're stunning. I look forward to seeing the final artwork."

Sandra handed the book back. Vanessa dropped it into the basket beside her and pulled a jumper over it, as if to hide it.

The car doors slammed, and Sandra wondered which of the guest would be first to appear. A tall, fair-haired man bounded up the steps ahead of the others. Kim's children ran to greet him. He stooped and picked them up and looked around, obviously searching for their mother.

"Kim's gone to change. She'll be here in a moment." Sandra said. "You must be Oliver."

He smiled and nodded. "I can't thank you enough for letting us come to Ol Essakut. I hope these two haven't caused havoc."

"Not at all."

"Any news?"

She shook her head. "No, but thanks for your concern."

She turned her attention to the family group that stood behind him. "Edward and Penny, so good to meet you both, and your budding zoologists. Vanessa told me all about the bug collecting. Sam and Emma are looking forward to showing you round."

Next, she turned her attention to the remaining trio. "Sean and Fay, it is lovely to put faces to the voices after all this time. And I'm guessing you must be Rosie?" The girl nodded, barely letting their eyes meet. She had an awkward nervousness about her, which was hardly surprising under the circumstance. Sandra looked towards Vanessa, wondering how she was going to greet them.

Sean made a move towards her. But Fay stopped him, and gently pushed Rosie forward, and said, "Vanessa, Rosie has something to say to you. Please hear her out."

The tension on the veranda was electric.

The girl looked on the verge of tears. But fixed her eyes directly on Vanessa, and said, "I'm sorry. I shouldn't have done all the things I did. Please forgive me." Her lips quivered as she waited for a reaction.

"I was told to think of a suitable punishment for you. Will you agree to do whatever I ask?" The girl gave a nervous nod. "Well, I want you to sit for a portrait. Will you do that?"

"Yes," she whispered.

"Good, we can start tomorrow."

Sean looked as if he was about to say something, but a slight shake of Vanessa's head made him swallow his words. "Fay, I hope that's okay."

Fay smiled. "Yes, I think that's a good plan."

Sean looked at Sandra and said, "We don't want to put you out by being here. As a group, we are good at entertaining ourselves, and a few quiet days will suit us fine. But if there is anything we can do, I hope you won't be afraid to ask us."

"Don't worry, we're used to having folk staying, and Kim has been an amazing help. Here she is. She's just helped deliver a baby, under rather difficult circumstances, so we're grateful that she could prevent a tragedy. Let's have tea before you settle yourselves in at the Ol Essakut house." Then, almost as an afterthought added, "I've asked Vanessa to stay on here. Having her in the house means Jenny can stop worrying about me and get some rest."

Sandra's wording made it impossible for Sean to protest, giving time for Vanessa to work out what she wanted to do.

Conversation settled into a gentle buzz. Rosie had joined the children who were at the far end of the veranda, playing with Rupee, who was loving the extra attention.

Jenny suggested it might be fun for the children to experience the same home schooling as Sam and Emma. "We rotate round the different farms, and next week, most of the schooling is here. They will get to meet lots of other children, and have fun."

Penny smiled and said, "That would be wonderful. The boys love mixing with other children. And it will help me too. I'm under doctor's orders to take things gently. I hadn't intended to tell you this and spoil the holiday, but I'm going in for an operation the day after we return." She turned to Edward and added. "I only told Edward yesterday and made him promise not to tell anyone, but it isn't fair to expect him to keep my secret. He needs support as much as I do. And to save you all the trouble of asking. I'm doing fine. What I don't need is to be treated like an invalid. I'll join in with what I can, and rest when I can't."

Edward touched her tenderly on the shoulder. Sandra could work out if it was wife's illness that made him so tense, or if there was something else going on? That she had revealed her medical details to the others didn't seem to have eased his tension. Maybe he needed a bit more time for it to sink in.

CHAPTER 35

Kenya – Saturday 28th September

Simeon braced himself to make the call. "Hank, I need your help."

"Sure. Sandra said you had rustled up some mates and gone off to see if you could find Martin. Any clue where he is? All our leads have gone cold."

"Yes. That's why I'm calling."

"Where is he?".

Simeon took a deep breath. He wouldn't reveal the location until he had stipulated some conditions. "I'll tell you once we have one thing clear."

"Go on."

"Me and my team are only interested in getting Martin out. Nothing more. We're not interested in his captives, and will leave their fate to your guys. We want no further involvement, and absolutely no publicity. Is that clear?"

"Yes."

"I'll send you a location for us to meet, and all the info I have. I'm going to check the place out. It's an old petrol station with a workshop on one side. While it's daylight, I'll go there and ask for help with my vehicle. I'll take as many photos of the place as I can, so you can see what you're dealing with. We're currently monitoring movements in or out of the building."

They arranged a meeting time, when they could complete details. He had picked a meeting place in a quiet spot outside the nearest village. And had Hank's agreement that no action would take place before nightfall.

Simeon, relieved that Hank had accepted his conditions, drove close to the garage. His colleagues were positioned on the only road leading to it. One beyond the garage and one on the approach road, so they could watch for any vehicle leaving in either direction.

Simeon put on a red t-shirt instead of the old army one he'd been wearing, to avoid looking anything other than a casual traveller. He drove closer, pulling over when the building came into sight. If anyone was watching, they could see him. He got out and walked round the vehicle, pretending to check the wheels, and let air out of his front passenger side tyre. Enough for it to pull the steering wheel, but not enough to do damage.

He grabbed an empty water bottle and set off to ask for help. He pulled out his phone, switched on the video mode, and pretended to be talking to someone as he approached the building.

He studied the facade. It was a solidly built, disused petrol station like dozens around the country. There was a single-story workshop attached with sliding garage doors on the left. The large window, to what would have served as the pay area and shop, was covered with newspapers. The door still had a glass panel in it, with a load of old marketing stickers covering most of the surface.

Simeon knocked on the door. No response. He peered through the gaps in the adverts. No sign of life. He moved over to the sliding doors and hammered on them. No answer. There had to be a back entrance because there were no vehicles in the front area.

Knowing there were people inside, he wasn't ready to give up. So, he hammered again and called out. "Can someone help me?"

He heard the scraping of a chair on concrete. But still no one answered.

He carried on round the side of the building. The workshop part had top windows. Too high for him to peer in. Maybe there would be a lower one at the back. He followed the rough track that ran alongside the building, leading to a solid metal gate. The high wall had broken glass cemented along the top. There was the distinctive smell of maize cobs over burning charcoal, and he could hear muffled voices. He retraced his steps and repeated his hammering on the garage door and shouting for help. Hoping that if Martin were there, he would hear him. Still no response.

He tried the shop door again and was taken aback when the tall man, who Martin had been following, opened it. Simeon recognized him from the photos Hank had shown him.

"What do you want?"

"My tyre is nearly flat. Do you have a pump?"

The man peered out of the door as Simeon pointed down the road to his abandoned Toyota.

"I noticed it was pulling to the left and stopped to check. If I don't pump it up, I'll damage the tyre." Simeon explained.

With a grunt, he turned and shouted out to someone to bring a pump.

Simeon took his water bottle and made as if to have a drink. "Any chance of filling this? He held out the bottle."

The man gave him a malevolent look, took it and said. "Wait here." He went to a door at the back. Called for someone, gave them the bottle with instructions to fill it. Simeon didn't move. The man was jittery enough as it was. At last, a scruffy individual appeared through the workshop door clutching a pump. He was given instructions to go with Simeon. His filled water bottle was returned, leaving him with no excuse to linger.

"Thank you." Simeon said. Further questions would be a dangerous move.

The man with the pump followed him in silence and inflated the tyre. Simeon offered to drive him back. He refused and sauntered back toward the garage.

Simeon started his engine, and drove on, waving to the man as he overtook him.

He met up with his colleagues beyond the garage to report his findings and to show them the video he had taken. "My plan is to go back after dark with a few bottles of beer and some food to thank them for their help. But it will depend on whether Hank agrees." He pointed to some faint tracks on the map. I'll take this route back to the others. And this will be our rendezvous spot.

Hank arrived at the chosen location and introduced him to an American dressed in black combat kit. "Joe will be in command. His men are waiting down the road for instructions."

Simeon studied all the information Hank and Joe had gathered, then shared what he had found. Joe had a detailed blown-up satellite image of the building and the yard. He talked through tactics he intended to use. Simeon's idea of returning with a thank you gift was approved.

"As soon as the door is open, we'll make a move." Hank's team leader said. "We'll push past you through the front door. Men out the back will scale the wall, and a third lot will force the garage door and enter that way."

"What about Martin? Won't that put him in danger?"

"There shouldn't be time for anyone to harm him. That's if he's still alive. We have enough men to overpower everyone in there. You needn't be involved."

Simeon didn't like this comment. “Sorry. We're going in. Our mission is to find Martin and get him out. We don't give a damn about what happens to anyone afterwards.”

He must have sounded forceful enough, because Joe shrugged, and said, “Fine, have it your way. Find him, and get him and yourselves out of there. Is that understood?”

Simeon nodded. Happy with the prospect of a quick exit.

CHAPTER 36

Ol Essakut--Saturday 28th September

Sean hid his disappointment that Vanessa wasn't at the airstrip to meet them when they arrived at Ol Essakut. What would he say to her? Sorry, was inadequate. He'd been a fool not to notice Rosie's behaviour towards her. He'd failed on so many levels, and wouldn't be surprised if she refused to speak to him.

Oliver rushed ahead, eager to see Kim and the children. Edward and Penny and the boys followed, while he hung back with Fay and Rosie. Vanessa was on the far side of Sandra with an older woman sitting beside her, and she made no move to welcome him. Which was his half-expected response to his letting her down so badly. Some serious grovelling was required.

Fay pushed Rosie forward to apologize to Vanessa.

Painting her portrait. Had she gone mad? What kind of punishment was that? He didn't get it, but Fay seemed happy, and gave him a look that told him not to interfere. This was between Rosie and Vanessa.

With the introductions done, they sat down for tea. Vanessa was silent and hardly glanced in his direction. After tea, the plan was to head to the Ol Essakut house to settle in before returning to Chui Farm for dinner. But Sandra had given Vanessa an excuse not to join them at the other house, which made it impossible for him to ask Vanessa to come without sounding like a jerk.

The Ol Essakut house was as Martin had described it. Old colonial style, a long low building with a veranda at the front. Inside, polished wood floors and furniture gleamed in the sunshine. Everything looked as if it had been there for a century, and probably had. But it was perfect. There were silver candlesticks on the tables. And dozens of photo frames filled with family pictures on the mantlepiece and on the side tables. The armchairs looked inviting, and fires had been lit in the reception rooms, which made it even more welcoming.

The group scattered to their allocated rooms, and reassembled an hour later to go back to Chui Farm for dinner.

Sean caught up briefly with Vanessa, hoping to make peace with her.

"I'm sorry I was so blind. You should have said something, instead of calling Fay." But she shut him down.

"Not here." Vanessa said firmly and turned towards Edward. "Tell me about your Tsavo safari."

Sidelined, Sean didn't feel he could contribute. Drinks were handed round and then they moved to the dining room to eat. The children, including Rosie, were at a smaller table at the far end of the room. They had finished eating and were busy plotting activities. Once again, Sean found himself seated as far from Vanessa as was possible. She sat between Amina and Jenny.

When the food arrived, Sandra tapped her glass with a knife to get their attention. "Welcome. I'm sorry Martin's not here, but I'm sure he'll be back with us soon to take you to explore. Meanwhile, I hope a couple of quiet days here will suit you all."

Everyone round the table nodded. "If you want to use the pool, take a walk, or go on a bike ride, please check with one of the staff before you set out. I hope you'll excuse me for not joining in."

There was laughter round the table as she stroked her bump.

"Oh Oliver, I have a message for you. Our vet called. He said you met in Tsavo. He'll drop round to the Ol Essakut house tomorrow morning to see if you and Kim want to see what work he's doing. That's if you're happy for your children to join the others for School. And Kim, you don't need to worry about me. You'll only be down the road. Plenty of time to get back if anything changes."

Conversation buzzed round the table, with people making plans for a day without children. Kim said she'd love to go with Oliver, as long as she could look in on the mother and baby she had delivered earlier in the day, first.

Penny wanted a day with her feet up reading and suggested that Edward go on a bike ride. "Maybe Sean can go with you?"

"I fancy a day doing nothing more than reading," Fay said. Which left Sean with no choice but to agree to join Edward, even though a bike ride was the last thing he wanted to do. He wanted to spend time with Vanessa, but she'd be busy with Rosie, and that invitation didn't include him.

When the meal finished, they rounded up their children. Leaving Sean and Fay facing Vanessa.

It was too public a situation for him to say what he wanted to say. So, Sean settled with the simple statement. "Sorry you're not coming back with us?"

Vanessa gave a tiny shrug. "Sandra is letting me use her studio here. You know what I'm like when I get into creative mode. And I'm keen to start on the portrait of Rosie."

Fay was about to say something, but Vanessa gave her a stern look. "You might not think it's much of a punishment. But for me, it's enough, and I hope you'll respect my decision."

Rosie stepped forward. “What time do you want to start?”

“After breakfast, when the light is good.”

Rosie nodded, tugged on Fay's sleeve to get her to join the others. With everyone waiting, he couldn't say what he wanted to say.

Back at their lodgings, he caught Fay when the others had headed to their rooms.

“Fancy a nightcap?”

Fay nodded and followed him into the sitting room, and sat by the fire, which the staff had tended while they were out. He poured her a drink from the array on the side table and joined her.

“What sort of punishment is sitting for a portrait? I couldn't believe it when Vanessa asked, and more staggered that Rosie agreed.”

Fay shook her head. “Don't you get it? Rosie refused to spend time with Vanessa. Now she's forcing her to do just that. It's brilliant. And far better than anything I could think of.”

“Should one of us go with her?”

“No. Vanessa would have asked if she wanted us there.”

He looked across at Fay. She had changed and lost weight, and her hair was shorter. She looked happier. Was it because she was no longer living with him? Had he been that difficult?

“Part of Rosie's problem comes from the feeling that Vanessa broke us up. I think my leaving resurrected memories of losing her mother and she didn't know how to deal with them.”

“No wonder she screwed up.”

“Anyway, I've told her Vanessa isn't to blame.”

“Isn't she?”

“No, I am. We should talk about custody.”

“Custody? I don't understand.”

"Rosie got it into her head that Vanessa had stolen you from me. When I told her Vanessa wasn't why I left, now she blames herself."

"That's ridiculous."

"To you maybe, but not to a teenage girl. And I'm struggling to convince her otherwise."

"But how and where does custody come into this?"

"In a normal divorce, the parents battle over custody. Because I walked away, we never discussed it. And that left her feeling that I hated her. That I didn't care enough to want to make a home for her. Basically, I..., no..., we slipped up."

"How?"

"Simple. Because we didn't take Rosie and Matthew's needs into consideration. A birth mother would never walk away. She'd have made you move out and fought to keep her children. Instead, because I'm not their birth mother, I chose not to disrupt their lives by breaking up their home that you had with their mother. I thought I was doing the right thing. But it was completely wrong. Wrong for them, wrong for me, and certainly not helpful to Vanessa."

"So, what happens next?"

"We have to talk to Rosie, like an adult, rather than a child. Make her understand why I left."

"If your departure had nothing to do with Vanessa, then why did you go?"

"It's simple. I married you for the wrong reasons. After their mother died and you weren't coping, I took charge and got a routine sorted and made a difference to the children's day-to-day existence. Slowly, you started functioning as a moderately normal human. The one bit that never really went back to normal was letting people into your life. Apart from the children, I mean."

"I wasn't that bad, was I?"

"Yes, you were."

“So, why did you stick around? Why did you agree to marry me?”

“The children. Basically, I wanted your family. It was not something I gave enough thought to, and I stayed because of them. I kidded myself that they were old enough to cope. I was wrong about leaving them, even though they didn't seem to care. Coming here was a chance for me to make amends.”

“Did you love me at all?”

“Of course, I did. But I loved them first, and maybe we never had heart-stopping passionate love, more mutual respect. I had an established role in your household, and it was far easier for both of us to keep it that way. Even if it wasn't the stuff of dreams.”

“But you could have left anytime.”

“No. You had the children. It was the children that made you so appealing.”

He knew she was trying to make a point here, but couldn't figure out what. “We could have had children of our own.”

“I couldn't.”

“I wouldn't have minded.”

“I said I couldn't.”

“You mean you tried.”

“No. I mean, I could never have children. My only hope of having children was taking on someone else's. And I chose yours.”

“Why didn't you tell me?”

“What? Say sorry I can't have kids, and admit I married you because you had two.”

“I don't believe that's how you felt.”

“Maybe not entirely, but there's an element of truth. You were still grief stricken and let me take over sorting out the children. Then we got closer. If you were happy, so were the children. I accepted your proposal because it formalized my position, even though I knew all along your heart wasn't in it. But it felt like the right thing to do."

"When you buried yourself in work, I knew something had changed, and guessed from the start that Vanessa was involved. I lived in dread that you would say something that would upset our little family. I loved Matthew and Rosie and was afraid I'd lose them, and couldn't bear the thought."

"What made you leave?"

"Matthew. He jolted me into reality. His friends had brought him home, high on pot. Not for the first time. But on that occasion, he was in a foul mood, and told me about your affair. Said I was a doormat, and that I was going to end up a childless divorcee. I knew it was the truth. One I had refused to admit to."

"So, you made it come true."

"Something like that. Sadly, I was wallowing in self-pity and forgot to take Rosie's feelings into account. She had been moody, and picking fights and self-harming. I tried to get through to her and failed. Matthew's remark was the final straw, so I let them get on with their lives. His poor exam results were my fault, as I stopped hounding him to do his homework. As for Rosie, I hadn't the strength to keep fighting with her. You were hardly ever home. I decided you'd all be better off without my nagging."

"I'm sorry."

"Sorry about marrying me?"

"No. I never regretted that." He meant it. "Sorry for not sharing your load. When you left, I discovered how tough parenting is." He held out his hand. "I even thought you'd programmed Rosie to be obnoxious, so I'd beg you to come home."

"No. Rosie wanted your undivided attention. That's what triggered her vendetta against Vanessa. From what the others have told me, the minute she realized how serious Vanessa's condition was, she reverted to the Rosie we all knew and loved."

"And instead of getting my attention, I ignored her."

"Exactly, and she's kept her distance from you because she's afraid of your reaction. She knows unless she makes peace with Vanessa, she'll never get you back."

"Did Vanessa tell you what she'd done?"

"No, just that Rosie might do something stupid. I didn't dare ask her what she meant. I assumed she was worried she'd try to commit suicide, or get hooked on drugs or something."

"So, how did you find out?"

"Penny told me. And without prompting, Rosie confessed. In two days, I've learned more about her, and it seems she needs me. Being her stepmother, I thought it made sense for me to move out, and never thought about having room for them. My focus was on becoming independent and taking control of my life. We have to make understand our separation does not make us love her less."

CHAPTER 37

Ol Essakut--Saturday 28th September

When the children had settled, Edward touched Penny's hand. "Come, we need to talk." He guided her towards the fire, which had been lit in their room, stirred the embers, and put a log on. Penny made herself comfortable and waited for him to start.

"Being here has given me time to think about the future."

Her eyebrows raised, as if that was an odd thing for him to do.

"I've neglected you all. And I promise I'll change." She shook her head, making him go on. "Not because you're ill."

"Are you sure?"

"Yes. Believe it or not. I had made a decision that the relationship that you don't want to discuss was over before I found out you had cancer. I've realized I'd been a fool."

She still didn't look convinced.

"The reason I am bringing it up is that there may be messy repercussions."

"What sort."

"Your being contacted. Or it becomes public knowledge."

"Trickier for you more than for me." Penny sounded more concerned than angry.

"When I told you the other day that I loved you. I meant it. And I don't blame you for not believing me. But it's true."

"Maybe it's a two-way thing. I let the disconnect happen. You can't take all the blame."

"But I took it a step too far. Did you know?"

"I had my suspicions, especially after you gave me that." She pointed to the red bag at her feet.

His cheeks went hot at the memory of Lauren insisting the bag would be the perfect gift. Had she hoped Penny would guess he hadn't chosen it and trigger her to kick him out?

"I'm guessing she picked it?"

All he could do was nod. This wasn't quite how he had planned this conversation. Get back on track.

"I've called work. I'm taking at least a month off, so I can be there for you and the boys."

"But..." she stammered.

"No buts. I know your parents will expect to step in. But that would probably drive you crazy. Mine will offer as well, not that you'd want them involved."

"I'm dreading telling them. Will you break it to them?"

"Yes. And I'll tell them that when we need help, we'll ask."

"You make it sound easy."

"I can be very persuasive." He touched her hand. "Will you let me try? You need to keep your sanity. I know you hate their fussing."

"They'll need time to take it in. And what shall I tell the boys?"

"Perhaps only minimal information for now. We can tell them more after your operation when you know what you're dealing with."

"Good plan." Her shoulders relaxed, making him glad he'd reduced a fraction of her load. She bent down, rummaged in the red bag, pulled out her phone and handed it to him.

"There are a few messages from a number I don't know. I haven't opened them. And don't want to. Can you deal with them?"

Edward read the first. His fears about Lauren were justified. She wasn't going to give up quietly.

Penny looked at him. "Are they from her?"

He nodded. "I'll deal with them."

"Good. I didn't want to tell you about my illness, because I wanted you to bond with the boys, in case the cancer has spread."

"Don't talk like that." He didn't want to think about the prospect.

"Okay, I won't, but I've allowed you to become disconnected from the boys. And you need to learn to read them, listen to the signs that a fight is about to erupt, know when they are putting on a brave face, or telling fibs about each other. See when they need a distraction, or need feeding to avoid them getting hangry."

"Hangry?"

"Anger caused by hunger. Usually, a biscuit or a bag of crisps is enough to stop it."

"You're right. I have a lot to learn. Watching you this week showed me how distance I have become. I promise I will be more involved, and as you say, learn the signs. I hadn't realized how little I knew about them. But we will get through this together."

CHAPTER 38

Ol Essakut--Sunday 29th September

Vanessa had worried that asking Rosie to sit was a mistake. But when Rosie turned up at eight thirty, minus her hideous nose and eyebrow rings, Vanessa relaxed. This might not be so bad after all.

Rosie was hesitant, lacking the defiant attitude shown the previous week. Vanessa tried to recall how she'd felt at that age. Had she been confident? No, that came later. Did Rosie miss the unconditional love a mother gives? Fay tried hard to fill that role, but from what Kim and Penny had said, Rosie had always stayed slightly aloof.

Rosie had a wide-eyed, timid look about her as she crossed the tiled floor, with her head sunk into her shoulders. A child in need of a hug. But fear made Vanessa hold back and pointed to the seat opposite her. A wide wooden coffee table separated them.

Rosie nervously sat on the edge of the cushioned day bed. Vanessa waited for her to speak. She wanted to let Rosie open the conversation. And if possible, draw her into talking without recriminations.

"I'm really sorry," Rosie said. Her chin quivered, and Vanessa picked up the sincerity in those words. Rosie was speaking from the heart.

Vanessa wanted to say it was fine, but she couldn't bring herself to do so. It wasn't fine. This kid had nearly killed her. Better to say nothing than lie.

"I didn't know it would make you so ill."

"Why did you do it? And why is forgiveness so important?"

Rosie picked at her cuticles as she considered the awkward question about her motive.

Vanessa picked up her pad and pencil and started sketching as she waited for an answer. She could see that Rosie was struggling for words, but she needed to find them. It could make all the difference to how her entire future shaped up.

The first sketch was done, and Rosie still hadn't found an answer to the question.

"It's hard to work these things out. Perhaps I can help. You want my forgiveness so that your father will forgive you." Rosie put her hand up to her mouth. Vanessa was on the right track. "I understand that, and I'm glad that his forgiveness matters."

Rosie wiped away a tear. Her shoulders still slumped, her head hanging. "Your need to please him is not enough for me?" Vanessa said. There was a tiny nod and Rosie bit her lip. "But I think that we have a good chance of sorting this out."

"You do?" Rosie whispered.

"Yes. I want you to talk to me. I know that will be difficult. I suspect that you rarely talk about your feeling to anyone. Am I right?"

Once again, she nodded.

Vanessa noticed a quick frown appear. "I'll ask you questions while I paint your portrait. Are you okay with that?"

Rosie's head lifted and looked Vanessa in the eye. "Yes."

"Good. I'll take some photos. And do a few sketches, asking you to pose in different positions while I work out the best angle and where the light comes from."

"What about my hair?"

"It's perfect as it is. What colour is it normally?"

They chatted about hair colour, and why she had wanted to go so dark, and whether she liked the change.

"I only did it to get Dad's attention."

"Did it work?"

"No, he never said a thing."

"What would you have done if he's said he hated it?" Vanessa knew Sean had. "Do you think he'd have allowed it, and if you'd asked him, would you have listened?"

She looked sheepish. "Probably not."

Vanessa stopped asking questions and focused on the sketches she needed before facing the canvas.

Rosie sat still, gazing out of the window at the cloud-covered mountain. Vanessa stopped for a coffee and suggested that Rosie walk over and see Fay, who was on the veranda with Sandra. "Come back in half an hour and we can carry on."

While she was gone, Vanessa sketched an outline on the canvas. She wanted to capture that vulnerability of a girl caught between two worlds. Childhood and adulthood. Such unfamiliar landscapes, with no guidebook for getting from one to the other. She had seen Rosie muck in with the little ones with total ease, and then sit with the adults, tongue tied, barely able to participate. If her brother had come, would she have been happier? Someone closer to her age in the group might have made a difference. Maybe, maybe not.

Somehow Vanessa needed to break the adult to child barrier and get the girl talking freely to her.

Rosie returned, more relaxed.

"Their dog, Rupee, is so cute," Vanessa said, hoping to ease Rosie into conversation.

"He's lovely."

"You've been so kind helping Kim with Alice and David. And with those two exhausting boys. I'm glad I don't have to put up with their bug collecting habit. You did a great job with those photos. Yours are nearly as good as your father's."

"Do you think so?" Shock in her voice at getting praise.

"Yes, have you taken many photos before?"

"Not many, but Dad showed me how to use the camera, and taught me what to look for."

They stuck to neutral conversations until lunch time.

Vanessa didn't need her there any longer, but after lunch, when everyone said what they planned for the afternoon, the only person with nothing to do was Rosie. Everyone assumed she would still be with Vanessa. So, the pair of them headed back to the studio.

Vanessa would keep her there until the others came back from school and then she could be a child again.

When Rosie sat down, she looked directly into Vanessa's eyes to catch her attention. "I've been thinking about why I did it." She fiddled with a thread from the rip in her jeans. "I didn't want you to replace Fay."

It was Vanessa's turn to nod. "I thought it might be." She held back on saying that no matter the excuse, the act was unacceptable. Best to drop that subject. And tackle an even trickier one.

"Rosie, it's lovely and warm in here. Can you take off that thick jumper? I want to sketch in your arms and hands."

She looked horrified. "Do I have to?"

"If you're worried about the scars, don't fret. I promise I won't paint them." Rosie blinked. Too taken aback to protest, she hesitantly peeled off the jumper and tried to hide the marks with her hands.

Vanessa moved closer to examine them. "Can I see? Did they hurt?"

Rosie mumbled, "Not much."

"Did it make you feel better, and are you likely to do it again?"

Rosie shrugged. "I don't know."

Vanessa wasn't sure where to go with the conversation. "There's oil you can rub in, that might make them less noticeable. Kim will know the name. Then you'll be able to wear short sleeves again."

She worked on in silence for a while, then heard a car coming up the drive. It was Jenny with Sam and Emma. Two hours had passed, and Rosie had been an excellent model.

"You can go now, but I need you back tomorrow." Vanessa said.

Rosie grabbed her jumper, pulled it on, and ran off to join the others.

CHAPTER 39

Ol Essakut--Sunday 29th September

Malcolm Scott, the vet, arrived to collect Oliver and Kim. He drove them over to the staff village, so Kim could check on Enuto's wife and child, and then took them up to Chui Farm to make sure Sandra was okay.

As they waited for her to come out, Malcolm started his sales pitch for the job.

Oliver cut him short. “I don't want Kim to feel pressured. I know there's a job available, but please don't mention it.”

Kim came back to them and said. “Sandra's fine, and Jenny promised to send someone to fetch me if anything changes. If I have to leave you two together, I'm sure you'll have a more interesting time examining animals without worrying about boring me.”

“Shall we carry on?” Malcolm asked.

Oliver guessed from Malcolm's grin that he would pull out all the stops to impress him, that moving to Kenya to work was a good idea.

The research centre was housed in a purpose-built complex. It had areas to deal with the varied projects that were going on. There was the lab that concentrated on identifying diseases and mutations. Which gave a fascinating insight as to the work they were doing. Then Malcolm took them over to the vet practice side, where a range of domestic pets and injured wild animals were being cared for. These aim with the wild animals was to treat them and then release them back into their natural habitat.

There were bushbabies, a pangolin, and a family of baby hyrax, creatures he had only ever seen in zoos, or in films. Kim seemed fascinated and asked more questions than Oliver expected.

Malcolm answered each one with a wealth of information about the animal's normal habitat, and how they came to be in his care. He also told them about the bigger animals that they treated, and how they handled those. He made it sound so exciting, as it involved extensive travel in a wide radius beyond Ol Essakut itself. And added that there were also rescue missions to treat injured wildlife, that usually involved planes, and occasionally helicopters if the terrain required it.

Spending time with someone as passionate as Malcolm really brought home how much he missed working with animals. He'd wondered if he could ever be content with gerbils, cats and dogs and parrots, which would be all that a job in England would offer. After seeing all this, that lacked appeal. And being courted to take a job rather than trying to chase after one felt odd, but exciting.

The more Oliver saw, the more he loved the idea of working with Malcolm. The opportunity was amazing, but Kim had to love the idea of living in Kenya before he could consider it seriously. If anything, she had to be the one begging to move. Her happiness mattered more than his job satisfaction.

With the tour done, Malcolm suggested they go to his house to meet his wife, who did admin at the research center, for lunch.

Kim and his wife got on well, chatting about their children, and Kim's work, and then Oliver heard Malcolm's wife say, "You'll love the house that goes with the job. I used to wish we lived there, because it has a nicer garden and a better view. But now my children have left for school, it would be too big and wasted on us. It's a perfect family home. I had it opened up so you can explore."

Kim gave him a puzzled look. Oliver wasn't sure what to say.

Malcolm intervened. "Sorry, I know Oliver hasn't had time to tell you. But I'm trying to persuade him to come and work with me."

Kim smiled at Malcolm. "No. He hasn't told me. But since we're here, I'm happy to look."

Oliver couldn't believe Kim's reaction. And was even more surprised when they toured the house.

It was a stone-built bungalow with a lovely veranda, with an enclosed garden full of trees and shrubs. It even had a play area with a swing and slide, and a big sandpit. There was a smaller house for staff at the back of the property.

Malcolm's wife had been right in describing it as a perfect family home, not that Oliver dared sound enthusiastic about it. He didn't want to make Kim feel pressured. She had to want to make the move without him trying to influence her decision. Moving away from her family might be too hard for her to contemplate.

"Newcomers to Kenya often struggle with the concept of having servants," Malcolm's wife said. "The cost is so low compared to what you would pay in England and provides much needed employment. It's a way of helping to support a family. Finding staff wouldn't be a problem, there are plenty of trustworthy people around who can ensure the smooth running of the household. Especially if you find work. Being a qualified midwife makes you very employable. I don't think there's anyone around with that qualification, and I'm sure the hospital would love to take you on."

Oliver could tell Malcolm wanted to stop his wife, but she was so busy telling Kim about the joys of living on Ol Essakut, there was no way he could shut her up. Kim listened, smiling as the woman prattled on.

Oliver hoped she wouldn't think he had arranged for this to happen. And was almost relieved when Malcolm took a call, which put an end to the tour.

“I've been asked to take you back. And told to say not to panic, Sandra is fine. But Enuto's family have gathered to thank Kim for her help, and they need you there.”

CHAPTER 40

Ol Essakut - Sunday 30th September

Malcolm drove them back to the Ol Essakut house. Amina was waiting there for them. All the others were standing on the porch.

"Great, I'll let Sandra know you're here. Then we can head to the village together. You're welcome to come too," she said to Malcolm and his wife. "Follow us, the more the merrier."

Kim couldn't work out why Amina seemed so keen for everyone to rush off. But didn't get the chance to ask. They waited while the others piled into the waiting vehicles and followed them over to the staff village.

Kim had been there to deliver Enuto's wife's baby. Oliver hadn't seen the place, but could tell he was impressed by the rows of neat houses.

What struck Kim as the vehicles came to a halt was the number of people present. On her previous visits, it had been quiet, almost deserted in comparison. Today there was a crowd mostly wearing traditional dress. The women wore heavily beaded neck collars, over predominantly red and blue fabrics draped around their shoulders.

Everyone was there, including her children, who were with Sandra and Jenny.

Kim sensed they were about to witness a tribal ceremony and were privileged onlookers.

Before she could ask Amina what was going on, Enuto came forward and singled her out, urging her to follow him.

Amina said softly. “Go, the tribe wants to honour you for saving his wife's life.”

Kim wasn't used to being the focus of attention, nervously stepped forward. An older woman came and draped a red cloth over her shoulders. Then a heavy beaded collar placed on her shoulders and fastened at the back. Enuto spoke for the first time. “My wife's mother wants to invite you to be a part of our tribe.”

Kim knew that this was an honour which she must accept, even if it felt strange. The women surrounding her took her hands and pulled her toward the semi-circle they had formed. Once she was in line with them, a chorus of ululations started. After a while, a single voice broke through the noise and the women joined in with a rhythmical hum. They rocked forward and back with each sound. Soon, the men joined in. The sound echoed off the buildings and Kim swayed with the women. Amina and Sandra, also draped in the traditional red fabric, had joined on either end of the line.

Even Jenny moved in sync with the humming. The children, including Rosie, had joined a smaller circle with some of the village children and were imitating the adults. Simeon and Vanessa were filming the event.

It wasn't long before the men started jumping. The height they achieved from a standing position was astounding.

Kim lost track of time. The singing, the rhythmical hum, and the swaying forwards and backwards with the beat, and the wide beaded necklaces bobbing up and down with the movement felt normal, as if it was something she had been doing all her life. The singing ended with a round of shrill ululations, and Kim wasn't sure what would happen next.

Enuto got Sandra to step forward. He said something to her. She looked shocked, but after some further conversation, nodded and translated.

"Enuto has asked me to say that thanks to your actions, his wife has survived. And that the council of elders has agreed that in future the women's coming of age ceremony will change. There will be no cut. Some of the other tribes have a adopted a ceremony without the cut, and now this tribe will do the same. And the women want to thank you for your part in making this happen."

The shrilling ululations resumed as the women celebrated.

Kim, with the wide beaded necklace and her red drapes, wasn't sure what to do next. She noted that Enuto's wife wasn't there and wondered why. Sandra told her that custom prevented the mother from being there.

"They are about to break a huge custom, but that one might last longer."

"It took me a while to realize this wasn't a typical tourist display."

"No, it certainly wasn't that. You have been truly honoured. But it is nearly time for us to leave."

Kim reached to remove the necklace. But Sandra stopped her. "No, keep it on. That is their gift to you. Amina and I both have them. We should have worn them today, only we didn't realize that it was going to be such a huge and important event."

Kim, still wearing the beaded necklace, went to check up on Enuto's wife and child.

When she came out, the others had left. Only Oliver and Amina had waited for her. She was glad. She was still trying to take all that had happened. When they reached the spot close to Amina's house, across a vlei from the Ol Essakut house. Kim said, "If it's okay with you, I'd love you to let us out here. I need to talk to Oliver, and could do with a walk."

Amina smiled. "Of course. I'll see you later at dinner."

Oliver took her hand as they set off. "What a day you've had. Two surprises in one day. Sorry I didn't warn you about Malcolm's offer of a job. I asked him not to say anything, but his wife hadn't got the message. I hope you didn't feel pressured by them. And being made a member of the tribe... Now that takes some beating."

"Yes, I never expected that, but more important is that the circumcision custom will change. That's a true reward." She stopped and turned to him. "Tell me honestly. Does Malcolm's offer tempt you?"

"I'd be lying if I said no. We haven't gone into any details, so I'm not absolutely sure what the job entails." Oliver kissed her hand. "And even if it is an amazing offer, I don't intent to put pressure on you to move."

"Find out what the offer is. If it's good, then I'd be prepared to move."

"But what about your family? And your job? I can't disrupt your career again."

"They'd have to visit us here. They still travel. And it sounds as if I wouldn't have a problem working out here."

Oliver stooped to kiss her. "You are an amazing woman. And I love you more every day."

"Let's not say anything to the others until we are certain that's what we are going to do. The offer might not be that great, and we still have a lot to work out about our house, and how long it will take to get the right paperwork in place."

"You're right, our secret for now."

Kim buzzed with contentment as they walked the rest of the way to join the others.

The children were still chanting and dancing. And the boys trying to beat each other with who could jump higher. Eventually, Edward intervened and persuaded them to play something else.

CHAPTER 41

Ol Essakut - Monday

Vanessa was finding it strange being part of a group, but being apart from them. After Kim's tribal ceremony, she finished the portrait of Rosie.

Now all she needed was to find a suitable moment to give it to Sean. Rosie hadn't seen it, and she decided she should see it before Sean did. So, after dinner, she had asked her to come over to the studio in the morning. Rosie had looked hesitant. But Vanessa reassured her, "I have something to show you. Nothing more."

It was always a nervous moment showing someone a painting that she had spent hours working on. Usually, it was the gallery owner's approval she sought. This time it was the subject of the picture, and far more nerve-wracking.

Rosie came in with a frightened look on her face.

Vanessa gestured for her to come round to the other side of the easel. "Do you like it?"

Rosie stared at the picture. It was impossible to tell if she liked it or hated it.

Eventually, she looked at Vanessa and smiled. A smile was enough to know she didn't hate it.

"You made me look pretty."

"Because you are, especially when you smile. Do you think your dad will like it?"

She nodded. "Are you going to come and live with us?"

"I don't think so."

"Because of me?"

"No. You didn't help, but I don't think it would work."

"Are you sure? I won't make any trouble, I promise."

"Sorry, but I won't change my mind."

"Have you told him?"

"I'm going to tell him when I give him your portrait."

"Can we still be friends?"

"Yes, I'd like that, but I want you to promise me that if you feel like harming yourself, you'll talk to someone."

"I'll try," Rosie said and bit her lip. "But I want to ask you something?"

"Go ahead."

"Everyone is so tense in the house. Is it because of what I did to you?"

Vanessa moved closer and put her arm around Rosie's shoulder. "No. Not because of what you did."

"Then what is it?"

Vanessa knew she could not fob her off with a trite reply. "Everyone is a worried about Martin. He hasn't been in touch, probably because his phone got lost, or his battery died, or he can't get a signal, but with Sandra about to have a baby, his not contacting anyone is odd. Please don't tell Sam and Emma. They don't need to know that anyone is worried."

"I won't. But is there something wrong with Penny?"

"She's having tummy trouble and is not looking forward to all the tests that she's due to have when she gets home. And her boys don't know about that either, so please don't mention it."

"Thanks for telling me. I thought it was my fault everyone was so tense."

"It is tough at your age, because people try to shield you from the truth, which can cause misunderstandings. Now scoot. I need to talk to your dad" Rosie surprised her by giving her a hug.

Telling Sean was going to be awkward. But she couldn't put it off any longer. He came into the studio with copies of the photos he took of the leopard draped over the tree. They were amazing.

"I thought you might use them to create a painting."

She wasn't sure. She liked to see the subject herself to get inspiration. But she didn't tell him that. She simply thanked him and turned Rosie's portrait round so he could see it.

He stared at it. "It's beautiful. I promise I won't let Rosie come between us again."

"Sorry Sean, it's over. My decision has nothing to do with Rosie. I've realized I value my independence too much. We'd stifle each other and end up being miserable."

"But..."

"No buts. It won't work." She said as gently as she could. "I've asked about staying on here for a while. I haven't been as inspired for years. Sandra says there's a little cottage I can use, and suggested I run some painting classes for their guests."

"What will you do about your exhibition?"

"That will go on as planned."

"Would you want this on display?"

"Only if you and Rosie are happy to loan it."

He stood and stared at it for a while. Took a step towards her, gave her a hug, and kissed her cheek. "I don't want to believe we're through, but I think I knew it was coming."

They stood silently for a while, and then he said, "Can I take it to show the others?"

Everyone had congregated on the veranda for tea at Ol Essakut house. Sean carried the portrait over. And held it up for everyone to see. “Vanessa's done a fantastic job. Even Rosie approves.”

Malcolm asked, “Do you do commissions? Because if you do, I know several people who might be interested. You should stay on for a while.”

Vanessa smiled. “I am thinking about it. Africa has worked its magic on me. I'm not sure I will ever want to leave.”

“I'm beginning to feel the same way.” Kim said.

Oliver stared at her, a look of total shock on his face. Vanessa wondered what Malcolm would say. She knew he'd been working hard to convince Oliver to come and work for him, and was so surprised that he stayed silent. Perhaps he was waiting to see how Oliver would respond.

She didn't have long to wait before Oliver turned to Malcolm and said, “Maybe we should talk about it.”

And Kim added, “I think that would be a good idea.”

At that moment, the children came running onto the veranda. All of them, including the smallest, were caked from head to toe in mud.

The shocked expression of their parents was priceless. Oliver was the one brave enough to ask what happened.

Sam came up with the answer. “They said you hadn't put sunscreen on them, and they remembered the keeper at the orphanage saying that the elephants covered themselves in mud to protect their skin.”

Kim roared with laughter, and said, “Perhaps we should leave the mud for the elephants.”

CHAPTER 42

Remote Kenya--Sunday 29th September

Earlier in the day, Martin heard the hammering on the door. There was a hiss from his captors. "Keep quiet or you're dead."

He recognized Simeon's voice, which was comforting, but he was no fool. Simeon had always been there for him, and would never act unless he was sure of what he was taking on. He would recce the place. Nothing more. Patience was the key. But now he had hope. Somehow, Simeon had found out where he was. There had been clattering and banging in the garage, doors opening and closing, and Simeon clearly thanking someone for their help.

When things settled down, he found the screw and continued working on breaking the ties that held his feet in place. Lack of mobility would put himself and others at risk.

As he poked away at the tapes that bound his feet together, he thought of Sandra. She'd be out of her mind with worry. And that wasn't good for her or the baby she carried. And he wondered how Sam and Emma were coping. Did they even know he was in danger? Probably not. They'd think he was busy in Nairobi. He hoped so. They didn't need that sort of stress in their lives.

He kept his spirits up by thinking of all the things he wanted to show his friends when he got out of this hellhole. They would be at Ol Essakut soon. Had his kidnapping messed with their plans, or had Sandra shielded them from the truth? He stabbed himself with the nail. A reminder to concentrate on freeing his bonds.

Success. He had broken through and could move his legs apart. He stretched them out to get his circulation going again. Next, he would try to stand, but carefully, he couldn't afford to alert his guards that he had freed himself. He twisted to get to a kneeling position, then to a stooped position.

There was a glimpse of light through the ripples of the corrugated iron that covered the pit. Afraid of making a sound that might disturb the men above, he sank back down and crawled the length of the pit. He found the water, took a swig, and made himself comfortable on the blanket, and thought about how he could protect himself if Simeon attempted to raid the place. Would his captors concentrate on defending themselves or try to run to safety? Or would they want to kill him before they got captured? The only things he had to hand were the blanket and a nearly empty water bottle. The blanket might help lessen the blow from a panga slash. If he wrapped it round his arm, he could use it to protect himself.

Keeping moving became his focus. He couldn't allow himself to stiffen up. Being ready could save his life. Every move made him aware of the battering his body had taken. Pain when he leaned against the wall kept his senses on full alert.

There was movement above. A waft of cigarette smoke drifted through the gaps. Without talking, his captors settled, and soon the steady rhythm of their snoring was the only noise they made.

He thought he picked up a vehicle approaching. Was he being super sensitive or letting his imagination go wild? It was real, and closer. Soon the engine stopped, a door closed, and then he heard the clinking of bottles in a crate, followed by hammering on a door.

The plastic chairs scraped on the floor as the men got to their feet, and a door creaked.

Then Simeon's voice. "I brought you some Tusker to thank you for your help." he sounded drunk and louder than usual. Knowing that Simeon seldom drank, Martin knew this was deliberate. He wanted to be heard.

Martin scrambled to his feet. Staying stooped so as not to move the tin above his head. What was Simeon planning to do? He heard the crate hit the ground with a thud. Seconds later, there was an explosion outside, and a smaller, closer explosion, followed seconds later by the noise of the garage door rattling open. Footsteps thundered in every direction. Men shouted. Martin wasn't sure if he should make his presence known, or if he'd be safer staying quiet with his head down in case bullets started flying. When he heard Simeon calling his name, he reached up and shoved the corrugated iron sheet that covered the pit to one side. The noise of metal scraping on the concrete seemed incredibly loud after days of near silence. He shouted, "Simeon, over here." And looked for the ladder they had used. He wouldn't be able to get out of the pit without it.

Simeon heard his shout and leaned over to pull him up, but realized he couldn't do it on his own. Martin pointed to the ladder. Simeon turned towards it, when the Somali refugee rushed into the garage, heading towards him, a raised panga in hand. Martin stretched out and grabbed the man's ankle. He yanked as hard as he could. The unexpected action caught the man off guard. He lost his balance and fell towards Martin, his panga still in his hand. Martin tried to duck out of the man's way, but the blade nicked his shoulder as the man plummeted into the pit. His other elbow caught the edge as he fell. There was a crack of bone breaking, followed by an agonized scream. He let go of the panga. It bounced off the wall and clattered to the ground, and the man landed heavily on top of it.

Simeon dropped the ladder in place and yelled. "Move." Survival instinct kicked in. Escape was the only thing that mattered. Simeon had risked his life to find him. It was too dangerous to stay. From the sounds out the back, there was fighting going on, and he was in no state to get involved. Martin scrambled up the ladder, steadied himself, and prepared to run. Another knife wielding captor came tearing through from the side door heading towards Simeon. Martin grabbed a heavy wrench off the bench beside him and aimed it at the man's arm. It connected with a bone crunching crack. The knife flew out of his hand and clattered to the ground. The man stared at Martin in shock. His momentum defused. Someone dressed in black combat gear came at him from behind and pushed him to the ground.

Simeon grabbed Martin's arm and pulled him towards the big garage doors and out to his Toyota. He sounded the horn. Two other men ran out of the building and jumped in.

"Good job," Simeon said, as they roared off.

About a mile down the road, he dropped off the two men. "Remember, the local cops will be angry they weren't involved. So don't say a thing, unless you want to spend weeks explaining yourselves."

"Don't worry. We don't want to get mixed up with whatever those Americans are doing. Is he going to be all right?" The taller of the two men asked.

Martin didn't have the strength to respond, even though he knew they were talking about him.

"I think so. I'll get him checked over before I take him home." Simeon said. "Once things have settled, you'll have to come up to Ol Essakut and we can talk then."

When they were alone, Martin asked. “Was Hank there?”

“No. His American buddies didn't want a civilian in the way. We insisted on going. Our mission was to get you out of their way. They were happy with that. Especially when I told them you wouldn't want any media coverage. I hope I got that right.”

Martin touched Simeon's arm. “Thanks. Glad you know me so well.”

“I've got a room at Blue Posts so you can clean up and sleep before we head home.”

Martin could hardly keep his eyes open, and was too grateful to be alive and out of that stinking hole to argue. The next thing he knew, Simeon helped him out of the Toyota, and guided him to the room at the hotel.

“I've called a doctor. He'll check you over. Then we can head home.”

Martin sank onto the bed. Exhaustion had taken over. He lay down and closed his eyes, only to wake in a sweat.

Simeon found him sitting on the edge of the bed, afraid to lie down again in case the nightmare came back. Now he knew how it ended and didn't want to relive that moment again. Maybe that was the problem. There was more he didn't know. Who had found him? The name of the girl and her family. It was unfinished business. Would knowing be helpful? It was worth a try. He had to do something.

“I can't go home,” he blurted out.

Simeon looked at him as if he'd gone mad. Maybe he had. But he wasn't in a fit state to face Sandra or the children.

“There's no rush. The doctor will be here soon. After he's checked you over, you can decide. Until then, we can stay here. I thought you might be hungry, so I've ordered for you.”

A tray of food arrived, and he got the waiter to put it on the table on the veranda. Martin was glad of the distraction and followed him out.

"I've spoken to Amina," Simeon said, ignoring Martin's earlier comment. "All your friends are at Ol Essakut. They cut short their stay at the coast and at the Tsavo camp."

Martin nodded and struggled to get his head back to normal. "Why? Didn't they like it there?"

"The younger kids were not coping with the heat. They flew back with Amina. Their mother, Kim, is a midwife, which has made Jenny happy. Sandra's doing fine. She's resting and relieved to hear you're safe, but she's keen to hear your voice."

Martin raised his hand and shook his head.

Simeon quit talking and picked up a sandwich. Martin did the same, not because he was hungry, but to give him time to work out what to do next.

The fear of the recurring nightmare was his major worry. Staying awake was one way of dealing with it. But unsustainable. He would have to sleep to function, but he couldn't risk it with the children around.

When Simeon stopped eating, he leaned back in his chair, waiting for Martin to speak.

"I need time alone."

"I guessed as much. How about Mountain View lodge? It's empty." Simeon peered at him to gauge his reaction. "And not too far from home."

Martin nodded. "Perfect."

"Good. I'll organize it. But you'll have to see Sandra first. She's always understood your need for solitude."

Martin wasn't sure about that. She had given him space before, but things were different now. The twins. The baby on the way. So much to consider. He'd never told Sandra about his nightmares. And wasn't sure he was ready to explain it to her now.

One of Simeon's army friends knocked on the door. Simeon looked at Martin. "Want to come to find out what happened after we left?"

Martin shook his head.

"Fine, stay here. I shouldn't be too long."

Martin sat staring out at the garden, which overlooked the waterfall. The hotel had been open for so long, everyone in Kenya who ever went through Thika knew about it.

He ought to sleep, but fear stopped him. Maybe he should take a walk. But he was too stiff and sore and lacked the energy.

He wasn't sure how long he'd sat there before a waiter came to clear the table and check if he wanted a fresh pot of coffee or something from the bar.

Martin declined. Alcohol was the last thing he needed.

Simeon returned with the doctor.

"I'll leave you to it," he said and walked away.

Martin let the man examine him. He prodded and poked and muttered something about cracked ribs. "Not much we can do about them. They will take a while to heal." He dressed the shoulder wound and commented on the old scar. Then offered medication to numb the rib pain.

"It's not too bad. I can probably manage without."

"I'll give you a prescription in case you change your mind. And something to help you sleep. The trauma of being kidnapped can disrupt your sleep patterns. I understand you've suffered trauma in the past. Do you have nightmares?"

"Sometimes, but nothing I can't handle."

"That's what most people say. But it isn't the best way of dealing with them."

“I'll be fine.”

“You need to talk to a professional therapist. Being open has proved to be the best way to deal with these things. I can recommend someone who can help.”

Martin shook his head.

“I'll give Simeon the information in case you change your mind. Rest as much as you can.”

Martin thanked the man, but was glad to see him go. He was probably right about needing help. But could he talk about his experiences? He didn't think so. He propped himself up on the bed to wait for Simeon to return.

The nightmare came back, turning him into a shaking, sweat soaked wreck, leaving him disorientated. It took a while to notice Simeon sitting in a chair by the bed, reading.

“You okay?” he asked.

Martin shook his head. “No. The bloody nightmare is back.”

“I'll get you a coffee.” Simeon returned with a cardboard cup. “When you're ready, we need to hit the road.”

“What's the rush?”

“Avoiding Hank.”

That reply was enough to spur him into action. He couldn't face Hank, now or soon.

CHAPTER 43

Monday 30th September

Martin swished water over his face, ran his fingers through his hair, and said, “Let's go.” He didn't really want to go anywhere, but had to make a move to avoid Hank.

On the way. Simeon said quietly. “I've spoken to Sandra. She gets your need to be alone. She's sent clean clothes and essentials to the lodge. But she wants to see you, even if it's only for a few minutes.”

Martin knew he owed it to Sandra to see her, but he was terrified. He didn't want to let her down, but he couldn't marry her. And he would have to find the words to tell her so.

“Okay, but is there any way of seeing her without bumping into anyone else?”

“I'll get Amina to organize it. I'll take you to the lodge, so you can shower and change first.”

Martin noticed the state of his clothes. The hoodie Jaz, the Indian shopkeeper, had purchased for him was bloodstained. The stink of sweat and goats lingered. He had become so used to the stench; it no longer nauseated him.

He ran his hand over his chin. Days without shaving had left him with scratchy stubble. Not something Sandra would appreciate.

“Good plan.”

Martin expected Simeon to launch into a detailed summary of his army friends' encounter with Hank and his support team. But he stayed silent. And Martin didn't ask. He wanted to blank the entire event.

Maybe later he'd be able to listen to the details. For now, he was grateful to stare out of the window at the familiar landscape and the little towns with their bustling roadside stops. Wide open spaces, with distant hills, and the cloud covered mountain. As they got closer to the base, the cloud lifted, giving a glimpse of the snowcapped jagged peak. His anxiety eased. Home was the only place he might find peace.

Simeon didn't linger at the entrance gates to Ol Essakut. He waved to the askari and drove straight through, heading directly to the lodge.

"I'll wait here. I'll warn them you're coming and tell them you're not ready to see anyone except Sandra."

As water flowed over his head in the shower, Martin wondered how he was going to tell Sandra he wasn't fit to marry her. Leaving that letter and the ring had seemed like the right thing to do. Maybe she'd turn him down and solve the problem. Or would it? He might not be fit, but he loved her and couldn't bear the thought of losing her.

He was drying himself when Simeon came barging in.

"Hurry. You need to get to the house. Sandra's in labour."

Martin dressed quickly and ran out to the waiting Toyota. Simeon put his foot down and sped to Chui Farm.

Martin ran into the house. He ignored everyone watching him and tore up the stairs to their bedroom.

Sandra was not alone. Jenny, Amina, and Kim were all there. Sandra was groaning. He knelt beside the bed, took her hand. She let out a yell and squeezed it so hard he thought she would break his bones.

"Come on," Kim said. "Martin's here now. Push."

Her panting slowed, and the pressure on his hand eased a fraction. He leaned in and kissed her forehead.

"It's okay, I'm here."

She moaned and clenched his hand even tighter than before.

"Breathe." Kim said, "Push. Good. Nearly there. Go on, one more push. Fantastic. The head is out, now another push. Come on, you can do this."

Sandra looked him in the eyes, let out a big breath, and relaxed her grip as the baby slithered into Kim's hands.

"It's a boy." She wrapped the baby in a towel and rubbed it firmly until he let out a scream. She clamped and cut the cord. And handed the baby to Jenny and said, "Okay, are you ready, Sandra? Time for the next one. Push again."

Martin was looking at the child, and it took a moment to register what she had said. He turned back to Sandra, who gasped. "Twins." And crunched his hand again and again. Until their daughter was born.

While Kim checked her over. Jenny handed their son to Sandra to hold. Martin wasn't sure where to look. At his son on Sandra's chest, or at his daughter who was being rubbed, and hadn't yet let out a sound. Finally, she cried. Kim told Martin to take the first baby while Sandra got to hold their daughter.

Amina whipped out her phone and photographed the precious moment.

"Martin, sit down," Kim said. He did so, clutching his son to his chest. "Put him in the crook of your arm, perfect." Martin did. And seconds later, Kim handed him his daughter. He was now trapped with a baby cradled in each arm, while Kim made sure Sandra was all right.

Sandra watched in silence as he planted kisses on their heads. He looked at her and mouthed; I love you.

He couldn't love her more than he already did, and now she had given him this precious pair.

Being there for their birth was not quite how he had expected it to be. Nothing had gone as planned. And he wasn't ready to face so many people.

Kim solved his dilemma. “I'm going to leave you two alone for a few minutes. And then I think you should let Sam and Emma in to see their siblings.”

Sandra nodded and turned to Martin and said, “Only if it's okay with you?”

“Here, let me take one.” Kim lifted their son out of his arms and placed him back into Sandra's. Then she left the room.

Suddenly, they were alone. He leaned over and kissed her. She had tears in her eyes. He whispered. “Thank you. They're beautiful.”

“Are you okay?”

“Battered, and exhausted. But I'll mend.” He didn't dare say more at this point. All he wanted to do was scoop her into his arms, but the bundles they held prevented him.

“Did you know?” he asked.

“About there being two?” She shook her head. “Not until Kim got here, and she noticed a shadow on the scan, and picked up the second heartbeat.”

He wanted to explain that he couldn't stay, but wasn't sure he could leave. But before he could say anything, Jenny knocked on the door.

“Shall I bring Sam and Emma in?”

Sandra looked at him. What could he do other than agree?

The pair rushed in and huddled round them, peering at the babies. They seemed pleased, and fired a load of questions at them, including, “What are you going to call them?”

Sandra took control of the response. “We haven't decided. Why don't you come back later for a cuddle? I need to rest now.”

The twins gave Martin a quick kiss, and their mother one, and hurried off to play with Kim's children, leaving Sandra and Martin alone again.

“I know you need to go,” Sandra said. “And my answer is yes. But I'm happy to wait until you are ready to ask in person, but I'd love it to be in time for that party you asked me to organize.”

Martin didn't know what to say. She had given him breathing space and permission to take time to get himself together. Maybe he should take up the doctor's offer of help. Or at least give it a chance.

“The nightmares are back. I'm going to get help.”

She touched his hand. “I was worried that they would.”

He wanted to hug her, but he couldn't move.

Kim knocked on the door, poked her head in. Jenny stood behind her. “Sorry to disturb you, but it's time to get this pair feeding.”

Sandra must have seen panic on his face.

“Go, I know it's what you need to do,” she whispered. She understood. She had always understood. He didn't deserve her love.

“Kim, help Martin. Let Jenny have a cuddle.”

Kim took the baby from his arms. He kissed Sandra and whispered, “I'll come back tonight.”

“Whenever you're ready. We're not going anywhere.”

He saw Sam and Emma on his way out. He made up an excuse that he had to meet some men, and would be busy for a day or two.

“Look after your mum for me.”

“We will.” They said and gave him a hug.

The staff had lined up to congratulate him. Juma and Wanjiru stood there with beaming faces. He knew he had to react. He walked towards them and took their outstretched hands. They'd all witnessed his dark moments in the last seven years, and were content to just shake his hand.

Only Juma spoke. "Pole Pole," was all he said as Martin approached his old Land Rover. Those two words, that simply translated as slowly, slowly, used for a multitude of situations, including dealing with a death, were nearly his undoing.

Simeon offered to drive.

"No, I can drive myself."

"Good. Perhaps you should have your phone back. Barnard will be up there with you at the lodge. Call if you need anything. Amina needs my help to entertain your friends."

Barnard greeted him with a big, gap-toothed smile. Bush telegraph had been working well.

Martin accepted his good wishes. He wanted to tell Barnard he didn't need to stay, but the consequence would be Simeon insisting on staying instead.

"I was told to give you this." He handed over a bag containing Martin's old Leica camera, along with a couple of rolls of film.

Sandra, that amazing woman, could read him better than he could himself.

There was also a note from Simeon with a blister pack of half a dozen pills. "The doctor suggested you take one of these to help you sleep. And this is the number of the doctor you should talk to."

Martin, who had been resisting help for so long, knew that now was the right time to take it. He owed it to Sandra.

He had to rejoin the present and face his friends and his responsibilities.

CHAPTER 44

Ol Essakut -Monday

There was much to celebrate: the safe delivery of twins, a boy and a girl, and the news that Martin was home was the perfect excuse to pop a champagne cork.

Dinner plans had altered. Simeon, Amina, and Vanessa had come down to join them at the Ol Essakut house, to let Sandra and Martin have time alone, and because Martin wasn't ready to face anyone.

"He's had a rough time, and needs to rest," Simeon said in answer to their questions. "Because of the sensitivity of the terrorist's involvement, his part in it has not, and hopefully will never, become public knowledge. It's safer that way, and what we all want, so I hope you will keep it to yourselves. His disappearance was unusual, but not surprising, as he had lost his phone and could not report his whereabouts. The lead he was following turned out to be of significant consequence."

Everyone nodded, they understood. "Maybe one day Martin will tell us the details of what happened, but until then. Please don't speculate."

With that information on board, Simeon and Malcolm came up with the suggestion of a trip to visit the animal orphanage in Nairobi, to see the rescued baby elephant they had seen in Tsavo.

"I intend going myself," Malcolm announced. "I always like to check up how the orphans are doing.

Especially ones I have had a role in rescuing. I could arrange special access, if you fancy coming."

The enthusiastic nods were all Simeon needed. "Tell me what needs to be arranged."

Penny asked, "What about the children? Can they come too? Nicholas and Timothy will be upset if we go without them."

There was a general discussion about whether Kim and Oliver's two would find it too tiring.

Everyone agreed. Kim had to go, and the children, because they had missed out on the Tsavo adventure. There was a slightly awkward moment when Sean asked, "What about Rosie?" He aimed the question at Vanessa.

She quickly responded. "Of course she should go. Her punishment is done."

Everyone agreed.

Simeon was pleased. This trip would take the pressure off Martin and Sandra. And with Malcolm as their guide for the day, he'd be free to deal with anything Martin might need.

A pleasant evening followed, listening to Malcolm extolling the joys of living on the ranch, and on his love of flying. "It's something I learned to do, almost as soon as I arrived, and never regretted the impulse. I love having the freedom to go where I want, without having to plan ahead. Well, there are some flight requirements, but nothing too arduous."

His enthusiasm was infectious. Simeon saw Oliver's eyes light up at the thought. Malcolm was doing a good job of winning him over. Kim might take a bit more coaxing. But they would both be very welcome if they made the move.

After dinner, Simeon drove Vanessa back to Chui Farm. And she queried if she should think about moving down to the other house.

"No, I think Sandra is happy to have you there. Although Martin is back, he's probably going to stay at Mountain lodge for a while. He's really struggling with being around people, so he'll be happy that there's added support for Sandra if he's not around."

CHAPTER 45

Ol Essakut -

Sandra was relieved when Martin appeared just before midnight. He looked more himself.

"Sorry, I should have come earlier," he said. "But I took the pills the doctor prescribed, and they knocked me out."

He gave Jenny a hug. "Go. I'll be here until morning." Sandra smiled and nodded to Jenny.

"As long as you're sure you can manage," she said, and placed the sleeping baby she had been holding into the crib, and picked up her glasses. "I'll be in the guest room if you need me."

Martin stood awkwardly beside the bed. He looked at the baby in the cot, then at Sandra, and the baby she held.

He obviously didn't know what he should he do. He hadn't been around when Sam and Emma were born, so he had no experience of being the father of a newborn, let alone two.

"Here," she said, "Take her for a moment." She handed the baby to him. "See if you can get some wind out of her. While I have a shower."

When she returned, she found him sitting on the edge of the bed, cradling the baby, talking to her.

He looked up and said, "Show me how to change her nappy."

That single sentence told Sandra all she needed to know. Martin was going to be a hands-on parent, something she hadn't expected to happen.

She handed him a nappy and a wipe and gave him a lesson in nappy changing.

He lay the baby on the mat and followed her instructions so efficiently she couldn't believe this was the first nappy he'd ever changed. But maybe it was just him being practical, the trait about him she loved. He undid the offending nappy and nearly gagged, but took the wipe and cleaned her bottom. Then slipped the clean nappy under her and pulled the tabs to seal it in place. The only thing he struggled with was the poppers on the sleep suit.

"How did I do?" he asked. Sandra kissed his cheek.

"Amazing. Thanks."

He put the soiled nappy in the bin and put the mat back where it had been before.

Sandra lay down. She needed to sleep, but there were so many things she wanted to ask him, tell him. But now was not the time. Tonight was just for the family. The rest of the world's problems could wait until another day.

"Lie with me." She tapped the bed. "They'll need feeding in a couple of hours." Martin lay down beside her, fully clothed. She didn't mind. He was here. That was enough for now.

She woke to the sound of a baby crying. Martin was cuddling him, trying to calm him.

"Sorry, I tried to keep him happy, but I think he's hungry."

Sandra sat up, adjusted the pillows to get comfortable to feed him. And reached out to take the baby from Martin. As he latched on, Sandra watched Martin, trying to gauge his mood.

He looked relaxed, which was good, but she had a feeling whatever he'd been through meant he'd want some solitude.

"We need to think of names." He nodded. They had not known the sex of the baby, so had not had the conversation before. "Any ideas?"

He shook his head.

"Family names, maybe?"

"Not sure I have any relatives I'd care to remember that way. Apart from my mother. What about you?"

"No, none spring to mind."

"Pass that note pad, let's jot down a few and see what stands out." She handed over the pad and pen. "What about Jonathan?"

He wrote it down. "Paul?" He wrote that, then they called out names until they had a long list.

They bandied names back and forth while the baby fed until he fell asleep at her breast. She stroked his head, amazed at how much hair he had. Most of the babies she'd seen before had been hairless. Martin had a thick head of hair, so perhaps that was the reason. She passed the baby back to Martin to wind so she could feed the other one.

With the babies fed and winded, Sandra sensed Martin was about to take off again. "Can you have breakfast with Sam and Emma before you disappear? I don't want them to resent this pair for taking up all our time."

There were sounds of stirring in the house. Martin said, "I'll see if they're awake, and bring them in to see you."

"Good idea. What will you do after that? I sense you aren't ready to face your friends, which is fine. They are off to the Orphanage today with Malcolm and staying at Giraffe manor tonight. We thought it best so you can have a few days quiet."

His relief was obvious, but he checked, “Are you sure you are okay with me ducking out?”

“Of course, I am. It isn't the first time, and I doubt it will be the last.”

“That predictable?” he said with a smile.

“Totally.”

He leaned in and kissed her.

After the children had cuddled the babies, Martin settled them in the cot, and took Sam and Emma down to have breakfast. On the way out, he blew her a kiss and said, “See you tonight.”

Sandra had an endless stream of visitors. Kim came to check on her and the babies. Jenny was in and out. And Amina popped in to give her an update of what was happening in the camps and with Martin's friends.

Sandra felt like moving after weeks of being stuck with her feet up. Being up and about was a joy. But a simple decision to leave the bedroom came with logistical challenges. Carrying two babies and all that they might need was not a straightforward task.

Jenny helped with carrying a baby, Kim the other, and Wanjiru carried down the wicker basket that the pair were sharing.

She had barely got herself settled when she saw a dust trail heading towards the house. Hank. He was the only person who drove that fast. And the last person she wanted to deal with, but it would be impossible to avoid him. How quickly could she get rid of him?

Juma came out and asked if she wanted him to bring coffee.

She said no. She didn't want to give Hank an excuse to stay.

Jenny asked if she should stay or go? Sandra decided that seeing Hank alone might make his visit shorter. Kim had already gone to find her children.

“No, I'll get rid of him quicker if I'm alone.” Sandra wasn't sure what tactics she'd use.

Hank stomped up the steps. Dumped Martin's holdall and camera case on the veranda, and called out for Juma.

Sandra was incensed. Not only had he come uninvited, but hadn't the courtesy to acknowledge her presence. And was expecting her staff to jump to his command.

Juma hesitantly stuck his head round the corner.

“Bring me coffee.” Hank demanded.

Sandra said, quietly but firmly. “It's okay Juma. No need for coffee. He's not staying.” She could see the conflicting instructions confused Juma, but he backed away.

Hank spun round to face her. “Where is he?” he snapped.

Sandra struggled to keep her voice calm. “Hello Hank. Martin's not here now, thanks to you. And I'd appreciate it if you'd leave.”

If he couldn't bother with niceties, why should she?

“I need his article.” Hank spluttered, barely hiding his rage.

“There is no article, and there won't be one now, or ever.”

“But he needs to tell his side of the story.”

“There is no story. And if you write one, you cannot mention his name.”

“But...”

“Forget the buts. He went to Nairobi, saw someone he'd photographed in a refugee camp, and followed him to see if he had any connection to the mall siege, and passed on that information. What happened to the man is of no interest to him. End of story.”

No way would she tell Hank how fragile Martin was, or that he hadn't spoken about his experience. All she knew was what Simeon had passed on to her. Hank didn't need to know about the panga injury, or the kicking he'd received that cracked his ribs.

Hank stood his ground. “But he promised me.”

“No Hank, you never gave him a chance to say no.” She realized she had raised her voice enough to trigger a demanding wail from the crib.

Hank looked puzzled, and then it registered. A baby. She had given birth. He opened his mouth to say something, closed it again without speaking.

Sandra stretched out to pick up the screaming child. “I need to feed this one, and I'd appreciate some privacy.”

Hank looked apologetic. “Sorry, I didn't know you'd had your baby.”

“Babies,” she corrected him. “I had twins. Now go. And don't attempt to contact Martin. You've done enough damage for now.”

Hank muttered, “Congratulations.” And retreated.

CHAPTER 46

Nairobi

Vanessa was amazed at how quickly the orphanage trip was organized.

Simeon told them to pack a small overnight bag, as they would stay at in Nairobi for the night. The flight would take off from Nanyuki late morning, and they would spend the afternoon at the elephant orphanage, and meet the keepers and the elephants. Then they'd go to their accommodation which was a nearby.

He said the airport was close to the orphanage, so they wouldn't be visiting the center of the city. And they would fly back the following day.

The children were so excited about going to see the elephants. Even the little ones who had missed seeing the rescue of the orphan in Tsavo had realized that this was a very special trip.

Everyone was ready when the vehicles arrived to take them to Nanyuki Airport. They were picking up Malcolm and his wife on the way, as they would be their guides for the trip.

Vanessa sat with Malcolm's wife, who pointed out the landmarks that they flew over. The Ngong hills, on the outskirts of Nairobi, rattling off names of the areas like Karen, named after the famous author, Karen Blixen, Langata and Dagoretti. The sprawling suburbs of Nairobi. Most striking was the contrast between the rusty tin roofs of the vast Kibera slum, with barely an inch of space between the houses, and the green oasis of a golf course right beside it.

She pointed out Mount Kilimanjaro in the distance as they flew over Nairobi game park on their descent to Wilson airport.

Transport was waiting, and it was only a short drive to the Orphanage. Malcolm had arranged for them to meet Daphne Sheldrick and her daughters, who gave them a private tour of the facilities and introduced them to the rangers who cared for the orphaned elephants.

Vanessa loved seeing paintings of the baby elephants, which Daphne's daughter did when new arrivals came to the orphanage. Copies of which were sent to the people who adopted them. Allowing people to adopt an elephant had become a huge part of their fundraising plan, with regular reports of each baby going out to update them on the progress of the elephant they had chosen.

The two most recent arrival, the baby they had a part in rescuing and one other were both doing well, but hadn't yet joined the rest of the herd for the daily walks so they went to see them in a small pen where they were adjusting to life at the orphanage. Edwin, the head keeper, told them how they were adapting and being slowly introduced to the others. It was easy to see the bond that he had formed with the pair. The little elephants had blankets over them to protect him from the sun, and they stuck close to Edwin, touching him frequently with their trunk. Soon they would go with the others into the park to learn to be wild.

The children were getting a little impatient to see the other elephants. They watched as the staff at base filled wheelbarrows with bottles of feed and followed them towards the visitor spectator area. It was time to wait for the fun began. Other visitors arrived, and on time elephants came hurrying back for their afternoon feed. The keepers had trouble making sure that everyone got a bottle. Some of the older elephants had learned to hold it for themselves, while the younger ones hadn't quite got to grips with the task, so the keepers had to help them. In no time at all, the bottles were empty, and they turned their attention to the mud pool.

One of the smaller orphans was trying to pick something up with its trunk, and getting frustrated that it couldn't do it. The older ones jostled each other loving rolling in the mud and pushing others into the water. Another group was pushing a ball around.

Vanessa felt she could spend days watching them and never tire of seeing their antics. She knew she would be back with her sketch pad and paints.

The children would have loved to have jumped into the mud bath with the elephants. They seemed to think that mud baths were the best things ever.

All too soon, it was time to go. No one knew where they were staying. They had been told it wasn't far away, and was a very special place.

They drove up the road and arrived at Giraffe Manor. Malcolm told them it had been the home of Jock and Leslie Melville, who had been involved in rescuing Rothchild giraffes, and created a sanctuary for them. Now their garden and forest surrounding the house was home to these creatures, who would stick their heads through the windows of the dining room looking for treats.

There was an education center to one side of the property with balconies at giraffe head height so one could get close to the animals. Which they would see.

CHAPTER 47

Ol Essakut -Monday 30th September

Martin slept during the day and returned in the evening to the house to spend time with Sandra. He arrived early enough to read to Sam and Emma, not because they couldn't read themselves, but from habit. One that the kids loved, and never hinted they were too old to be read to.

He was pleased that Hank had returned his camera equipment, but preferred to use his old Leica to take pictures of the family. Jenny and Amina were the only other people he was communicating with, though they left him and Sandra alone when they could.

It was a small circle, but a growing one. Each day, it got easier. But he was still a long way from being comfortable around people.

Simeon sent texts, telling him what his friends were doing. And checking if he wanted company.

The pills had helped Martin get over his exhaustion, which enabled him to call the doctor that Simeon's friend had recommended. They had lengthy conversations during which Martin eventually shared details of the recurring nightmare, hoping that by doing so, he might reduce the impact it had on him.

They decided he needed to find out who found him, and what happened to the child. Which meant he had to talk to Hank.

Barnard waited while he slept and followed him when he took a walk. He was getting used to being shadowed, knowing he couldn't send him away, or Simeon would replace him. And soon almost forgot he was there.

Sandra was coping with the string of well-wishers who had dropped in. She'd told him about Hank's visit and how she'd sent him packing. Which made him laugh. Something he hadn't done for a while.

Sandra had commented that she'd do it again, if only to make him laugh. And confessed she had enjoyed the moment, even if she felt slightly guilty afterwards. Especially when Hank's driver arrived with a huge hamper and a rocking horse for the nursery.

"Should I invite Hank over?"

"Actually, I need to speak, and will go over today. Don't feel bad about how you treated him. And don't worry, I'm ready to fight my own battles."

As he was leaving that morning. Kim caught him and said, "You'd better meet up with the gang soon, or they'll come and track you down." He knew they would and decided it was time to reconnect with the world. After he'd seen Simeon and Hank.

As he drove to Simeon's house, he thought about how he'd been wallowing in self-pity. Yes, Westgate had stirred up memories that were hard to deal with. But he was blessed with an understanding partner, newborn twins, and his other two children. And friends who didn't deserve to be neglected after travelling so far to spend time with him. It was time to stop wallowing in self-indulgent isolation and act on the advice given.

He knocked on Simeon's door, wondering what sort of welcome he'd get. Simeon was holding a piece of toast in his hand, and ushered him in, and sat down to finish his breakfast. Amina was at the table. She reached out for a mug and poured him a coffee, just as she had on many occasions.

“Sorry, I've got to dash off. Catch up with you later,” she said and hurried off.

Martin wasn't sure if she was being diplomatic or if she really had to be somewhere else, but it suited him to be alone with Simeon to make his apology.

“Sorry, I've been a pain.”

Simeon shook his head. “No need. What you went through was tough. I'm sorry I didn't get you out of there sooner. Sandra's the one you need to thank. If she hadn't mentioned that wrist band tracker, we'd never have found you.”

Martin rubbed his wrist. The silicone band was still there. He hadn't realized that the cheap-looking device had saved his life.

“If those guys had found it, things might have been different.” Simeon said.

“I have a lot to be thankful for. It's a good thing the kids customized it so brilliantly. I need you to tell me what went on at the Mall, after I went missing.”

“Sure.” He went off and returned with a stack of newspapers. “These might help.” He sifted through them and pushed one forward. “Probably best to begin with this.” Then he turned on his laptop and pulled up a recording of a news broadcast for that date. He spun the screen round to face Martin. “Watch this, then read the report.”

Martin watched and read. The reports were conflicting. Some said four gunmen had attacked. Another said between ten and fifteen. There were disputes over whether the guns were fired first or if there had been an explosion. People had been gunned down; some had hidden behind shop counters. Civilians and brave security guards had rescued others. With more explosions, a fire had started and billowing black smoke was coming out of the building.

The battle with the police raged for forty-eight hours, during which the attackers seemed to have taken hostages in the supermarket in the basement. No one was sure how many. A few lucky people were still escaping from the building.

Later reports stated that three fighters had been killed and ten soldiers wounded.

On the Monday there was a lull in the firing. Soldiers were sent in and there were images of them looting the shops. But eventually, after part of the building had collapsed, the building was declared secure.

With a loss of seventy-one people. Of which sixty-two were civilians.

There was some doubt whether all the attackers had been killed. There was speculation that a few had escaped early on during the attack. Islamic militants from the Al Shaabab group had claimed responsibility.

When they reached the end of the reports, Simeon made fresh coffee.

"After you went missing, Hank was able to track your phone to where it stopped moving. It was found it on a market stall in a little town on the outskirts of the city. They arrested the man who ran the stall."

"Sandra reminded me of the running tracker connected to your phone. And asked me to check if it was working. That's how I found you."

"How did Hank get involved?"

I had to get his help in the end because of the numbers involved. But I insisted on going in myself to get you out. I wasn't sure his American friends would have the same objective. They were, as I expected, rather heavy-handed with their tactics. But as I had no interest in getting involved with anything other than getting you out safely. I was happy for them to deal with your captors, some of whom were terrorists on their wanted list. I've steered clear of Hank ever since."

"So, you don't know what happened to the kidnappers?"

"No. I made it clear we wanted no part in their capture and that you would not want any publicity. It seemed to suit them."

"Good, it's best that way."

They sat and sipped their coffee. Martin broke the silence. "Kim kicked my butt and made me realize I need to spend time with my friends. I wondered if you'd join us. It's time I took Sean, Edward, and Oliver out to see why Ol Essakut is so special."

"Nice idea. I was going out to check the lodges today, anyway. And it will be good for the staff to see you. I know they all want to congratulate you on the birth of the twins."

Simeon was right, connecting with the staff was important, and it was one more step towards normality.

"I need to talk to Hank first. Then I'll head to the house and see if they are up for a tour. I'll call you and you can meet me there."

He set off to Hank's house. Wondering if Hank would remember Sandra's instructions. He doubted Hank would. But it would be interesting to see. She had been right. He had no intention of writing anything about the past week. And no amount of cajoling from Hank would make him change his mind. This trip was about something far more important.

Hank and Beverley must have seen his dust trail because they came out to meet him. Beverley gave him a hug and said. "So glad you are back. Congratulations too. Come on in."

"I won't," he said, I just need some answers from you both.

Beverley looked puzzled. "Of course. What do you need to know?"

Who gave permission for that award-winning photo to be published?"

Beverley's expression changed. She turned to Hank and said, "You can answer that."

Hank took a moment before speaking. "No one. I saw the picture in amongst some that Beverley forwarded to me. It was so captivating, I had to use it. I was under pressure to get something out that day and assumed that you were okay with me using it."

Martin could tell he was uncomfortable, and stood silently waiting for him to say more.

"I had no idea that you had problems with it until we turned up at that award ceremony, and you ducked out on me. I couldn't work out why you reacted so badly, so I looked at the other photos in that batch and saw the context of the pictures."

"How did you get them?"

Beverley said, "That was my fault. When you were recovering in Paris, you told me you were going to wipe all the photos off your computer. I copied them off before you did so. I'm sorry."

"Did anyone recognize her?" Martin asked.

"I don't know. It was a difficult time over there, as most of our staff pulled out at the same time as you." Hank said.

"Can you ask? I need to know her name, and if she had surviving family."

Beverley touched Hank's arm. "We will do everything we can to find out for you."

"Good. And I'd like to see the pictures that relate to it, too. Call me when you have something for me."

He got back into his Land Rover and drove away, stopping briefly when he was far enough away to be out of sight, to let the peace of the bush ease the tension of the morning's revelations. He had to be calm to face his friends.

His tension eased, and he continued his drive to Ol Essakut. As he walked up the steps to the Ol Essakut house, he had a moment of panic. Could he handle all the questions they'd fire at him? The temptation to turn and leave was strong. But his resolve was stronger. He could hear laughter and children chattering inside. He had to go in. Kim's threat that they'd come to find him was real.

He took a deep breath and pushed the door open.

"Hi, Anyone in?" Kim was the first to react. She came over and gave him a quick kiss on the cheek and said softly, "Glad you made it."

He couldn't believe that it was over seven years since he had been with this lot. Within minutes, they were talking as if they had been together the day before.

He went over to Penny. Gave her a hug and said, "Sorry about your news."

She squeezed his hand. "It's fine, but I'd rather not dwell on it." He understood there were lots of things he'd rather not deal with.

After a round of friendly banter, Martin said, "I was wondering if I could persuade Edward, Oliver and Sean to come out with me today."

Jenny arrived to pick up the children. He stood and watched the chaos of trying to round up the four children. All born since their last reunion. The kids had enjoyed going to school and persuaded their parents to let them go every day. Rosie, Sean's daughter, was the only one he'd met before, but she wasn't around. She had already gone up to the main house to sit for the portrait Vanessa was painting.ms Martin plied them with questions about their flights. How much they had liked the house at the coast, and the Tsavo camp.

They gave him the sanitized version. No mention of Rosie's behaviour. No mention of Penny's pending surgery. No mention of Oliver's state of unemployment.

No explanation of Sean having his wife and his mistress here at the same time.

Were they all holding back because they saw him as fragile? Or were they all afraid to talk about how they really felt? Open discussions had never been an issue in the past. Why now? And what could he do about it? He was hardly in a good frame of mind to air his problems.

Simeon arrived in a vehicle that they would all fit in more comfortably than in his battered old Land Rover. Would having Simeon there make it harder for them to get back to the easy camaraderie shared since college? He hoped not. Simeon had spent time with them all since their arrival, so introductions weren't necessary.

Martin let Simeon pick the direction that suited his rounds of the camps. Edward was in the front and Martin in the back with Sean and Oliver. "Okay, spill. How come Fay and Vanessa are here at the same time?" No point in being subtle.

"Didn't anyone tell you about Rosie?" Martin shook his head and listened to Sean's version, which ended with, "Thankfully Rosie seems to be remorseful and behaving well."

There was a general feeling of sympathy for Sean, with both Oliver and Edward, saying that he had handled things better than they expected.

"Not that well," Sean sighed. "Vanessa will never forgive me. And to be honest, I don't blame her."

They reached the first camp, and everyone was keen to explore and see what an Ol Essakut camp offered. The staff, as Simeon had predicted, were keen to clutch his hand and congratulate him on the birth of the twins. They all said it was good to see him back. He guessed that Enuto and Barnard had given them an idea of what had gone on in Nairobi.

They had coffee and then set off for the second camp. Sean sat in the front seat, probably hoping that no further interrogation about his love life would come up.

Martin asked Edward how he was coping with the news about Penny.

"I'm struggling. But I must keep going. The boys don't know, telling her folks and mine will be tough. They will either rally round, or fall apart, and neither of us can cope with the latter. It will be easier once the boys are back at school. I'll take time off work while we discover if she needs further treatment. The biggest complication is that a woman I had an affair with isn't happy that I ended things. She's been texting Penny. It could get very messy."

This information took a while to digest, and none of them seemed able to respond with anything more than "Tough. Tricky. Good luck."

Simeon had organized a curry lunch, Kenya style, with all the trimmings. After they had eaten their fill and were having coffee, Oliver said, "I guess I'm next."

They all nodded.

"I lost my job a few weeks before we left. I kept it a secret from Kim, who thought I was having an affair."

"She wasn't the only one." Sean said with a sardonic grin.

"Yes, complete fail. But she shocked me with the news she had updated her midwifery qualifications and was going back to work."

"And now Malcolm is piling on the pressure for me to fill a vacancy at the research centre." Oliver said. "And I'm tempted. Working with animals again after years behind a desk would be amazing."

"Did you know that he's been asking around to check if Kim could work here?" Simeon said, "He's been trying to find out what permits she'll need."

"I know, and believe it or not, I think might be happy to make the move."

Oliver obviously didn't want to carry on with the speculation about his future, so switched the subject.

"What about you and Amina?" He looked directly at Simeon, who shifted uncomfortably in his seat. Was he ready to share personal stuff with these newly made friends? Or would he bluff his way out of answering?

Simeon took a deep breath. "I've asked her to marry me several times, but she always says no."

There were understanding nods, with Oliver looking guilty at triggering a tough topic.

"Events of the last couple of weeks have made me want to try again. Our problem is not that we don't want to, but that our families will struggle with marrying outside our respective tribe and nationality. The Westgate siege will make the prejudice even worse."

Then, to deflect from himself, he turned to Martin. "Your turn. Perhaps it is time for you to tell them what happened to you this week."

Martin knew he wouldn't get away with brushing this off. He would have to say something.

"I was persuaded, against my better judgement, to cover the story of events at the Mall. I really don't want to talk about it. And I am sure Simeon has already told you his part in rescuing me." He turned to Simeon and asked, "Do you know if the woman who helped me is okay?"

"Yes. I checked with the shopkeeper, and she got her money. They're glad you're okay."

Martin was pleased to hear this, and said, "I'll thank her next time I'm in Nairobi."

"We get that you'd rather not talk about it," Edward said, "But are you okay?"

Martin shook his head. “No. Being in that situation stirred up memories I've tried to suppress for the last seven years. The honest answer is that I'm a mess.”

He looked round. “I've finally accepted that I need help to sort myself out.” Then, to lighten the atmosphere joked, “By the sound of things, you could all do with therapy too.”

Then Edward dealt the final blow.

“Penny will never forgive you if there isn't a wedding. Sean told us you hadn't proposed. What happened?”

“It's all a matter of timing. You'll just have to wait and see. What I do know is that there will be a christening.”

That sparked a conversation about names. Suggestions made. The mood was much lighter for all the confessions made.

CHAPTER 48

Ol Essakut

Martin was all set to propose, but wanted to do it when they were alone. The twins had other plans. Both were being demanding. He took one and walked up and down, patting his back. Hoping to get some wind out of him. That failed, so he held him on his knee, and gently wiggled him the way Kim had shown him and finally got a burp. Jenny took that child and handed over his daughter. He did the same with her. And by the time she obliged with a burp. Sandra had fallen asleep. With the babies settled, he lay down beside Sandra, thinking how lucky he was to have her in his life.

When he woke, she was lying so close he could feel her breath on his cheek. She put a finger to his lips. The babies were sleeping. She moved her head and their lips touched. A light, tender kiss. He pulled away. He had to do it now.

"There's something I should have told you years ago," he whispered. "It's about the nightmares..." She nodded. "I couldn't talk about them, but until I do, I can't marry you."

He watched her reaction. Expecting her to say something. She didn't.

"I worked in some harrowing situations for so long, and to do the job, I somehow switched off all emotion. It was the only way to keep taking those pictures. My aim was to get in and get the hell out as fast as possible. You get the drift?"

She nodded.

"One day, I got trapped by crossfire, not sure if I would make it to safety. When dawn broke, I risked moving. I ducked from one building to the next, taking photos on the way, capturing the destruction. A sniper spotted me and fired. I was wearing a bullet-proof vest, which saved me. I had dived through the nearest doorway for cover and lay frozen in the dust, hoping that the sniper would think he had killed me. As it got lighter, I faced the worst carnage I had ever come across in all my years of reporting."

Sandra kissed him and whispered. "You don't have to tell me if you don't want to."

"That place is what the nightmare has been about for the last seven years."

Sandra gently kissed his cheek. "Why are you telling me about it now?"

"Until last week, I only remembered part of that day. I have spoken to a trauma specialist, who said I had blanked it out, which is a common reaction. But now the rest has come back to me. My nightmare takes me back to what happened later, as clearly as if it was yesterday. I can't describe it to you., and probably never will be able to. But it ended my career. It broke me. I don't know how I got out of there. Or much about the months that followed. Until Hank tried to get me to attend an award ceremony for a photo I had taken."

"What happened?"

"He badgered me until I agreed to go, and as we walked into the hotel lobby where the function was being held, I saw a massive blow up of a tear-stained child with a sparkling green shawl covering part of her hair. Seeing it made me freeze. I wasn't sure why. I knew I had seen her before and probably taken the photo, but also knew I would never have given permission for it to be used. I felt physically sick and dived into the nearest cloak room and spewed my guts."

She stroked his arm. "I remember that picture."

"You do?"

"Yes, Nick kept copies of all your work. I still have them."

"I couldn't accept an award for it. It should never have been published."

"Why?"

"When working in tough places, I'd take photos on autopilot, trying not to absorb what the camera lens recorded. That child was in that building. In my recent nightmare, I've relived the part where she died in my arms."

She gently wiped a tear from his cheek.

"It's left me with a lot of questions."

"Such as?" she whispered.

"Who was she? What happened to her and her family? It's silly, but I need to find out."

"Not silly at all."

"I went today to ask Hank how that picture got published without my permission. I've asked him to find out who she was, and if any of her family survived." After a while, he added, "Can you find that photo for me?"

"Yes. I'll find it tomorrow."

"It might help to look at it again now that the memory has returned. Apparently, I deleted most of those photos from my computer."

She kissed his forehead and whispered. "Enough talking. Let's enjoy the quiet. We can look for it together in the morning."

The next thing he knew, the sun was streaming in through the window, with the curtains billowing gently. Sandra was beside him, cradling a baby, the other baby was snuggled in the gap between them.

"Good morning, sleepyhead," she said, and leaned over to kiss him. "We need to talk baby names."

He stroked the little one beside him and said. "Paul?"

"Paul's perfect. What about this one? I wondered about Lucinda, but that's likely to be shortened to Lucy or Cindy.

"Lucy suits her."

Sandra laughed. "Both names were on our initial lists. I can't think why it's taken us so long to decide?"

"Other distractions," he said, "Like the unresolved issue of a wedding."

She looked him in the eye. Stretched out and pulled the ring box off the bedside table and handed it to him.

He opened the box, took the ring out, and said, "Sandra, will you marry me?"

"Did you ever doubt it?"

He shook his head. "No. Only myself." And he slipped the ring on her finger.

Later, they sat waiting for Hank to come. He had sounded hesitant when Martin phoned him. And had asked Martin to apologize to Sandra for his rude behaviour on his previous visit.

"He sounds terrified of you," Martin chuckled. "I think that's him approaching. He's driving like a snail. You really shook him."

Hank's wife came ahead and congratulated them both, and bent to look at the babies in their basket beside Sandra. "I hope you'll forgive Hank for his awful behaviour. That Mall siege made him so bad tempered, but he's calmed down now."

"Nothing to forgive. He caught me on a bad day, too."

"Ah, but it was good for him to have a wake-up call." She said in a soft voice.

Hank had joined them, and waited to speak.

“For heaven's sake, sit down Hank.” Martin said. “Sandra promised not to bite you head off today.”

“That's a relief,” he said, and looked at Sandra. “Sorry, I was being a jerk the other day.”

“Forget it.” Sandra said, “I understand Martin has asked you for some information.”

Hank nodded. “I checked with the local office there. And you were right, the image attracted a lot of attention. She had surviving relatives. One of them found you and got you to the hospital.”

Martin looked stunned, as if he hadn't expected to get answers, and now he was getting more than he had bargained on.

“They are going to let me have all the information they have. It should be available later today. I'll bring it over as soon as I get it. There is also the matter of the royalties accumulated. I know you said you didn't want them, but we arranged for them to go into a special account in case you changed your mind. It has grown to a sizeable amount.”

Martin put up his hand to stop Hank. “Enough for now.”

Hank looked across to Beverley. Sandra couldn't ever remember him looking so unsure of himself. He knew he had stuffed up, and the consequences were something he hadn't had to deal with before.

“Would you like us to go?” Beverley asked.

Martin swallowed and shook his head. “No. Stay for coffee.”

Sandra leaned forward and filled the cups and handed them round.

Beverley broke the silence. “Is it true that Malcolm has persuaded one of your guests to join the team at the research center?”

“I think he may have.” Sandra said, “Which would be amazing, as his wife is the midwife who delivered this pair. Another of the group is planning to stay on for a few months. She's an artist, and has agreed to run some art classes for our guests if we can arrange them. Which might be a good draw to pull tourists back."

Before they had time to discuss that in more detail, cries of hunger became an unavoidable distraction.

Hank looked uncomfortable and said, "I really do think it's time to leave."

Sandra smiled and said. "Thanks for coming over." Martin had picked up the baby and was trying to calm him. But the wailing was relentless.

As soon as they had gone, she settled herself to feed the baby. Martin sat beside her, looking very pensive.

"Does it help to know that relatives survived?" she asked.

"Would it be strange for me to want to meet them?"

"Not at all. But could you bear to go back?"

"I'm not sure, but maybe."

"If you go, I want to go with you. You can't do it on your own."

He leaned over and kissed her. "I think all the royalties should go to the family. I am sure they could make better use of it than I could."

"Do you still want me to find that picture?"

He nodded. "Yes, I think I am ready to see it. I presume if she had relatives, they gave her a decent burial, or at least know where she was buried. No. Finding the picture can wait." She seemed happy with that answer.

Sandra sensed a shift in his mood. He seemed calmer for having made that decision. She hoped it was the first of many steps in his recovery process.

"You did a real number on Hank. I can't believe he sat there and never said a word about the Mall attack. "

"I am sure his silence won't last long."

"Probably not. I got Simeon to tell me what went on while I was missing. He wasn't sure what happened to the guys who held me. But Hank is bound to tell me as soon as he feels I can handle it. But it's not important. I'm more interested in your plans for the wedding?"

Sandra smiled. "I started off with a traditional ex-pat sort of party. But since that celebration in the village the other day, I've had other thoughts."

"Sounds interesting."

"Now that I know it is our wedding, I've been thinking about who really matters to us. There are the obvious contenders, family, close friends, and our regular social contacts. But I can't leave out our Ol Essakut community. To have such an important a celebration without including them would be unthinkable."

"Go on."

"I don't know if it can be done, but I want the ceremony and the festivities to be held here. I know it will be huge, and far bigger than you imagined. But I hope you like the idea."

"If you're talking about a tribal affair, you realize I will expect you to walk a few paces behind me?"

Sandra laughed and punched his shoulder. He flinched, and she realized she had hit his bad arm. "Sorry, I definitely I won't follow that tradition."

He pulled her close and kissed her.

"Your plan sounds amazing. Can we pull it off in the time we have?"

"With our amazing team, of course we can."

*****

I hope you have enjoyed this book. The second book in the African Adventure Series. **Feast of the**

Antlion is where Sandra and Martin's adventures at Ol Essakut began.

You might also enjoy a crime novel **Smoke Screen.**

Here are the first two chapters for you to read.

1

Luke Tanner's phone buzzed in his pocket. He slowed down, pulled it out, and read the message. They needed him to clock on early. Adrenaline surged. He'd never figured out if it was fear of putting his firefighting training to good use, or the thrill of the unknown that triggered a rush of blood to course round his body.

Owen, yards ahead of him, was already turning his bike back towards the fire station. Luke assumed he'd received the same message. No words were necessary as their routine pre-shift bike ride became a race back to the station. The sound of the station bell ringing in the distance added a sense of urgency.

One pump was easing out of the building. The second would go as soon as the crew boarded.

Luke abandoned his bike against the wall and tore into the building. He pulled on his trousers and slid his feet into his boots. Owen, already fully kitted, was on his way to the door. Luke grabbed his jacket and shirt and ran to catch up. The moment he and Owen clambered onto the vehicle, the station manager raised his thumb and the engine pulled out onto the main road, with sirens blaring.

"What are we in for?" Luke shouted.

"Warehouse fire," James, the newest recruit, answered.

Luke pulled off his cycle top and searched for his regulation t-shirt. It wasn't there; he must have dropped it in the rush. He tugged the top back on and donned his bulky jacket over it and stuffed his hands into his gloves.

The tension on board was palpable with the anticipation of a tough shout ahead. Warehouse fires were notoriously tricky, making Luke regret the extra pint he'd consumed after his shift the day before.

Eye-stinging acrid smoke filled the pump long before they reached the address. The first crew already had their hoses unrolled, ready to drench the front of the building.

Flames and thick black smoke poured out of a window, licking the walls of the second floor.

"What's in there?" Luke asked the officer in charge.

"No idea. They let the storage space on the different floors to a mix of customers. No one has a clue what they store," he answered. "I want you and Owen to go around the back and check for any nasty surprises we need to be aware of."

Luke gave him the thumbs up and signalled Owen to follow him.

He led the way along the metal fencing round the side of the building, then cut down a narrow lane leading to the rear of the property. At the end, he turned off onto an overgrown path beside a ragged chain-link fence. He pushed forward through arching brambles and nettles, stepping over abandoned bottles, cans and soggy sleeping bags; evidence of rough sleepers using the space. There were no obvious breaches to the fence. Then Luke spotted a break higher in the wires, which he pointed out to Owen.

"We could try to get in here."

"Damn, I forgot the wire cutters," Owen said. "I'll go back for them." Luke turned to tell him not to bother, but Owen was already running back the way they'd come.

Luke scanned the fence again. This appeared to be the only weak spot. He heard banging and looked up.

Silhouetted against a second-floor window of the blazing building was a figure hammering at the window. Luke studied the hole in the fence and wondered if he could pull himself up and use it as a foothold.

He spotted a discarded milk crate, which would give him the step up he needed. He dragged it into place, grasped the pole that supported the fence, and hoisted himself up. Wedging one foot into the hole, he swung the other leg over the top of the fence. For a second, he balanced on the top wire, then as he eased his foot out of the foothold, his grip on the post slipped. Gravity pulled him over the top. The collar flap of his jacket caught on the jagged metal support and slowed his descent, leaving him dangling with his nose pressed to the wire.

Before he had time to figure out how to release himself, he registered a loud ripping noise and hit the ground with a thud. He caught his breath and got to his feet. Still no sign of Owen. If he waited, it would be too late. The figure by the window had vanished. He sprinted across the yard to the only door on that side of the building.

Could he get it open? Would it be flimsy enough for him to force it with his body weight? He rattled the handle. Nothing happened. He tried again. No luck. He stepped back a couple of paces and ran forward, shoulder first, aiming at the height where he thought the lock would be. With a splintering crash, the door gave way, propelling him into the smoke-laden space at the bottom of a staircase. He grabbed the handrail, using it as a guide as he tore up the stairs, two steps at a time, up to the second level.

The higher he climbed, the denser the smoke became. Eventually, he stepped into a corridor with doors on either side. He figured the window was about four rooms away from the downstairs door, near to the end of the building where the blaze raged. Groping his way along the wall, counting the doors as he progressed, he entered the third. It was empty. One more, then he'd turn back. The roar of the fire above had a terrifying ferocity. He'd come this far. He couldn't leave now. He pushed the door open. The man lay slumped on the floor by the window. Luke ran over and stooped to lift him.

A deafening thud and the scary creak of failing timbers added urgency to his mission. Seconds later, the ceiling caved in. An enormous beam crashed down through the hole. Hot embers sprayed the room amid the clouds of plaster dust. The floor shook, and the blast of heat nearly knocked him off balance.

Years of training and experience kicked in. He was here with a purpose: to save a life.

He ignored the shower of embers, grabbed the man's coat, stooped lower and lifted the inert figure as near upright as possible. Then he shoved his shoulder under the sagging body, wrapped one arm around the man's legs, and straightened up.

Kicking burning debris out of the way, he staggered back to the door with the dead weight on his shoulder. Finding the stairs and getting out of this hellhole was his only focus. The thick smoke made breathing nearly impossible. He held his breath and stumbled on.

Everything seemed to happen in slow motion. How many rules had he broken by entering the building without his breathing apparatus? It didn't matter. He had done what he needed to do.

The stench of burning changed. What was it? The man's coat? No chance of checking—he had to get out of this inferno first.

Ignoring the smell, he kept going, down the corridor, down the stairs, through the disorientating thick, black smoke. He clung to the handrail to guide him to the ground level. The door he had broken through earlier was somewhere on his left, but not visible. He lurched forward, feeling his way along the wall until he touched the door jamb. He pulled the door open and almost fell into the fenced yard. Staggering under his load, he kept going as far away from the burning building as possible before he collapsed on his knees, lowering his load gently onto the weedy gravel.

Intense pain and the stink of burning flesh brought him back to his senses. It took a moment to register where it was coming from.

The area from his neck to his chest was alight. Flames licked his face. Like a slow-motion replay of a horror movie, he registered the flames were real. He was on fire. How? He looked at the man lying on the ground beside him. Smoke was coming from the man's coat. Smouldering embers had become embedded in their clothing. The ripped fastening of his jacket had enabled the glowing embers to touch his cycling top. Air had got in, setting his top alight and melting the synthetic material onto his skin. He tugged his coat off and yanked the burning top over his head, cursing at his stupidity. How could he have gone on a shout with a nylon shirt on? No time now for beating himself up. The man on the ground beside him needed his help.

Why hadn't Owen come back? What was holding him up? He rolled the man over and brushed off the burning embers. The man moaned. He was alive but struggling to breathe. Luke had run out of strength. His shoulder and chest felt as if it was still on fire, but there were no flames now, just a sickening stench of burnt flesh and melted nylon.

He retched and then muttered to his companion, "Sorry, this is as far as I can help you." He retched again. His brain went into overdrive. How the hell would Amy react? His being injured had been her worst nightmare. How would she tell the girls?

2

Luke wondered when the fog of pain would lift, and he would find the strength to react. The clatter of a laden trolley drew closer. He waited for the swish of curtains, which would bring pain relief with an injection. People spoke to him, but he hadn't the energy to reply. The burns were deep and painful, and he trusted those around him to make the right decisions on his behalf. He didn't want to know the details; he'd rather float through this ordeal in a drug-induced haze.

The smell of burning flesh stuck with him. Sometimes a whiff of Amy's delicate perfume kicked in and she'd take his hand. He loved her so much and would attempt to respond by gently squeezing her fingers and force open his eyes. He wanted to tell her how much he loved her, and the girls. But his mouth was too dry. The fact he'd tightened his grip on her hand was enough to soften her worried expression before he drifted off again.

His waking moments became more frequent, and he knew when Amy was there from her scent. When she wasn't there, he'd lie there wondering how she would cope with him being scarred.

Sometimes, when he woke, Owen would be in the chair by his bed. And Luke knew he was waiting to reprimand him for going into a burning building alone, which he deserved. Owen was right. His pain was a constant reminder of his foolishness, and he wished he had the energy to tell Owen to skip the lectures.

Gradually, the fog lifted. The drawback being that the jumbled flashbacks had more clarity. The man clawing at a window. The chain-link fence. The locked door. An acrid smoke-filled staircase. The roar and crash of burning timber falling. Each episode was so vivid he felt as if he could touch and feel the heat. But worst of all was the revival of the stench of burning flesh that seemed to hit the back of his throat and would linger throughout the day.

On one of his more lucid days, he dared to ask the doctor the question dominating his thoughts.

"When can I go back to work?"

The surgeon raised an eyebrow. "Not for some time. Your burns are deep. You'll need more surgery. When that's done, we'll talk again. Until then, I can't possibly promise you will be fit for such a physically demanding occupation."

"When will you operate?"

"When the current grafts have healed. Follow the discharge team's instructions. They will tell you when you're ready." With that, the man turned on his heels and marched out of the room.

Amy returned later, rather remote and distracted, as if she didn't want to be there. Her perfume was different, too cloying for his liking. She fussed about at his bedside, moving his water jug and glass to one side, making the place tidy, but not easier for him, and he didn't know how to stop her fiddling.

"Can you bring the girls in?" he asked to distract her.

"Sorry. This is no place for children." Her tone was a distinct 'don't-bother-trying-to-persuade-me-otherwise' one. He wasn't ready to give up. He needed to see them.

"I could come down to the cafeteria. No need for them to come on the ward."

"Absolutely not." Sometimes Amy's stubborn reactions went too far, and this was one of those occasions. He didn't know why she was so adamant. Perhaps she would be less against the idea another day.

Ten years of marriage had taught him to be patient, to win her over to his way of thinking.

Every time she came, he asked again. But nothing changed her mind.

He wasn't sure if he was imagining it, but her visits seemed to get shorter and shorter. The excuses varied, from having to pick someone up, or drop something off, work, school events, or some other vital chore she had forgotten. These came up the moment she sensed his wound was about to be dressed. He saw fear in her eyes. The realization that she couldn't cope with seeing his damaged skin hit hard. Was that what was making her behave so differently towards him? What would life be like when he went home?

Owen was more stoical. He would sit there for hours doing a crossword or reading some snippet out of the paper he brought with him.

Luke sensed the uncomplicated relationship they'd enjoyed since their schooldays had become strained. Owen was happy to talk about recent shouts, but would not discuss the warehouse fire, which resulted in Luke's injuries. If Luke brought the subject up, Owen would change the topic or find an excuse to leave.

What was it about that fire that made him reluctant to discuss it? The lack of answers niggled, and Luke tested Owen by asking about it every day.

"Did they find out what caused the fire?" he asked.

Owen shrugged, and muttered unconvincingly, "Possibly electrical. Hey, did you see the Exeter Chiefs match on TV last night?"

Next time, Luke asked, "Who headed the investigation?"

"Oh, some new chap came down from Somerset. He didn't stick around," Owen answered, and again diverted the conversation. "Did Amy tell you when she was coming in?"

“Later, I think she and Tamsin were having a spa session.” Owen frowned, as if it was the first he’d heard of his wife’s plan, and got up to go. Luke had never really connected with Owen’s wife. He thought she was rather self-absorbed, but she had introduced him to Amy, and for that, he was grateful.

The surgeon was due on his rounds. The nurse drew the curtains around his bed and removed his dressing so they could inspect his wounds.

She chatted merrily as she worked. "This is healing well."

"Can I see?"

"Yes, I'll get a mirror."

While he waited for her to return, he peered down at his chest. Up to now, he had resisted the urge to look at the damage. He was as cowardly as Amy. The bumpy swathe of scabs that he could see were not pretty.

The mirror enabled a closer inspection of the skin round his neck. Amy's insistence that they work round his neck first had paid off. While still rather red and lumpy, it was closer to normal than the rest of his chest and shoulder area.

The nurse let him examine himself without comment. Then, judging that he was ready, explained the difference between the grafted skin and the untouched areas.

"See, now there are no oozing gaps between the newly formed scabs." The nurse pointed to a big scab in the middle of the cratered landscape of skin. "This is the worst spot where the deepest damage occurred."

When the surgeon arrived, he also pointed to the same place and said, "I presume that's the most painful area?"

Luke nodded.

"Be prepared. The pain won't go away for some time, the nerve damage is permanent. This area here," he said as he pointed towards Luke's armpit, "is where the next round of surgery will be done. The scars have tightened the skin, causing restriction of movement. The aim will be to improve your arm mobility."

"Is that why they have trussed me up like a chicken?"

"The sling helps to stop you from disturbing the scabs that have formed. Those need to heal and drop off naturally, or you will risk getting an infection in the wound. The new skin is too tight, you won't be able to lift and stretch your arm very far. Doing so could cause more damage. The aim is to let the new skin form, and then graft skin from your thigh to give this area more movement. The operation will be painful but should give enough flexibility to get you back to work. Until then you must take care to avoid infection. Nurse Brook will give you all the instructions you need to deal with this at home. As soon as she feels you're ready, you can go."

When he left, Luke asked, "What do I do about the pain?"

"Keep taking the painkillers. The nerves are so close to the surface, the slightest touch is going to trigger pain. I believe that gradually your brain learns to cope, and the sensitivity will lessen."

She talked him through the skin care regime, making him apply the creams and watching as he took those first steps of touching and caring for his damaged skin.

As he put the first dab of ointment on the least nasty looking area, his stomach lurched, but he continued. Overcoming revulsion was the price he must pay to get out of the ward. He took his time, discovering which areas were more sensitive than others. Touching one spot triggered a flashback of the fire. He pulled his hand away.

"You okay?" the nurse asked.

He didn't answer. He couldn't explain that it wasn't just the pain; touching there brought back fresh memories of the nauseating smell of his flesh burning. A smell that overpowered all the antiseptic creams he was using. He forced himself to continue applying the cream. At last, the task was over. He checked the clock on the wall. It had taken him almost an hour to cover the burn area. He looked up for reassurance.

"You've done really well."

"I'm wondering how my wife will cope," he said.

"You mustn't worry about that. I'm sure she'll deal with it. But you realize you'll have to do this three times a day, no skimping."

He nodded.

"If you have any breaks in the skin," she continued, "or you have any discharge at all, you must come back in. Please don't do the macho thing of shrugging and saying everything will be okay because all you will do is set your progress back."

"What about dressings?"

"No dressings. The best thing is getting air to the wound. Go shirtless if you can, but otherwise a soft cotton t-shirt is your best solution. Your wife brought some in for you. Here, try this on. Cotton can go through a hot wash, and you must change your shirt often. Try to do it every time you put the cream on. Good hygiene is the key to recovery."

"Understood."

"How does that feel?" she asked once she had helped slip the t-shirt over his head.

"Fine."

"Here, take a peek." She held up the mirror.

"Not bad. The scar is barely visible."

Amy would be pleased. Appearance mattered to her.

Once he had his sling back in place, the nurse continued. "The physiotherapy team will be along shortly to run you through a set of suitable exercises. Very gentle ones to start, and they'll tell you what you must avoid at all costs."

The physio work began and reality hit. If he didn't follow their instructions, he might never work again. He put on a brave face and agreed to make the effort.

It took a few more days before his discharge details were in order. They would release him from the hospital with enough medication to last him for a fortnight.

This news came with a mix of joy and fear. How the hell was he going to deal with being back at home? More importantly, how would Amy manage?

He was longing to see the girls again but was terrified over how they would react.

Amy came to collect him. She suggested dropping him off at home before going to fetch the children from school. He wasn't sure if this plan was for her benefit, a plot to keep him out of sight of her friends at the school gates, or because she thought it was what he wanted.

When she offered him a smart new coat with a high collar, along with a silky scarf for him to wear, he was sure it was the former. She wanted to keep him, and his scars, hidden from sight.

"Thanks," he said, "too hot for those. I don't need anything."

She still hadn't looked him in the eye.

"Okay, forget the coat, but at least wear the scarf." She held it out for him to take. He stepped backwards.

"Please."

He couldn't believe she would do this to him.

"Amy. Look at me." It took an age for her to turn and face him.

"I have injuries. That's something I have to live with. But no way am I going to wrap myself up in winter woollies, because you don't have the guts to look at my scars."

"Sorry, I thought you'd want to cover up." She had her eyes locked on his. He had to make her see what was visible was not stomach-churning.

"Look at my neck."

She took a deep breath, and her gaze lowered. She went pale. He knew then that to ask her to touch his scars would be a step too far.

"Not so bad?"

"No," she mumbled, but turned away from him.

"The rest are still grim, so I'll do my best to keep them covered up. All I ask in return is for you to stop treating me like some sort of freak. Deal?"

His nurse was standing in the doorway behind Amy. She stuck her thumbs in the air in a supportive gesture.

Amy wasn't smiling. "Fine, if that's the way you want it," she said, as she shoved the offending garments back into the carrier bag she'd brought them in and strode to the door.

As they walked through the endless corridors to exit the building, he half regretted the stance he had taken. How long would she hold it against him?

To find out more about the author and to learn about new publications and special deals or order copies of my books, please visit my page.

www.caroayre.co.uk

MHM Photograpy

Caro Ayre

A childhood in Kenya provided lasting memories of hot sun filled days, vibrant coloured birds and flowers, armies of insects, roaming wildlife in vast expanses of open spaces and warm waves lapping on silvery sands.

I now live in rural Somerset where family, gardening, running a Bed and Breakfast, in an amazing rural setting, along with painting and writing fill my days.

The Feast of the Antlion

Sandra Harriman is out of her depth. Widowed and keeping control of her stepchildren's inheritance, a huge wildlife ranch in Kenya is her priority.

An attack on the ranch by an armed gang, and the appearance of poachers are complications that threaten to destroy everything she is striving to save.

Who can help her? If what she reads in her dead husband's diaries is true, no one can be trusted. Who will it be? The man he once shot? The distant relative who has a right to live on the ranch? The childhood friend who she appointed as manager? The woman he was having an affair with before he died?

Buy this now to discover the magic that Africa has to offer and learn who Sandra turns to for help.

www.amazon.co.uk/dp/B006PZBXCI
www.amazon.com/dp/B006PZBXCI
ISBN 978-0-9572224-0-3

Breathless

How would you cope knowing your genes gave your child a life-threatening disease?

Clare is exhausted coping. Her husband has been in denial for 15 years. Her daughter is rebelling against her cystic fibrosis treatments. And her son is overwhelmed by guilt at being spared from the disease.

Clare is determined to keep the family communicating with each other, while trying to create an independent life at Dovedale's. Will finding out her husband's secret change anything? Does accepting help from an old flame hurt her family? There is no choice as it is not just her family that will benefit.

www.amazon.com/dp/B00DFOT5VI
www.amazon.co.uk/dp/B00DFOT5VI
ISBN 987-0-9572224-1-0

Never too late

Love, loyalty and a lie leave Fiona vulnerable to blackmail

Her home and office become places of torment.

Can she keep her true feelings secret?

Will making the ultimate sacrifice, be enough to save her life-long friendship?

Who else will be hurt by her actions?

Read this if you enjoy an emotional page turner.

www.amazon.co.uk/dp/B0866BQXD6
www.amazon.com/dp/B0866BQXD6
ISBN 978-0-9572224-5-8

The Mallaig Link

When you can't trust your boss, who can you trust?

When surveillance of a mysterious house in Mallaig exposes a weak link within D I Gavin McKay's department, he pretends to drop the case.

Will solving the identity of a woman with amnesia provide the cover needed to hide the fact that he has not given up on solving what went on in that house. Can he find answers before someone else dies? Will his personal relationships suffer because of his determination to get to the truth?

Buy the first book in the Detective Inspector McKay series now. The sequel is coming out soon.

ISBN 978-0-9572224-3-4

Smoke Screen

Devon firefighter, Luke Tanner, gets caught in a fire. His injuries could end his career and his marriage. Will he be able to save them both?

Doubt about how the fire started creeps in. Is there an arsonist at work? His colleagues say he's paranoid. Can he prove them wrong?

The deeper he digs the more complicated his investigation gets. Tension rises as his search for proof puts others in danger, including his family.

He's not a quitter. The arsonist must be stopped before someone else dies.

This thriller will keep you on the edge of your seat.

www.amazon.co.uk/dp/B0C8VBMDHX
www.amazon.com/dp/B0C8VBMDHX
ISBN 978-0-9572224-7-2

Printed in Great Britain
by Amazon

56297589R00179